Elsha's fire . . .

"I have not changed . . . just because I burned my mining clothes and wear your sacred sign. I am still Elsha. Elsha of the Quelled. How can I ever forget it? It's branded on me, burned into me, stamped into my flesh. But it doesn't touch my soul. And my soul is the same, whether I live in a goatskin tent or a grand house, whether I live with a harsha friend, or a Chosen youth, or you. None of you touch me. You don't make me anything. I am me. Myself. Elsha. Woman."

point

WINTER OF FIRE

SHERRYL JORDAN

SCHOLASTIC INC.
New York   Toronto   London   Auckland   Sydney

ISBN 0-590-45289-4

12 11 10 9 8 7 6 5 4 3 2 1   1   5 6 7 8 9/9 0/0

Printed in the U.S.A.   01

For Jean,

who has loved this story
from the first elated telling
through to this final form,
and who, next to Elsha, has been
my greatest encouragement

With love

CONTENTS

Tribute to Elsha

Winter of Fire is a special book to me. It was written after I had been told that I had RSI (Repetitive Strain Injury), and would never write again. It was while I faced that, and fought the greatest battle of my life, that I wrote Elsha's story.

Her story had been inspired more than a year before, and Elsha herself had lived in my life as a character for all that time. She was inexorable, charismatic, and a warrior at soul. It was because of her that I refused to accept that my writing days were over — because of her that I picked myself up out of despair and grief, and wrote again. We were warriors together in our battles against the impossible; and this book exists only because of her, and the love and inspiration of God.

S.J.

WINTER
OF FIRE

PART ONE

FIREBRAND

1

High Dreams

Always at the heart of my life there has been fire.

Fire heated the brand that marked me with the sign of the Children of the Quelled. And with the Quelled I toiled in the dark mines of Siranjaro for the black fuel we call firestone. Fire it was that gave me heat when all else was wind and ice and killing cold. Fire cooked my food, warmed my frozen clothes, and was my life's light. By fire at night I dreamed my high, heroic dreams.

From when I was a child I had my dreams, though I did not often talk of them. While my parents worked in the mines, the other children and I were looked after by the caretakers, the ones too old or ill to work. We grew vegetables, carried water, wove clothes from goathair and wool, tended the tiny flocks, and kept out of the way of the Chosen.

The Chosen were our lords, our masters. My earliest memory of the Chosen was of a man with tall boots dyed gold and green, and a fur-lined coat and trousers of blue wool. He carried a short whip. I had been crouching in the garden, singing to my cabbages to make them grow, and a darkness had fallen over me. I looked up and saw the man. He said nothing, for the Chosen had convinced themselves that we Quelled had no intelligence and no speech. He looked across the stony frozen earth, past the hard-won rows of withered vegetables, the wizened beans, and the spindly, precious wheat; and he made a sound like a laugh. Then he put his boot on my cabbages, ground them hard into the dirt, and turned to go.

Fury overwhelmed me. I picked up a stone the size of my fist, and threw it hard. It landed with a dull thud in the small of his back, and he stopped and slowly turned around. He came back, smiled, and wound my hair around his hand. Then he lifted me by the hair until my feet swung above my crushed cabbages. I was so angry and shocked, I hardly felt the pain. I lashed out with my feet. He gave a yell, and with the whip handle started hitting me.

I don't remember how it ended. I do remember that for a long time afterwards I lay on my sleeping mat by the fire in our black goatskin tent, with a soft darkness all around, and voices that whispered and faded, and whispered again. I heard the quavering voices of the old caretakers, hushed and grave.

"She's not moved for five days. Her nose is broken, and her eyes are swollen shut. She's learned the hard way, not to cross the Chosen."

"She'll never learn, that one. Only four years old, and already her spirit is all spit and fire."

"Not anymore. I think he hurt her spine. They won't allow her to live, poor child. They'll break her father's heart."

And I remember my father's voice, distraught and imploring: "Don't give up, little Elsha, joy of my life. Don't give up."

I did not. But to this day my nose has a hard lump high between my eyes, and is slightly bent. My back is fine, else I could never have survived a single day in the mines. And they tell me that my eyes never quite look in exactly the same direction.

I was five when next I saw the Chosen. I knew, that fateful day, that something terrible was going to happen. My mother hugged me close before she went to the mines, and I remember the smell of firestone dust in her grey Quelled clothes, and the heat of her tears on my cold cheek. "Be brave, child," she whispered, and would say no more.

The caretakers did not take us to the garden that day, or out to move the goats to new places in the mountains. They gathered us five-year-olds together, washed our faces carefully, and rubbed ointment made from herbs on our fore-

5

heads. The others thought it was a new game, and laughed. But I knew evil hung in the air, colder than the wind.

That morning we were allowed only a little water. About halfway through the morning a cart came for us, drawn by four Quelled youths. The other children clapped, delighted, and climbed up by themselves; but me they had to force.

Five Chosen marched alongside our cart, roaring with laughter at something one of them had said. Their heads were thrown back, their teeth gleamed in the pale grey light, and their fine-spun gold and scarlet cloaks swung radiantly as they walked.

The four Quelled youths pulling our cart were harnessed to it with leather halters and chains. Their clothes, like ours, were of dull grey and brown, though theirs were blackened and torn, while ours were clean. They moved in that restrained, solitary way of all the Quelled, silently and without vigour.

I remember one of them clearly. He must have moved when he was being branded, because his mark, instead of being a perfect circle in the centre of his forehead, was a wavering oval across his right brow and down across his cheek. The eyelids were puckered, the eye itself dried up. There was no flame symbol within the circle of his brand — only that terrible sightless hole. He would have had a striking face, without that withered eye. In spite of his bowed head and the demeaned way he walked, there was something sensitive and strong about him, as if a secret inner life burned in him of which the Chosen knew nothing. I felt akin to him.

We came in our little wooden cart to a lonely hut in a barren, stony place high above the mine. The hut was low and long, and built of mountain rock. A small fire blazed outside and a man stooped over it, turning something in the flames.

I should have known — we all should have known — what was to come. We all had seen the brands on the foreheads of other Quelled, all seen our older brethren go away unmarked one day, and come back Quelled. But it was never spoken of, and no one warned us. It never occurred to us that our turn would come. So we submitted when the Chosen blindfolded us, though I was stricken with terror. And we waited while, one at a time, we were taken to the man by the fire.

I have never forgotten that agony, the shock and outrage and blinding pain. And I remember well the long walk home. I refused to be thrown on the cart, and some mad, unyielding pride made me walk. The Chosen thought it was a joke, though one of them swore at me.

I walked beside the youth with the blinded eye. His presence comforted me. Even through the throbbing haze of pain I could tell he kept his good eye on me, and several times he caught my anguished gaze, and smiled. He was strong under the chains and leather straps that bound him with the others to the cart, and there was a steadiness about him that gave me strength.

We dared not speak, not with the Chosen so close. The Chosen forbade us to speak in their presence, perhaps because they believed that by stopping our tongues they stopped our minds. But when they had gone on far ahead, the Quelled youth smiled again and said: "What name do they call you by, young lionheart?"

I tried to smile, and winced with pain. "My name is Elsha," I said. "What name do you have?"

"Lesharo," he replied. He walked in silence for a while, and then he said very softly: "They cannot put their stamp upon your soul, Elsha."

We did not speak again until I was twelve years old, when we became friends; but those few words from him had more influence on my life than anything else I ever heard.

Time diminished a little the anguish of that day. There were days when I even forgot the scar, since I never clearly saw my face. But sometimes when I was lying by the fire at night I lifted my hand, pushed back my heavy yellow hair, and traced the pattern of the brand.

It seemed an inoffensive thing. I even liked the feel of the perfect circle and the shape of the flame within. But it bewildered me. I did not understand then why such a mark was necessary: there were Chosen, and there were Quelled. The Chosen owned the mines, and we laboured for the firestones in the mines — and we all were kept alive by the fires we made. It was only later, when I understood injustice and the shame of slavery, that I knew why they branded us.

Out of all the Chosen, there was only one I loved. We called him our Firelord. He was our great firestone diviner, by whose sacred sight fire and warmth were kept alive in our world. My father told me stories of him, and visions of him illuminated my life. I used to sit with my father by our firepit at night, snuggled close to him on the dirt floor, and look into the flames, and listen.

"Once, long ago, when my father was a boy, the firestones in this place were hidden deep in the mountain," my father told me. "The people did not know where they were. There was no mine, and there were no firestones for fuel, and everyone was in danger of dying from the cold. In all our land, there was only one man who could help — one who had the power to look upon the mountains and see the firestones deep inside, and tell the people where to mine. He is the Firelord. He alone has the gift of inner sight, the great divining power."

I remember how my heart used to beat like a wild thing at the thought of that power, and I asked eagerly: "How did he see the stones, Father? *How?*"

My father used to laugh and stroke my hair. I loved the sound of his laugh. "No one knows how he sees them, child," he said. "But he came to this place, and he saw the stones, and he told my father's people where to dig their mine. He still divines for firestones, and tells people where to mine. He is an old man now, though some say he is very strong, and still looks young. His soul is full of firestone power, and has all the strength and light of flame. And in the time of the great Fire Festival, he goes back to the sacred flame and renews the fires there."

"The Firelord can touch fire, and not be burned?"

"I don't know, child. He is a man apart. No one knows him very well, except the highest-born woman of the Chosen, who is his hand-maid."

"I'll see the Firelord one day," I said.

My father's voice became husky then, and full of sorrow. "No, Elsha. You will work in the mine this year and next year and all your years until you die. Because that is the fate of the Quelled. And the Firelord won't be coming here again. Our mine will last a hundred years."

"I'll see him," I said. "I love the Firelord. And I love his sacred flame. I love the way it burns high on a mountaintop, and never goes out."

"How can you know such things?" he asked.

"I've seen them, Father. I've seen them in my dreams."

My father gathered me up in his arms then, and kissed my hair and face. "You are strange, my little love," he said, laughing. "The strangest Quelled child ever born."

2

Dark Realities

The Siranjaro mine was one of the largest in our mountains. Seven hundred Quelled worked there, besides the old women and men who were the caretakers in our camp. For us there was no other life but mining. We were branded and easily identified, so there was no escape.

The mine was a single shaft straight down into the mountain, and we descended into its utter dark by a series of long wooden ladders. I worked the fifteenth seam down, one of the narrowest and wettest. It was also warm there, deep as it was in the bowels of the earth. I worked wearing only my skirt, lying on my back in the water on the tunnel floor, picking at the firestones in the roof directly above my head. My shoulders and elbows suffered in the confined space, and the fine, black firestone dust filled my eyes and throat. I carried no candle, but worked by touch in the total dark. I had heard explosions caused by candle-flame in the tunnels that seeped gas, and seen the people carried out.

One day for me stands out beyond all other days. It was the day I was sixteen years old. In celebration of my birth, and because an inexplicable joy had taken hold on me, I worked slowly, and rested often. It was partly in defiance of the Chosen — a small defiance, true — but sweet just the same. And so I worked hard for a while, lying on my back in the narrow place; then when my arms ached I rested, placing the pick across my chest. I felt the dank water seeping through my skirt, and slapping softly against my bare arms and sides. It filtered through the rags I had bound about my long hair, and felt warm and gentle on my scalp.

I listened to the sounds of the other Quelled at work, muffled and faint in the far passages. I heard the dull thudding of their picks on the firestone face, and heard people groan as they hoisted their full baskets onto their backs. Somewhere a child hurt itself and wailed, and I heard the soft voice of a man comforting it.

"Hush, little love," he said. "There — I'll tear my shirt for a bandage and stop the blood. You sit here awhile. I'll fill your basket with stones from mine, and the overseer will never know."

I heard a woman weeping quietly as she laboured, heavy-laden with her basket of stones, up the long creaking ladders to the mine surface.

Sometimes I heard conversations echoing weirdly in the blackness; sometimes I heard tender whisperings and sounds of agony, or joy. And sometimes — some blessed, awesome times — there was a brief space where no sound was. Then I'd hear the soft breathing of the darkness, the throb and hum of the deep earth itself, the power of the firestones all around. Sometimes then it seemed as if my heart beat with the firestone heart, and I felt a oneness with the rock. And then far in the darkness a pick would start up again, and the flow of power would be broken. But those silent times, those times when I was one with the mountains, earth, and the black stones that held fire — those times were the strength and joy of my life. I didn't understand it then, and when I told my mother how I felt she said I was half crazed. "Keep it to yourself, Elsha," she said, smiling but earnest. "Your father is troubled enough by your mad ideas." Only one other I told: my one true friend, Lesharo.

I thought of him often on that strange, slow day, while I lay enfolded in darkness and my enigmatic joy. Perhaps that day I first knew I loved him, and the wonder of it took my breath away, left me dazed, dreaming, in the velvet dark. Perhaps destiny was watching me, and made my limbs lazy and my mind dream. I did not know it then, but our history changed because I was slow that day.

At last I heard the gong that signalled evening and the time for the return home. I groped blindly in the water for the last few firestones I had chipped out, and placed them in my basket. I crawled backwards down my narrow tunnel, dragging the basket after me. I came to the end of my seam, stood upright, and felt for my heavy outer clothes near the foot of the ladder. I stripped off my soaking skirt, dragged on my thick grey goathair overdress, tied my belt, pulled on my sheepswool boots, and hauled the basket onto my back. Staggering under the weight, I felt for the ladder, and put my foot on the lowest rung.

The air grew colder as I neared the surface. The pitch-blackness glimmered sooty black, then frosty grey as I came up into the evening light. A freezing wind slashed across my face, and my wet hands and feet turned blue. My heart sank when I saw the long line of us waiting for our last baskets to be weighed. I struggled down the stony track to where the overseer checked our loads, and stood at the end of the line. We did not all have our loads weighed. Most of us the Chosen trusted, and left to work without supervision or inspection. But there were some of us whose every load was weighed, every day's work recorded, assessed, and answered for. We were the troublesome ones, the offenders. It was ever a grief to my father that I was one of them.

About fifty of us waited; fifty silent, grimy souls, our burdens at our feet, our backs and heads bent from cold and fatigue. We were all grey, our icy garments tossing stiffly in the bleak wind, our faces and hands wrapped in rags for warmth. Our flesh was black with firestone dust; our eyes were haunted. Remembering now how we looked, I realise the horror and hopelessness of our poverty. And I marvel that I was the only one who questioned it.

We did not talk while we waited; we had no strength to talk. A few others came up and took their places behind me. Hundreds more, the trusted workers, stumbled past us, dumped their final loads into the carts that waited to haul the fuel to the homes of the Chosen and to our tents, and went on home. Looking back towards our camp, I noticed that already some of the fires were lit, and the smoke hung in a gritty haze over the black tops of the tents. By morning the smog would be so thick, the tents would be totally obscured.

Opposite our camp, across a deep valley, and scattered high across the rocky mountain slope, were the mansions of the Chosen. Built out of rock they were; huge rambling structures that seemed to climb out of the mountainside itself, their ancient walls and buttresses and towers the same dull brown of the earth they sprang from. Today was special to the Chosen, and they had hung splendid banners over their balconies, and crimson flags from their uppermost windows.

The line shuffled forward again, and I picked up my basket and dragged it over the stones. The wind had dropped by now, and our breath made mists in the dusky air. Our hands and faces ached and became numb. Slowly we moved forward, and after a time I saw the fire of the overseer's torch, a tawny flag against the smoky sky.

At last it was my turn. I hoisted my basket onto the weighing-hook and stood respectfully aside while the overseer read the scale. I showed him my family sign on the board, and he made a charcoal mark beside it. I took down the basket, heaved it onto my back, and started to walk over to the carts.

"Harsha!"

The overseer called me back, using the Quelled word for female slave. We had no names, with them. I turned and slowly lowered my basket to the ground, and waited with my head bent.

"Harsha, yesterday you brought up seven-and-twenty full baskets. Today, twenty."

I dared not look at him. That was forbidden. I looked at the gold embroidery on the shoulder of his emerald coat, and arranged my face into a look I hoped resembled contrition. I knew he looked at the air over my head, for no Chosen ever looked into the face of a Quelled. We were not worthy.

"Those seven loads will be made up," he said. "They will be made up before you begin tomorrow's work, and will be counted separately. Altogether there will be four-and-thirty loads. Do you understand?"

My mind whirled. Four-and-thirty loads! That

was not asked even of the strongest men. It was a sentence of brokenness, or death. For an instant, shocked and questioning, my eyes met his. He strode over to me, and raised the small whip he carried. I did not move. I looked at a point beyond his left shoulder, at a far calm mountain peak, and the lash burned a line on my face.

"There is defiance in you, harsha," he said, his voice shaking and low. "You I have watched."

The mountain peak was wreathed in mist, and the shadows were purple below. In my soul I flew to them, for calm.

"Do you understand?" he spat.

I fought the urge to answer him. I nodded, and bent my head low.

"Be here in the hour before the dawn," he said loudly. "You will work at the pace I decree, and not stop until I have weighed four-and-thirty loads. If you fall, you will be forced to your feet. If you refuse, you know the penalty. Next."

Dismissed, I picked up my load again and took it over to the carts. It took all my strength to lift it over the wooden side and pour the firestones out. I left my basket on the piles of other empty ones waiting for tomorrow, and started walking home.

I crouched over the bowl of lukewarm water on the stones outside our tent, and splashed the greying liquid over my face and arms. My swollen cheek stung where the whip had cut. I pretended not to notice. The steam from the bowl rose in silver drops into the chill evening air; rose too in a mist from my hands and arms. I leaned over the bowl and peered at my reflection, wondering whether on this day I looked suddenly older, more mature. The murky ghost of my image stared back, shadowed, with its dull halo of hair.

I had never truly seen my face. If Lesharo had not told me, I would not have known that my eyes were blue and grey like smoke, and that my hair, when I had washed it, was the lighter shade of flame. He had told me, too, that I had a solemn look and did not laugh enough; but when I smiled, he said, my face was all light, and beautiful. He lied, I think, because he was my friend. I did not know my face; always the reflections in the water were too dark to see.

The sky was thick with the smoky shadows of the night. I did not know then what the stars were, or the moon. I had never seen them. Always in our world there was cloud, a dark wintry haze of smoke and floating ash from tens of thousands of fires. Our skies during the day were vaporous and grey; at night they were as black as the inside of the mine.

I stood leaning over the bowl, staring hard at my reflection, disappointed. Then Mishal, my youngest brother, jostled me aside. He was seven, and had worked in the mine only two years.

"Mother calls you," he said in high, imperious tones, plunging his hands into the sooty water.

"The water's filthy! You're supposed to wait till after me."

I dried myself on the frosty towel already used by my other four brothers and my parents, and draped it around Mishal's blackened neck. "First here gets the clean water," I said, lightly.

He kicked backwards with his foot, and missed. "Men before harsha," he said. "That's the law."

I made a rude gesture with my hand, not to him but to the mansions of the Chosen high on the opposite mountain slope, and to all the men who made the laws. Then I turned and went into our tent.

Mother was squatting by the fire making wheat cakes on a flat buttered stone in the embers. The smoke rose in ragged circles, tossed by the night breeze that came in through the joins in the black goatskin walls. We were luckier than most; our tent was erected against a low stone wall, and was protected from the icy northern gales. But tonight's breeze was from the south, and brought with it the smells and smoke from the whole camp. It brought too snatches of song, music from flutes and pipes, and the occasional throb of drums. Those I loved. We Quelled rejoiced in our music, and all the oppression of the Chosen could not beat it out of us.

My father and brothers were sitting on a mat of bullock hide against the stone wall, talking. There was no furniture in our tent. We rested, ate, and slept on the dirt floor. Little Mishal sat with them, pretending to be a man. He mimicked my father, slapping his right hand on his knee and frowning.

My father was a handsome man. He had golden-red hair and a long beard, and his hair shone in the dark shadows. He wiped his hands over his face often, and sometimes I saw in him a haunted, sorrowing look that tore my heart. He did not share my strange love for the fire-stones we mined, but he told us grand Quelled myths of a glorious past when all the world was filled with warmth and there was no need for fire or mines, Quelled or Chosen. My brothers smiled at the stories, and my mother shook her head. Sometimes our singers sang the myths and we danced to their music, laughing and clapping our hands. But mostly we were too tired to dance.

My father looked up at me as I came in, and a look half anger, half sorrow crossed his face. "I heard talk of you, Elsha," he said, in that deep, quiet voice of his. "And I see your face. They say that tomorrow you must bring out four-and-thirty loads. Is this so?"

I shot him a dismal grin, and nodded.

"It will kill you, child," he said, with heavy quietness.

I crouched by my mother near the fire, and warmed my hands near the flames. My fingers trembled, and I clenched my fists to make them still.

My father sighed. "Five sons I have," he murmured, "and from them not a shadow of a bother. But you, Elsha — you bedevil me with your fiery soul. Why did you work so slow today?"

"Because today I am sixteen," I said.

He said: "So?"

I looked through the flames at him, and tried to find the right words. "The Chosen don't own all of me," I said. "I kept some of me today, for resting in the dark, and for joy."

"God, Elsha," he said, " — joy?"

He covered his face with his hand, and I thought he laughed, or wept. But he took his hand down and said in a low and tender voice: "Help your mother, child."

I took the turning-fork from her hand, and she gave me a fleeting, weary smile. She was not yet forty years old, yet her face, once vibrant and beautiful, was deeply lined and ingrained with firestone dust. Her hair was totally grey. Her hands shook all the time, and she sobbed sometimes when she straightened her back. She was old by Quelled standards. Soon, I hoped, she would be permitted to stay at camp as a caretaker.

She noticed me looking at her, and smiled. "No matter what happens tomorrow," she whispered, "they can never take away today."

I finished cooking the wheat cakes, then made a salad out of kohlrabi, onions, and other vegetables the caretakers had grown. I served the meal to my father and brothers, and sat with my mother a little distance apart, and waited while they ate. We never dreamed of eating with our men; it would have been a sign of greatest disrespect.

Our men were our lords. They slept on the softest sleeping mats in the choicest places near the fire; the finest goathair and wool went into coats and trousers for them; and they had first choice of all our food. Our men, though Quelled, were still called men; but we, being both Quelled and female, were not called women. We were called harsha, a name made up from the old Quelled words for oppression and earth. Only females of the Chosen were called women, and it was a term of respect. I dreamed sometimes that a man, faceless and tall and with a tender voice, did call me woman. It was my finest, maddest dream.

After the men had eaten, my mother and I ate what was left. My father always left the choicest bits for my mother, but my brothers were not so kind to me. I think they were jealous of me because I was my father's only daughter, and though I grieved and worried him, he favoured me. My brothers all were older than I, except Mishal.

After the meal I collected some water from the trough outside, heated it over the fire, and washed our bowls. My brothers spread their sleeping mats on the earthern floor, and started playing a game with a bone die. Mishal played with them, though he did not fully understand the rules, and howled when he lost.

I finished washing the bowls, then pulled on my heavy hooded cloak. "I will go and see Lesharo for a while," I said.

"Don't be long," said my mother, with a gentle look. "You need a good sleep tonight, Elsha, and all the energy you have, tomorrow."

3

My Calling

Lesharo's tent was not far from ours. Sometimes at night if the camp was quiet and the wind
was right, I could hear him play his pipes.

Shivering in the frosty air, I stood outside the
skins of his dwelling and called his name. The
tent entrance was flung aside and he stood there,
smiling, welcoming, his blind eye a black pool in
his shadowed face.

"Welcome, she who is called Elsha," he said,
with his quiet laugh, and he put his hand behind
my neck and kissed my cheek. His face was warm
from the fire, and his hand behind my hood was
steady and strong. Always I had loved that
strength in him, that silent energy. He laughed
often, and I had never seen anger in him. It was

his joy, I think, that was his strength. It was like an endless spring in him, finding expression in his music, his voice, his smile, his gentle ways.

All his family had been killed years before in an explosion in the mine, and I marvelled that even that had not destroyed his spirit. He was a man apart, a lord among the Quelled. It was Lesharo who was called if there were difficulties or accidents in the mine. He had an amazing way with people, of dispelling discord and fear.

I pushed back my hood and sat on the floor by him, the toes of my sheepskin boots on the stones of his firepit. I sipped the hot mint tea he gave me, and for a while we did not talk. I knew he watched me out of that one blue eye, and that he saw the whip mark on my cheek.

"I look so different, now that I am sixteen?" I asked, glancing sideways at him. It was a game with us, that if one of us was whipped, the other never mentioned it. It was our small denial of the power of the Chosen.

He grinned, and his eye glittered. "No. You look the same. Almost. You are still Elsha. You will always be Elsha." He put his left hand on the back of my neck, and gently rubbed the aching muscles there. "You won't be defeated, lion-heart," he murmured.

I finished the tea, and put the bowl down on the hearth. It rattled on the stone, and I was appalled to see how my hands shook. Lesharo must have noticed, but he said nothing. He finished massaging my neck, and folded his hands across his knees. Out of the corner of my eye I saw the sooty brown of his coarse woven sleeve, and the strong tendons of his hands, pale under the everlasting firestone dust. His nails were deeply edged with black. I looked at my own hands, paler still than his under their dust, and smoother, and trembling. I said: "Tomorrow I must bring out four-and-thirty loads."

He said nothing, but his folded hands were tense.

"The Chosen have a saying," I added. "They say a dead Quelled is better than a defiant one."

"Then defiance is not worth its price, is it, lionheart?" he said gently.

I did not agree, but said nothing. I cursed my brand, without which I might have escaped, might have gone to live another life, might even have pretended to be Chosen.

Lesharo reached into a pocket in his shirt, and took out his reed pipes. He polished them slowly on his sleeve, then blew softly into them. I stared into his fire, dreaming. The music made me think of high places, of triumph, and of joy.

When he had finished playing I said: "Tomorrow is the first day of the great Fire Festival. Lesharo, don't you ever wish you could go with the Chosen? Don't you wish you could make that pilgrimage to the holy mountain, and see the Firelord?"

Lesharo smiled, all amusement and gentleness. "You're a strange one, for a Quelled," he said.

26

I felt my face flush. "You sound like my father," I said.

Lesharo leaned forward, and threw some firestones on the fire. The flames leapt, shooting gold and scarlet lights across his face. "Your father speaks a truth," he murmured. "You are not like the rest of us, Elsha. You have a feeling for the Firelord that is not normal for a Quelled."

The words were soft and said with love, yet still they hurt. Sometimes I despaired over my thoughts and dreams. They caused me only pain, and my family stress. Yet I could not live without my dreams. Without them, my life was firestone dust and darkness. With them, I held a world of hope. And in the centre of that hope was the Firelord, our life-link to the warm, the highest person in our world. To the other Quelled he was a god, impossibly remote, a vague and distant power beyond their daily lives. But to me he was a kindred soul. When I lay in the silence of the mine and listened to the firestone heart, I thought of the Firelord and wondered if this unity with stone, this fire, this inner force, was what he felt. It was sacrilege — mad, outrageous sacrilege — and only Lesharo knew of it. And it made him afraid. I was never afraid. Not of the Firelord, anyway, or of firestone power. I looked into Lesharo's fire, and all I saw was a mountain I had seen only in dreams, a high and sacred place, and an everlasting flame.

Lesharo put his hand against my cheek, gently. "Look at me, Elsha," he said.

27

I turned to him.

"I wish your eyes would meet," he muttered, taking my chin. "I could swear you are having visions."

"Not many," I said, "only one."

He dropped his hand as if it were scorched, took up his pipes again, and played a short tune. I noticed that his fingers trembled slightly, and was amazed that he who could calm people's fear and dispel trouble, could be unnerved by me. He played a longer tune then, a haunting one. I moved closer to his fire and bent my head on my arms, and listened.

When it was finished he put his pipes away, got up, and took something from inside a rolled rug at the foot of his sleeping mat. He came back to the fire, sat down, and gave the thing to me. It was a piece of firestone, wonderfully shaped. It was like a small woman, with head and shoulders, breasts, hips, and folded arms. The legs were formed in one piece, but that was the only fault.

"It's almost as I chipped it from the mine," he said, his eye alight with pleasure at my face. "I did only a little shaping on it, and polished it."

"It's beautiful," I said, and flung my arms around his neck. "I'll keep it until I die."

I drew back a little, and kissed his cheek close by his lips. We stayed close for a moment or two, and his face slowly became grave. The flames made black shadows in the hollows of his cheeks and scarlet lights on his mouth. He had a fine black beard and his hair was long and thick. It was streaked with grey above his crooked brand, for he was much older than I.

"You are my dearest friend," I said, kissing his cheek again. "You are all my joy, Lesharo." An emotion I had not seen before crossed his features. We did not move, but his warmth flooded all my soul and blotted out the world.

"Go home, lionheart," he said hoarsely, bending his forehead to mine, and stroking my hair. "Go home. Your mother will be waiting for you."

"I'd rather stay here awhile," I whispered.

He moved away, and threw unnecessary fire-stones on the fire. "The whole camp is asleep," he said. "Take your woman-stone, and go. I'll find you in the mine in the morning, and help you all I can."

I tucked the woman-stone inside my dress. My rope belt would stop it falling through. Then I pulled my thick hood over my head, and went to the tent entrance. He came with me, and we stood for a while in the bitter smoky air, looking out across the camp towards the mountains. We did not have seasons in those days, and it was always winter. At that time there was no snow, and the bare brown rocks of the mountain ravines and peaks were savage and bleak. Lesharo and I saw nothing of the wild heights, as we stood there that night; we could see only the dim glow of fires within the tents of the Quelled, the lightless black of the valley beyond, and then, scattered on the nearest mountain slope, the mansions of the Chosen. They were preparing for their pilgrimage to the festival. We saw their torches as they rushed to and fro, loading up their donkeys and carts in readiness. Torchlight leapt along the narrow winding mountain paths between their houses, and crawled along stairs cut deep into the rock. It gleamed on painted doorways and gold-tipped towers, and on high, ancient stone walls. Most of the Chosen had already gone, and these last were the families of the mine overseers.

"They'll all be gone tomorrow," Lesharo said. "Only ten Chosen left in all of Siranjaro, to oversee the mine."

"A fine time to revolt," said I.

I heard his sharp intake of breath, and felt his body go tense. We were standing close for warmth, and his arm was around my waist. He withdrew his arm, and stood in front of me and took my face in his hands.

"I never heard those words," he said gravely. "For lesser words than those I have seen men have their tongues torn out."

"I'm not a man," I said. "I am a woman."

"You are harsha," he said. "A harsha with a lion's heart, and a spirit that frightens me — a harsha whom I love. Now go." He kissed me on the mouth, quickly, and pushed me away.

I ran all the way to my father's tent, stumbling and laughing in the dark, singing inside for joy, for that first kiss on my mouth, for the music, and for the woman-stone I loved.

I had no idea what hour I awoke. I rolled out of my sleeping mat, careful not to disturb my mother next to me, and threw several handfuls of firestones onto the embers of last night's fire. I put a bowl of water in the glowing ashes, and hoped it would soon warm. I had no time to eat, of that I was certain, but I needed a hot drink before the long day's labour. We slept in our clothes, so there was no need to dress. But I pulled on my wool-lined boots and my heavy cloak.

Outside, the earth and sky were black, and the wind cut my face like a knife. My feet moved by feel on the frigid stones. I climbed the narrow rocky track up behind our camp, and stumbled into the damp, musky soil of the cultivated land. I stooped down and felt in the darkness. My fingers moved across cabbages, the smaller leaves of beets, and found the mint. I picked some, then went back to the path. I looked down the rocky slope towards our camp. Fires were being rekindled, and the light gleamed through the cracks in the tents. The smell of smoke wafted up to me. I looked along to my right, past the camp to the place further on where the mine was. There were no torches blazing in the blackness, so I was early yet.

I stood in the early dawn, sniffing my mint leaves, and the most terrible despair swept over me. For all my courage last night, I dreaded today. I sank to the frozen soil, and covered my face with my hands. Why, why was I not like other Quelled? Why did I have this fire in me, this mad rebellion burning? It would be my death, in the end.

Slowly, slowly like water seeping through rags, or the smell of smoke wafting on the wind, I became aware of a presence all around. I lifted my head, listening, my ears and eyes straining in the darkness. It was a vibration, a sense of deep and vibrant power, such as I felt in the silence in the mines from the firestones all around. I gazed up at the sky, totally black still, but alive. And *warm*. I thought wildly of the stories I had heard of a powerful God who lived in times long past, sung of in our great Quelled myths. Was this him? I wanted to speak — my whole being cried out to him — but I had no words. How did one who was forbidden to speak to a Chosen, address a god?

"Are you there?" I whispered, terrified, peering into the dark. I waited, trembling, for an answer. Nothing. The power ebbed and faded, and all was only blackness. It was like a death — worse than a death. It was a forsaking, a withdrawal of all dreams, all promises, all hope.

"You're a lie!" I screamed inwardly, to the empty dark. "You're weak. Powerless. If you are real, come out and show yourself. They say you called forth the mountains, that you spoke and the world was formed. If you live, do something. Rescue me from the mine today."

The darkness was silent, passionless, and bitterly cold. I realised I had been crying, and my tears turned to ice on my face. Shivering from cold and fury, I stood. So, I had challenged God. The feeling pleased me, gave me a wild, cool kind of satisfaction. I said aloud to the forsaken sky: "If you are listening, it is the woman Elsha who speaks." I smiled defiantly, and started on the downward path to our camp.

There was a movement in the blackness behind me; a grating like a footfall on a stone. I hesitated, and stood still. There were wolves in the mountains, and I had heard reports of lions.

Slowly I turned around. A man stood there, a little way beyond the garden. He was holding a flaming torch, and his robes were vivid blue where the flamelight fell on them. His clothes were different from any I had seen. He wore a long tunic down to his knees, trousers of the same fine weave, a wide belt, and high painted boots. I could not see his face; it was all leaping shadows and scarlet light, and his hair was a golden river down to his shoulders.

"Woman?" he called, and my heart leapt and my knees turned to water. I looked behind me, and all around. I was alone. He had addressed me. Me. Woman.

"God," I said, and collapsed on the ground. I was trembling uncontrollably, and my head spun. My wits left me.

"Come here, woman," he said.

In a spinning, dazzling, glorious daze I got up

and went to him across stones, cabbages, kohl-rabi, and icy dirt. I stood at last before him, and he held the torch out between us and examined my face.

Even in the torchlight, I saw the colour go from his. "You are Quelled!" he cried, astounded, seeing my brand.

I looked into his brilliant eyes, blue and mauve in the light, and I wept. "My lord," I choked, "I lied. I didn't know you were listening. I am harsha. I am sorry."

He smiled, briefly, as if amused. "I think there is a misunderstanding," he said. "I was looking for a woman."

I bent my head. Never had my soul gone so far so fast, from ecstasy to desolation, heaven to deepest hell. Still he looked at me, and the only sound in all that dark, still morning was the crackling of his torch, and the high singing of the wind in the distant mountain peaks.

"I was sent to find a woman," he murmured, "and I find you. How do you explain that, Elsha, daughter of the Quelled?"

"I do not know, lord." My voice sounded small and despairing. I felt vegetable leaves rustle under my boots, and was distressed. I remembered my place, my trouble, my work. I looked along the mountain path towards the mine. A single torch burned on the path, moving, and I knew it was the overseer. My head dropped further, and I murmured, "I have to go, lord. I must work today." I began stumbling backwards away, as quickly as I dared.

"Wom — harsha!" he called. He took a step towards me, his face agitated and flushed. "Harsha, I must speak with you!"

I looked towards the mine again.

"Are you alone in this place?" he asked. "Please. This is of the greatest importance."

I tore my eyes off the mine and the distant waiting torch. "I am alone, lord," I said.

"Do any of the Chosen women ever come here?"

"Here, lord? To our cabbages?" The thought was ludicrous.

He smiled again. His face was beautiful. "Yes," he said quietly. "To this plot of earth right here, among your cabbages."

I smiled back, in spite of my apprehension and fear. "No, lord. Never has a woman of the Chosen been here. Even we harsha don't come here this early, usually."

"Then how is it that you are here?"

"Because I must work early at the mine today, lord. To make up work I did not do yesterday. The overseer waits. I must go, please. This delay is death to me."

"No — stay!" He came nearer, and held the torch closer to my face. I saw that he had tiny tongues of fire embroidered on his coat, and on a chain about his neck he wore an oval plate of gold engraved with a single human eye, and in the centre of the eye was the shape of flame. I looked up at his face, and it seemed sculpted in the firelight, stately and powerful. His eyes, wide and compelling, were of the clearest, strangest blue; and his mouth was finely shaped, and strong. He had a golden beard shaped to a point, and he would have looked severe had he not smiled a little around his eyes. He looked straight back at my face, at my trembling mouth, my eyes, my brand.

"I am Amasai," he said, "steward of the Fire-lord. I know custom demands that I do not look on your face, harsha. But custom has been already broken here today, and by one far greater than myself. Besides, it would have been a sin not to have enjoyed your face."

I flushed wildly. The truth dawned suddenly on me, and I almost laughed with relief, and at my own stupidity. "I thought you were God," I said.

His smile widened. "I am not so high, harsha. Though he who commands you is high. You must accompany me to him." He turned to walk away, not toward the camp, but to the mountains behind, away from Siranjaro.

Panic swept over me. "Lord!" I cried, ago-nised. "I cannot go! I must work at the mine! It is almost day! And there are my parents — and Lesharo!"

He turned back, not smiling anymore, but inexorable and commanding. "Your days at the mine are over," he said. "You no longer dwell

in Siranjaro. It is not I who commands you, Elsha, daughter of the Quelled. It is the Firelord.
It is he who asks for you."

I stared at him, barely comprehending. He
came back, took the golden disk from about his
neck, and placed it around mine.

"It is his sign," he explained, solemnly. He
gazed at me as if uncertain what to do next. I
was incapable of doing anything, except stare at
his face, which was forbidden. We both were
breaking laws.

"I think I must explain," he muttered, passing
his hand through his hair. The torch leapt in a
sudden wind, and then I saw that he was as bewildered and fearful as I was. He took a few deep
breaths, and said: "Three days ago my high lord
gave me this command. He said I was to go to a
place called Siranjaro. On the day of the great
festival, in the hour before the dawn, I was to go
to a garden place behind the tents of Siranjaro's
Quelled. He said I was to wait there, in that hour
before the dawn, and that a woman would come.
That woman is to be his handmaid. All these
things he said to me, and all he foretold has come
to pass. This is the hour before the dawn, and
the garden place, and you — you are the female.
So in his name I command you, Elsha of the
Quelled, to come with me now, and to be handmaid to the Firelord."

He hesitated, then added more gently: "I cannot begin to understand why you are the elected
one. Always he has called his handmaids from

among the highest-born women of the Chosen. Perhaps he has a special knowledge of you, beyond the knowledge of ordinary men. It is not for us to question, only to obey." He turned and began to walk away, holding his torch to one side so that I, too, could walk by its light. And so I followed him, up over the mountain ridge beyond our camp, away from Siranjaro, the mine, my home, my family, and Lesharo.

One thing more this strange man said to me: "Don't look back, Elsha of the Quelled."

4

Fire on My Mind

For three days I travelled with Amasai, steward of the Firelord. We travelled on foot, though he had a mule waiting just outside Siranjaro, laden with brightly coloured travelling bags. For the first time in my life I saw beyond Siranjaro; saw the vast world of our mountains, range upon cloud-topped range, rocky and desolate and beautiful. Often, far up in the misty heights, we saw snow, almost white against the sooty sky. We passed beneath huge stone cliffs, sheer to the clouds; crept along razor-edged tracks where, a step away, the world vanished into mist; and crawled like ants along ridges swept with icy winds, where eagles soared. Once we saw, far below on a windswept plain, a pack of wolves tracking a solitary deer; and once on a high and rocky place we startled a small herd of ibex, and they leapt away before us on the sheer rocks as if they were winged. I did not know what the creatures were, then; the man told me.

Though we travelled through desolate places, all our paths were marked on either side by rounded stones, many of them carved with words I could not read. At times the stones were so many, they made a low wall on either side, and we were sheltered from the bitter winds. I asked the man what the carved words were. "They are travelling prayers," he told me. "The paths through these mountains are dangerous, handmaid, and the carved stones are our protection. Every time our shadow falls across a prayer, it is as if we speak it, and God listens and watches over us."

"But who placed the stones, lord?"

"Hundreds of travellers, over hundreds of years," he said.

Sometimes, when the wind dropped and our path was smooth, we looked out across vast wilderness places, ashen grey and hoary with mist. The hugeness of the icy wastes appalled me, yet at the same time I found them strangely comforting. They gave me space to think, and their cold was a cleansing thing. I could not have borne then the turmoil of the town we went to later. I needed this peace, barren and desolate though it was. And there was joy in being all day outside on the mountains.

It was a pleasure to walk tall and free with no load on my back; pleasure to be always in the pale grey light of day; pleasure, in a strange, exhilarating way, to be in the company of a Chosen, and know that he enjoyed my face.

Ours was an odd relationship. Sometimes we seemed almost equals, both of us in the service of the same high lord; yet at other times there was that great gulf fixed between us, because he was Chosen and I was Quelled. He found it almost impossible, I think, to come to terms with me. I guessed he had never spoken to a harsha before, let alone travelled and eaten and slept in one's company. Sometimes he forgot there was that gulf between us, and he looked in my face, smiling, and listened while I answered him. Those were the times he showed me how to light our fires with the strange flints used by the Chosen, and how to cook his unfamiliar foods. But at other times he seemed confused, remote, and there was a deep conflict in him. Then, he looked past my head when he spoke to me, the way the Chosen always did with the Quelled, and he gave instructions that did not need replies.

In my own confusion and inner conflict, my emotions swung between exultant joy and overwhelming grief. I could not think clearly, and even the simplest tasks the man asked me to do, I managed to bungle. At times he must have wondered if he had made a most appalling mistake. I wondered it myself, many times. Yet he was never impatient with me, never harsh or rude. He was totally unlike the Chosen who owned our mine.

Towards the end of the second day we came to a small cave high in the mountains. It was almost hidden under a low overhanging rock, and was similar to the cave in which we had spent the previous night. There were many of these caves, Amasai told me, all used by the Firelord on his journeys between the towns. He travelled all the time, sometimes going great distances to places needing new supplies of firestone, divining in the nearby mountains for the vital fuel. In the towns the Firelord stayed in the great houses of the Chosen, but out here in the mountains he had his own dwellings.

"It is my task, Elsha, to travel these ways twice a year, bringing a loaded cart, and to replenish his caves." Amasai waved his hand towards the shelves carved deep into the cave walls. These were packed with blankets, clothes, flints, cooking utensils, dried meat and fruit, and water jars. On the floor near the back of the cave were several baskets filled with firestones.

"He travels with a donkey, as well as with his handmaid," Amasai went on, arranging kindling grasses in the firepit in the cave floor. "He takes fresh clothes, some food, wine, and the things needful for his divining rituals. But much that is necessary is already here, waiting for him."

I handed him the flints, and watched while he lit the fire. He had beautiful hands, smooth and pale and incredibly clean. I hid my own black-stained fingers in my ragged sleeve, and asked: "Does no one steal from these caves?"

He glanced across the curling smoke at me, and smiled. "Look on the outside of the cave, Elsha."

I went out, stooping under the low entrance, and looked back at the overhanging rock. In the evening dimness it glistened with ice. On the rock face, carved deep, was the shape of a human eye, and in the centre of it was the sign of flame. My hand went to the golden disk about my neck. Wondering, I returned to the cave.

"That sign is enough to stop all but myself and the Firelord entering," Amasai said. "And you, now."

We were crouching together near the fire, both of us holding our hands towards the warmth; and he looked sideways into my face, and kept his eyes on me a long time. Under his gaze I felt vulnerable and afraid, and was more than ever aware that this was his world, and I was a stranger here.

"The Firelord's sign is sacred, Elsha," he explained quietly. "There is not a soul in the world would pass beneath his sign without his knowing. And there is no soul would lay a hand on you, as long as you wear his sign. Wear it always. It is your shield and your guard. But without this sign, you are shelterless. Do you understand?"

I nodded.

"There is much you have to learn, Elsha," he

said lightly, smiling again. "Tonight you will learn how to cook hezzin, our dried bullock meat. You are not too tired? You have walked all day."

"I am not tired, lord," I said, giving him a small smile tinged with pride. "I could walk twenty days on end, and still it would not equal one day's toil in Siranjaro mine."

He looked startled for a moment, and one fair eyebrow rose. "So. He chose you for your strength, did he, Elsha of the Quelled?"

I blushed again, and shook my head. "I do not know why he chose me, lord," I said.

His lips curved, and he stood up and went outside to unload the mule.

Under his instructions I washed my face and arms and hands, and cooked our meal. Then I sat in the cave entrance and waited while he ate. I faced the deepening night, and felt the evening wind cold as ice on my face. The cut from the whip still ached. I put my hand inside my dress and drew out the woman-stone. It lay on my palm, black as the night against my skin, humming with firestone power. Now it was all I had, of Siranjaro, my home, and him. I lifted it to my face, pressed its smooth surfaces against my cheek, and sobbed. I tried to cry quietly, so the man in the cave would not hear. But he came out, crouched in the cold shadows at my side, and put his hand on my shoulder. "Come in by the fire, Elsha," he said softly. "Come and eat. I've finished now."

Blindly, I followed him into the cave and sat down by the fire. I was still crying, the woman-stone still clutched in my hand. No man had seen me weep before, except Lesharo. I was ashamed and angry. Amasai said nothing, but after a while he got up and brought me a bowl of stew. I put the woman-stone on the dirt floor and took the bowl, though my appetite was gone and my stomach churned. He waited, crouching the way Lesharo did, his elbows on his knees, his hands folded quietly in front of him. But this man's sleeves were brilliant blue and edged with gold, and his hands were clean and beautiful. And he did not give me strength, as Lesharo gave me strength. This man drained strength out of me.

I bent my head over the bowl, and scooped out some of the stew with my bone spoon. I made myself eat. When I looked at Amasai again, he was holding the woman-stone, turning it over in his hands. I resented his touching it, but said nothing.

"This was a gift?" he asked, smiling at me. We looked into each other's faces all the time now, as if there were no longer laws for Quelled and Chosen.

"Yes, lord."

"From your husband?"

"No, lord. The Chosen had not yet designated me to a man. The woman-stone is from my friend."

Amasai looked at me strangely, as though something I had said saddened him. "You will never know covering now, Elsha," he said.

Confusion flooded me. I watched the fire, and my face grew hot. I suffered in these times he said things I did not understand. The Chosen language was very like our Quelled dialect, but they used words sometimes that were alien to us. He must have known my confusion, because he looked away quickly, and sighed. But he did not explain. The woman-stone turned in his hands, over and over, and he smoothed its rounded surfaces with his thumb, gently. I bent my head lower over my food, and forced myself to eat.

He got up and rolled out his fine sleeping mat on the other side of the fire, and lay down to read a small scrolled book. I watched him over my steaming bowl and through the fire, and listened to the howling of wild animals in the valley below. I thought of the silent shadows of the wolves, and was afraid. But if the man heard them, he took no notice. He glanced across at me after a while, and smiled.

"Can you read, Elsha?"

"No, lord," I said. "But I know my family sign. We have to show the overseer at the mine our sign, and he marks on the board beside it all the loads we bring out. I can read my sign."

"What is your family sign, Elsha?"

"The lion."

He drew a small knife from a leather sheath on his belt, and handed it to me. "Scratch your sign on the wall for me," he said.

I did; the circle for the lion's face, and the wavy lines going out from it, all around, that were the lion's mane. I cleaned the knife on my robe, and handed it back to the man. But his eyes were still on my family sign, and his face had a strange, deep look. "Are you sure that is a lion, Elsha?"

"Of course, lord. It has been my family's sign for generations. It is marked on the outside of my father's tent, and on our bowls and belongings. It is a lion."

He gave me a faint smile. "For the Chosen, that sign is a symbol for something else," he said.

"What else, lord?"

He took his knife and sheathed it, and did not tell me. But his eyes were on my face, and he was deep in thought. I sat and picked up my stew and began to eat again.

"The Chosen think that you Quelled cannot even talk," he murmured. "They think you have no intelligence, no mind."

I chewed my stew, and said nothing.

"You have a mind," he added quietly, his amazing violet eyes aglow. "Tell me what is in your mind, Elsha of the Quelled."

A moment I hesitated. Then I said: "Fire."

He rolled up his book, placed it on the mat beside him, and sat up. Being on opposite sides of the fire, we faced each other, and our faces were well lit. I wished mine were in the shadows. I did not like his quiet appraisal of me, as if he measured all my soul. I put the last of my meat aside until morning, stood up, and heated some water to wash our bowls. Always, his eyes followed me. It seemed an age before I sat down again, and I picked up the woman-stone and pretended to polish it. Still his eyes burned into me.

"So, there is fire," he said, as if no time had passed since last we spoke. "What else, Elsha?"

I looked straight into his face and said: "My mind is my own, lord."

"It is not your own," he said softly. "Not now. You are the Firelord's, now. Tell me what is in your mind, Elsha, besides fire."

"Love," I said, tearing my eyes from his face, and looking at the woman-stone I held. "Love for myths and legends, music and song, and firestone power, and dreams."

He leaned forward, his face solemn and intense. "Ah — there we have it," he said quietly. "Firestone power, and dreams. Those words the Firelord says to me. Firestone power, and dreams. And you mentioned legends, Elsha. What legends are there, of the Quelled?"

I lifted my head. "Legends of a world filled with light," I said. "Legends of a huge orb burning in the sky, that gave warmth and light and life, and there was no need then for our little fires. No need for firestones, mines, or Quelled. In those days, all were Chosen. We Quelled were lords, then. We lived in great dwellings high in the mountains, with vast gardens that hung there in the shining light, gardens of green trees and fruit and many-coloured flowers. And our children played in the light, and were naked, and were not cold. Because the light was warm."

He was leaning forward still, his eyes fastened on my face, his own face frowning and intent. "What changed the world, Elsha, to make it cold?"

"Men were evil, lord, and God regretted that he had created them. So he made death come out of the sky and shake the earth, and he smote his fist on the land, and covered it with dust and dark. And the light withdrew behind the darkness, and cold came."

I blushed, suddenly self-conscious, thinking myself mad for talking so earnestly of fantasy. "They are only myths, lord," I mumbled. "My father tells them to us, and our musicians sing of them."

Amasai said nothing, but got up and threw more firestones on the fire. The flames spat and leapt, and I thought I had angered him. I asked, to placate him: "You have legends, lord?"

He sat down again, picked up his book, and unrolled it. He read for a while, and I thought he had forgotten me. Then he began reading aloud.

"These, Elsha, are the words of our great Prophet, Tharan: *In the time at the beginning of the new world, there was found a race of people left over from the old. The people of this race were hidden in the earth, and were without minds or souls, and their hearts were dry like the dust from which they came. And God looked on that race, and saw that it was evil, and he*

49

called it Quelled. Then God saw the beasts that were left, and the great cold that afflicted them. And God called forth a new race that was wise and good, that would restore the world. He called the new race his Chosen ones, and they were highest of all, and had wisdom and knew all truth; and God gave them dominion over the birds and beasts, and over the secrets of hidden fire, and over the race called Quelled. And the Chosen shall rule for all time."

I stared into the fire, and did not dare open my mouth.

"This is from our sacred writings," he said. "What do you think of them, Elsha?"

The temptation was overwhelming, but still my lips were sealed.

He laughed softly, rolled up the book, and threw it onto his pile of belongings at the back of the cave. "Come, Elsha," he said, "I know your tongue burns with words. Spit them out."

I looked him straight in the eye and said: "Your prophet is a liar."

The smile died on his face. Still I looked at him, though my palms grew wet with sweat, and my heart thundered. Slowly he smiled again, and I could have sworn that his eyes looked almost admiring.

"God help us," he said. "I have found a firebrand."

An icy wind blew into the cave, whirling up dust and ash, and making the flames dance. I shivered, and pulled my robes closer about me.

Amasai got up, went over to his scarlet travelling bag, and took a leather bottle out of a deep pocket in the side. He brought it over to the fire, uncorked it, and drank a few mouthfuls. He sat beside me, close to the fire as he could get, and offered the bottle to me.

"It is our best Chosen wine," he said. "It will warm you like a fire inside."

I took the bottle, shot him a curious look, and drank. After a while he grabbed the bottle from me, spilling the tawny liquid down my chin.

"God, Elsha — a sip or two, I meant!" he cried. "Have you never drunk before?"

"Often," I said, wiping my hand across my chin, and licking off the fiery drops. "Water, though."

He wiped the bottle carefully, and replaced the cork. He put the bottle back in its special place in the bag.

The fire flared up, dazzling, and the flames had never seemed more beautiful. A glowing warmth enveloped me; a deep, rapturous feeling that all the world was wonderful. I watched the flames, saw visions in them, and could have wept for joy.

Amasai, oblivious to the miracle that was happening, spread his furs across his sleeping mat, crawled in, and closed his eyes. I sang, I think; but I do not know whether it was to myself, or aloud. After a while Amasai opened one eye, half smiled, and asked: "Are you sleeping tonight, Elsha?"

"It's too marvellous a night to sleep," I think I said.

He got up and spread my sleeping mat out for me, and placed my furs on it. My furs. Last night my furs had been an unfamiliar luxury, soft and strange. Tonight they were pure deliciousness. At some time I peeled off all my clothes and squirmed naked into them, and the feeling flew my mind away. I had a dream that I danced by the fire, naked and shining, with my furs half draped about me.

I hope it was a dream.

5

My Strange Philosophy

The town sprawled below us — a bustling, dusty, noisy turmoil of animals and people. Stone huts clustered about the tents and awnings of a busy marketplace, and above rose the majestic houses of the rich.

"It is Jinnah, the centre for all our trade," explained Amasai, checking the ropes and leather straps of the mule's travelling bags. "It is the hub of all the roads through the mountains. Here are sold cloth, pottery, metal utensils, clothing, and things of wood. And they buy in firestones, since here there is no mine." He straightened up, and gave me a meaningful look. "And there are no Quelled," he added.

I looked down the winding track between the rocks, down at the dust and noise and turbulence, and my heart sank. "No Quelled at all, lord?"

"Only you. I am meeting the Firelord here, now that the great festival is finished." He hesitated, his marvellous eyes looking down across the town. "It will be difficult for you from now on, Elsha. Put out of your mind the way things were between you and me, on this journey. You are Quelled. All in this place are Chosen. Never has a Quelled set foot on this road or in this town. We must not be parted."

He came close to me and put his hands on my neck, feeling for the chain. He drew the Firelord's sign from under my robes and hung it outside, where it shone. "I will not let them harm you, Elsha," he said gravely, "but I cannot stop their hate. Stay very close to me."

He picked up the reins of the mule, and together we stumbled down the steep track. We went down past the first stone huts, and children playing on the road stared, curious and horrified, at my brand. One of them ran into a hut. A man came out, looked at me, and spat. "Quelled!" he shouted. He called other things, things I didn't understand, and more people came out and started yelling. The children threw stones, and Amasai roared at them. We walked on, Amasai pulling the terrified beast as well as me. He held my right hand hard, but still with every step my fear and apprehension grew.

I pulled my hood low over my forehead and covered my brand. But the people knew, and threatened and taunted me. They swarmed near, and some threw stones and swore and spat. Something tripped me and I fell, helpless, dragging Amasai with me. He pulled me up and shouted something in my ear, and walked with his left arm tight about me.

We came into the marketplace, and I saw brown and yellow awnings over stalls of vegetables, clay pots, and cages piled high and filled with screaming birds. The tumult was deafening. The air was full of dust and confusion, the mob pressed close, though not close enough to touch me; and rocks and sticks struck me from behind. Amasai crushed me to him, half dragging me through the turmoil. At times I closed my eyes, too terrified to look; and when I did look, I saw a multitude of faces all shouting, hostile and savage. Something struck me in the face, hard, and my head snapped back. Light splintered across dark, and the world spun. I heard, as if far away, Amasai roaring in anger, and felt him grip the Firelord's sign I wore, and raise it high until the chain cut my neck. "She is his handmaid!" he cried, and for a moment the crowd moved back.

We pressed on, and I could hear Amasai swearing awful oaths, and our mule snorting with fear on the other side of him. Then the shouting started again, and the mob closed in. They hit me from behind, where he couldn't see, and a woman rushed up with a bucket in her hands and emptied something foul over me. It missed my face, but the stink made me retch. I tripped and fell, and Amasai's arm was wrenched away.

Heavy boots smashed into my ribs and legs, and something hard and sharp cut across my back. I fought for breath. I heard screams, and wondered whether they were mine.

Then I was on my feet again, being dragged, half carried, through the chaos. There was a sound like thunder; a door crashed shut, a bolt shot home, and there was quiet.

I tried to stand. My legs were like water, my whole body trembled, and a red darkness swam before my eyes. Someone lifted me, pushed back my hair, and fingered the welt on my face. My vision cleared.

Amasai alone was with me, as dusty and dishevelled as I was. "That was an impressive beginning, Elsha," he murmured, with a pale smile. "You caused a riot. I don't doubt you'll cause worse."

I must have shown my dismay, because his face softened, and his fingers on my cheek grew gentle as they brushed away the dirt. "But for now, you are safe. We are at the house where my high lord stays." He looked at me straight, and his eyes were deep and full of fervent things. He added very quietly: "More than any other woman's, Elsha of the Quelled, I have enjoyed your company."

He sighed, turned to the mule behind us, and smoothed its wet and trembling neck. He took a waterskin out of one of the travelling bags, and washed his face and hands. He was obsessed with cleanliness. Our first night in a cave he had made me wash, all over, while he waited outside in the freezing wind.

I looked at the place we had come to. We were in a large courtyard with walls on three sides. On the fourth side was a high, long building, painted white. It had ten rows of windows going up, and many doors leading from the courtyard to the lowest floor. The doors were all painted around the edges with vivid greens and golds, and the windows had richly carved shutters of metal and wood. Brilliant banners hung from the windowsills, and bright flags fluttered from the high roof.

"Stay here while I find my lord," said Amasai, when he had finished his wash. He looked pale and apprehensive. "When I have spoken with him, I will send out a servant to bring you." He strode away across the courtyard, and vanished through one of the painted doors.

I could hear my heart drumming, and the sounds of the distant marketplace. I could hear children laughing, and men shouting. They were fierce, bold, brazen sounds, unlike any I was used to. More than ever before, I felt alone — utterly alone.

A door opened at one end of the house, and a man came out. He came to me across the blowing yellow dust, gazed into the air above my head, and commanded me to follow him. As we neared the house I realised how high it was, how huge and overpowering. Never had I been inside any place except the mine, and our tents. Now, as I stepped across the threshold of this place, darkness swallowed me, and a deep musty silence. There were smells of sweet incense, ancient woven hangings, and old wood. I followed the man through vast rooms painted white and hung with immense flags and tapestries. The rooms were dim, and through the cracks in the carved window shutters came shafts of pale light, and shimmering clouds of dust. There were dark, twisting passages, smaller rooms containing statues and wooden furniture, and steep shadowy stairs. All the floors were wood, and some were covered with carpets.

The servant took me to one of the smaller rooms high under the roof, and said to the air above my head: "Women will bring water so that you may wash, harsha, and they will help you dress in clean garments."

I looked straight into his face, and thanked him. He flushed with anger, still without meeting my eyes, and went out.

I turned around slowly, and examined the room. It was small, compared with some of the other rooms through which we had passed; but still it was ten times bigger than my father's tent. There was furniture: a bed, covered with silken quilts and cushions, and several splendid furs; a carved wooden chest inlaid with ivory; a low table with a huge tasselled cushion on the floor beside it; a cabinet with latticed doors; wall hangings of glowing saffron, green, and vermilion; jars of bronze and cups of silver; and thick, dark-coloured carpets. A huge fireplace stood in one wall, backed and surrounded with sooty stones. I did not know at that time what all the things in the room were called; a woman told me later. All the wooden furniture, and the house itself, was made hundreds of years before in the days when there were trees, and wood was plentiful.

It all was wonderful to me, and mysterious. I went over to the wooden cabinet with latticed doors. The catch on the cabinet confounded me for a moment; then it fell open, and I pulled back the doors. Scrolls. Rows and rows of scrolled books, all the colour of clean bone, smooth, and smelling of great age. I lifted one out, carefully, and unrolled it. The parchment was thick, and covered with beautifully even black writing. I could read none of it, of course; but I held the book high and said solemnly: "These are the myths of the Quelled, spoken by the wise woman, she who is called Elsha. In the beginning God created all men and women equal, but the women were a little higher than the men; and God was good and loved all his people. But one day in a desperate time, some wicked men rose up and overpowered the peaceful ones. And the wicked ones called themselves Chosen, and the peaceful ones they called Quelled. Those were not the names God gave to the people: those were the names given by the oppressors, and those names were not true. But the Chosen were not always strong, and the Quelled were not always subdued."

There was a slight cough behind me, and I spun around, hot with terror and guilt. Behind me stood a man.

He was tall, and wore all red. His clothing was different from that of other Chosen; his robes were long down to his feet, and fell in thick folds. He had a pointed black beard, and thick hair receding from his forehead. He was old, yet his face seemed strangely young, and he was dark-skinned, noble, and strong. His eyebrows were black and straight, and almost joined above his large hooked nose. His mouth was strong and well-formed, his upper lip coming out a little over his lower one, giving him a distant, dignified look. His cheekbones were high and prominent, his eyes heavy-lidded, the lashes thick and black. I had seen no other man like him.

I stared at him, entranced, the scroll crushed to my breast, my voice lost. I forgot I was harsha and he was Chosen, and that I was breaking laws. If he was angry, he did not show it. Besides, he broke the law himself, staring as he was intently at my face.

"You *are* harsha," he murmured. His voice was incredibly deep, sonorous, and powerful.

I nodded, my mouth hanging open, stupidly. His eyes fascinated me.

"I heard you reading from a sacred book," he said, crossing the carpet between us.

I swallowed nervously, and blinked up at him. His eyes, black and gold like burning firestones, smiled down on me. I smiled back. "It wasn't really your prophet, lord," I said. "I can't read."

"Oh." He took the scroll from me, smoothed it flat, and rolled it up again. "I thought the philosophy was strange," he murmured.

"It was mine, lord. My philosophy."

"You do have one, do you, harsha?" he asked, frowning and smiling at the same time, tapping the scroll against his strong chin. His beard, in parts, was streaked with grey. Like Amasai, he looked into my eyes. "What is your philosophy?" he asked.

A warning buzzed in my head, urgently, but I ignored it.

"I think you Chosen have it all wrong, lord," I said. "I think your myths are wrong, your beliefs are a curse on the whole world, and your prophet is a liar." I looked into his face. It was grave, attentive, and he nodded slightly. Astounded and encouraged, I poured on him the pain and humiliation of eleven years in Siranjaro mine.

"Look!" I cried, holding out my hands. "Two arms, two hands, the same as you. I have a mind, a language, feelings, myths, dreams. We Quelled are the same as you Chosen. The only difference is the mark of the brand — the mark you forced on us. We weren't born with it. We're equal. Equal with you. Yet you treat us worse than your animals. You brand and enslave and kill us slowly in the mines. Your treatment of us is wrong, evil, and unendurable." I paused, breathing hard, and suddenly realised we were not alone.

At some stage Amasai had come in. He was staring at me in disbelief, his face white with horror. Suddenly he turned to the man I had been talking to, and flung himself full-length before him.

"My high lord," he said, his voice muffled against the floor, "high lord, I grieve most deeply my mistake. I brought the harsha here to be your handmaid, and find she is depraved. High lord, I crave your pardon. I crave . . ."

Whatever else he craved, I never knew. I fainted.

6

The Firelord

Freezing water struck my face, and furious hands shook my shoulders, lifting me. I groaned and tried to pull away. My head ached.

"You have disgraced me!" cried a man's voice, wild with rage and despair, and I looked up and saw Amasai bending over me. He let me go, suddenly, and I fell against the stone wall. He began pacing the floor, his fine boots leaving flattened marks on the soft mat. He swore, and ran his hands through his long fair hair, and turned on me with a look that terrified.

"You have destroyed everything!" he shouted, and for a moment I thought he would strike me. "You have destroyed my standing with the high lord, my honour, his trust in me. You have made a mockery of me, my service, our Chosen laws, our religion. You have mocked the high lord. Mocked everything — everything Chosen! You are a fool, harsha! You had everything within your grasp — the highest hope of every highborn woman — and you destroyed it."

He turned away, breathing heavily, and tried to calm himself. I sat crushed against the wall, weeping.

"I thought," he said, in a low, passionate voice, "I believed I knew why he had chosen you. I believed there was a strength in you, a flame, that set you apart from every other woman, Quelled or Chosen. I thought I understood that strength, and why the Firelord wanted you. I was wrong. He was wrong. You are wrong. We all are wrong. You're a fool. I don't know if you can even go back to your mine. Sedition is dangerous. People with words like yours have their tongues torn out, or are killed. I couldn't endure — "

He went over to the window and leaned on the ledge, looking down. His breathing was uneven, and several times he passed his hand over his face.

A servant came in, bowed low to Amasai, and said: "The high lord would speak to you, master, about the fate of the harsha you brought."

Amasai nodded without looking around, and the servant went out. For a long time Amasai stood there in the window's sombre light, looking down. Then he sighed and, without glancing at me or speaking again, went out.

It seemed an age I crouched there, tortured with grief and remorse. My head ached intolerably, and I wanted to vomit. With everything in me I hated my madness, my blind stupidity, my own accursed tongue that had destroyed my dreams. I wept and wrung my hands, anguished. That I could have seen *him* — could have looked into his face and heard his voice, and not recognised him — that was the cruelest irony of all. I crushed my fists into my eyes and pretended this was all a nightmare, and I was still in the mine at Siranjaro, my dreams intact, unspoiled.

The door opened and closed behind me, and I pressed harder against the wall, shaking and sobbing.

Someone knelt behind me, and I felt a hand on my shoulder.

"Elsha," said Amasai, softly.

I shrugged his hand off, and hid my face. He was gentle now, come to tell me that I was to die.

"Elsha, I was wrong. You are still to be his handmaid, and there will be no punishment. You are to have a bath and put on clean garments and eat and drink, and after that the high lord will speak with you." His hand was on my shoulder again, and I felt his smooth cold fingers brush my cheek. "Elsha, do not weep anymore. All is well."

I cried harder, from confusion and relief and nerves stretched way too far.

"I confess, I do not understand," he sighed, standing up. "I am all confused."

"*You're* confused?" I choked. "You told me I'd be killed, or have my tongue torn out. Now you say I'm just to have another wash."

"I know, Elsha." He was laughing, quietly. "Here — let me help you up."

He helped me to my feet, brushed back my tangled hair, and wiped my face with his hands. "I don't understand anything anymore," he muttered. "A rebel is vindicated, heresy is excused, and a harsha is the highest female in the land. You'll drive me mad, Elsha of the Quelled."

But he was smiling as he left.

If I had any false pride, any illusions about my worth, they were dispelled that day. Amasai had called me the highest female in the land. And so I was: but I was also Quelled, and I learned now what that meant to the Chosen.

Several women came and lit a fire in my room, and brought in a massive copper tub. They filled it with hot water from large clay jars, which they must have carried up countless stairs and passages. Then they told me to strip and get in. They spoke to me slowly, with many gestures, as if I were unintelligent. Their attitude nettled me. "I washed yesterday," I said. "All over. I'm already clean."

My voice startled them, blew away generations of belief. They stared, astounded. Then one of them, tight-lipped, commanded me to do as I was directed.

I was too tired for a fight, so I took off all my clothes and stepped into the scalding bath. Never had I been totally immersed in water, hot or cold. The heat scalded me, made my skin pink, my fingers look like boiled grubs, and my head throb. The steam filled the room like a mist, and I felt suffocated. But it was a pleasant sensation, once I was used to it; and the heat eased the bruises I had got with Amasai on our struggle through the town.

The women gave me a cloth, a large rough piece of soap, and a small hard brush made of animal hair. They told me to scrub myself until every black speck and stain of the mine was gone. It must have taken me most of the afternoon. The water was cold when I finished. Even my nails were clean, and the soles of my feet. My hair was the colour of wheat in the firelight, cleaner than it had ever been.

The women spread out clothes for me, taken from the large carved wooden chest. One at a time the garments were handed to me: a fine woven underdress, pure white, and falling loosely to the floor; a crimson long-sleeved overdress, split from neck to waist, the embroidered hem falling just short of the white hem underneath; a wide yellow sash made of silk; and black fur-lined boots reaching almost to my knees. Over it all I wore a long sleeveless tunic of pure black fur. The crimson dress had a deep pocket in one side, into which I placed my woman-stone. The women, curious and whispering, watched me all the time.

The overdress had silken cords in front, but I did not know how to lace them up. I asked one of the women to help, but she became confused, uncooperative, and angry with me. She tried to explain how the lacing went, but I ended up with the cords in knots. "Show me," I said, exasperated. "I've not worn clothes like these before. Do it for me, please."

She took a deep breath and came close, and unwillingly, as if it caused her distress or pain, she lifted her hands and untied all the knots I had made. She did it all correctly, so that the scarlet cords crossed in a design all up the front, a brilliant pattern against the white beneath. Then she backed away, her hands held out in front of her, her eyes downcast. The other women moved aside, and one of them poured some clean water into an unused copper bowl, and placed it beside a new piece of soap and a towel I had not touched. Then the woman who had touched me washed her hands, meticulously, with a painstaking care that was almost a ritual. I watched, at first curious and bewildered; and then I realised why she washed, and humiliation swept over me.

She had touched me. Me, the harsha, unclean, low-caste, of the race of slaves. None of the other women in the room that day had actually touched me; she alone had. And now she washed, thoroughly, as if to cleanse her whole being.

I turned away, sick to my soul. In the year to come, I would know all forms of rejection and scorn; but nothing hurt as much as that simple, ritualistic washing of a woman's hands.

Those eyes again. I glanced at them, my heart leaping, then looked down. I remembered what I had been told, and bowed low, then lay full-length on the carpet in front of him. I smelled wool and rope, and the polished wood beneath. I waited.

"You may stand, handmaid," he said.

I rose with as much dignity as I could, caught my heel in my long hem, and heard something rip. Cautiously I straightened, my eyes on the floor at his feet, my face burning.

"Have you eaten?" he asked gently.

"Yes, high lord. Thank you."

"The women — they were considerate?"

"Yes, thank you."

"You are not wearing my sign," he observed. "The sign Amasai gave to you."

"I . . . I think I left it in my room, high lord. I took it off when I had my bath."

"Wear it always, even when you sleep."

"Yes, high lord. I'm sorry."

"Has Amasai told you what your tasks will be?"

"He said I was to be your handmaid, lord. I am to cook your meals and wash your clothes and accompany you on your journeys to divine for firestones. He taught me how to cook hezzin, and how to light fires your Chosen way. He told me I had to keep clean. He said things would be difficult for me."

"And are they, handmaid?"

I hesitated. "High lord, I find it hard in your world . . . being harsha."

He chuckled quietly, and I looked into his face, surprised. He was watching me. I dropped my gaze again, quickly.

"That much I understood," he said.

He was silent for a while, and I had the unsettling sensation that his eyes were moving through my mind, reading my fears, my hopes, and all my most terrible rebellious dreams. It was to become a familiar feeling when I was with him. After a long time, when I was sure he knew every last burning secret, he said: "Why do you carry a firestone, handmaid?"

I was surprised, and guilty for being surprised. My heart raced. "It was a gift, high lord."

"May I see it?"

I took the woman-stone out of my pocket, and held it out towards him, flat on my outstretched palm. He picked it up, and his fingers brushed mine. I waited for him to go away and wash, as the woman had when she had touched me; but he stayed where he was, relaxed and princely in his carved chair, examining my woman-stone. His hands, like Amasai's, were clean and beautiful. But the Firelord's hands were dark, like his face, and his fingers were delicate and fine, with long nails that shone like dark polished bone. He gave me back the woman-stone, and said: "When I am divining, make sure you do not carry this. It will be a distraction to me."

"Yes, high lord."

"And now, there are certain things you need to know. Lift your eyes when I speak to you, harsha. No — not to my face. But lift your head. I cannot abide people who feign humility."

I looked at his left shoulder, and saw that he wore a thick black cloak over his robes, fastened on his shoulder with a large red stone.

"That is better," he murmured. "You know a little of the way in which the Chosen regard the Quelled. There are laws which must not be violated. The basic laws you know, from your dealings with your overseers at Siranjaro mine. You understand that, to the Chosen, you are less than an animal, unclean. They believe you have no intelligence, no rights, no soul."

"Lord, I think — "

"I am very much aware of what you think, harsha. But in your thinking you are alone. Now every other person in your life is of the Chosen race, and of the opinion that you are a lesser being. I cannot overnight alter this discrimination. It is ingrained in centuries of Chosen thought, as much a part of us as our love of fire and freedom and the strength of men. Always for the rest of your life you will bear the burden of that prejudice.

"You will remember the things of the Chosen that are sacred, that you must not touch: you must not touch a Chosen himself, not his skin or garments, or his bowls or cups or knives, or his food or the places where he eats or sits or lies down. Neither may you touch the women, for they, too, are sacred to you, though not so sacred as the men. You may not walk in front of a Chosen, or beside him; you may not walk in his footsteps if he leaves them in the dust. You may not look in the face of a Chosen, since his eyes are the windows of his soul, which you are not worthy to see. No Chosen will look on your face, and he will not speak with you unless it is necessary.

"I know there will be difficulties. When you are travelling alone with me in the mountains, it will be necessary for you to handle my bowls and cups and prepare my food, and to wash my garments. You are permitted to speak with me at any time, unless I speak with a Chosen, and then you may not interrupt, even though you are my handmaid. At all times you will wear my sacred sign, and will be permitted to speak with the Chosen when necessary. At no time will you look in the face of a Chosen, or be in any way disobedient, arrogant, or defiant. Being my handmaid does not lessen your being Quelled in the smallest degree. Do you understand these things?"

I shook my head. "Lord, I am confused," I said. "I'm sorry. You say there are laws that must not be violated, and times when they will have to be broken. Lord, wouldn't it be easier if I didn't remain Quelled?"

"It is not a question of remaining Quelled, harsha. You *are* Quelled. You bear the mark of the Quelled on your forehead. There is no skill, no power on earth can take that mark away. I cannot suddenly declare you Chosen. You are Quelled. I cannot change that. I can only, in special circumstances, suspend our laws, and make life as easy for you as I can."

He lowered his voice, and added gently: "I know your nature, Elsha. It grieves me that you must remain Quelled, alone in a world that despises you. But there is nothing I can do about that. Yet."

Not all of it despises me, I thought thankfully, remembering Amasai.

"Amasai confessed that he has broken all the laws," went on the Firelord, and I was so startled, I looked at his face. It was very grave, and his eyes burned through me. I dropped my gaze again, and felt guilty and afraid.

"Amasai was deeply shocked to find that you were Quelled. Others, too, will be shocked, but they will not be so sympathetic. We have a long fight ahead of us, handmaid. While we are guests in this house you will learn from the women here all the duties that you will perform. In thirty days we will leave for the mine of Talbar, across the western range. Ask the women of this house anything you need to know."

"Yes, high lord."

"You may go."

"High lord? May I ask you something?"

"You are permitted to ask anything of me, handmaid."

"High lord, why is it that no Chosen will look on my face, but you do?"

"The Chosen believe that to look on your face is to risk defiling their souls."

"But you take that risk, lord?"

He hesitated. When he did speak, his voice was rich and warm, and I could have sworn he smiled. "My soul is strong, handmaid, and cannot be defiled."

I half smiled, myself. "My soul, too, is strong," I said.

"You have no soul, harsha."

"That, lord, is for God to decide."

I heard his chair creak as if he leaned forward, or stood. I dared not look at him.

"Go, handmaid," he said.

I bowed low, and remembered to walk backwards out of his presence.

Those thirty days at the great house were extremely difficult for me, and I think I broke at least one law every time I moved or opened my mouth. I spent my days in the vast, cold kitchens on the bottom floor. Dark, busy, smelling of damp stone, rancid meat, grain, vegetables, live fowl, fowl freshly killed, drying pork, blood, ash, and fire — the kitchens were my great learning place.

And I had much to learn: a whole new life. What was easy routine to the women was often bizarre and difficult to me. The women were always patient and courteous; but there was warmth between themselves, and coldness towards me. I longed to join in their laughter, to chatter with them around a big bowl of wheat cakes hot from the ovens, chase the chickens with them, or crowd with them close to the blazing fire. Always I was left apart, standing separate and alone. I lived in fear of accidentally brushing against the women's clothes, or touching their fingers when they gave me things. And always, always, I had to remember not to look at their faces. I felt alienated, and the house oppressed me.

There was only one place I loved, one place I was liberated and happy: out in the mountains behind the house. There, out in the wind and lofty heights, I went with the house-owner's son and I learned something fine. I learned to fly a falcon.

I alone, of all the women in that great house, was permitted to go to the mews and choose a falcon for myself; and I alone was allowed to own such a bird, and train him to respond to my commands, and to have him hunt for me.

Kallai was my falcon's name.

He had eyes blacker than firestone, though

sometimes in the light they burned deep gold; soft creamy feathers marked with brown on his breast and legs; and his head and wings were dark. He wore narrow leather straps attached to his legs, by which I held him when he was on my fist; and he had a long leather leash attached to the ends of the straps. He had two brass bells tied to his legs, by which I knew his landing place if he went down out of sight among rocks or tussock grass. He never tried to leave my fist unless I removed his leash and held my wrist high into the wind, so he could take flight. And when he flew . . .

Oh, when he flew, he moved so fast and fine, he took my soul with him. So high he flew, spiralling upwards almost out of sight; and then he'd spy his prey — a raven maybe, or a rook — and he'd dive, and with his great talons strike it down. Then he'd come back to me. And we'd walk, a long way sometimes, to pick up the quarry and take it back to our kitchens for fresh meat that night.

Kallai and I became inseparable. Always, when not in the kitchens or involved with other household duties, I wore on my left arm my leather glove, and Kallai. Flying him was the only thing that I did well; it was my one joy, my triumph.

I managed, after a while, to live fairly well within the laws, though I longed for the time when my high lord and I would leave. I was more comfortable with him than with anyone else. Except Amasai.

I saw Amasai again, just one more time.

We were all working late one afternoon, getting ready for the evening meal. I was preparing my own meal, which I would eat alone later in my room. I worked in a far corner of the kitchen, away from the windows and the main door, out of everybody's way. It was dark where I was, and smoky, and the only light came from the fires. The first and second cooks were arguing over which herbs to put in the stew, and several of the younger cooks were chasing hens around the benches, trying to catch one for the pot, and shrieking with laughter. Noise and smoke filled the dark air, and the place was warm from work and hot stone ovens and the open fires. I loved these times, when they were all half crazy and I could laugh and forget I was not one of them.

Suddenly it was quiet. I looked behind me and saw a man standing in the far doorway, dark and tall against the afternoon light. Immediately, the two chief cooks smoothed back their hair, straightened their red aprons, and knelt and touched the floor at his feet. The younger women ignored the hens, pushed back their tumbled hair, and rearranged their rumpled skirts. I saw that several of them blushed, and whispered behind their hands. Whoever their rare male visitor was, he had a startling effect on them. I smiled, amused, and turned back to my vegetables. Then I heard the name Amasai, and my hands were still.

"The handmaid!" someone said, and the silence deepened. All their eyes were on me. I bent over my bench, and pretended I had heard nothing. If he wanted me, he could come to me.

I heard boots stride over the stones, and stop a little way behind me. The women were silent, watching, wondering.

"Elsha of the Quelled," he said, and it seemed a hundred years since I had heard that voice. "I would speak with you."

I washed my hands in a small bowl, dried them, and turned around. I bent and touched the shadowed floor at his feet. "Welcome, lord," I murmured, and stood up again. I longed to look at his face, but risked only a glance at his right shoulder, near his face. He looked at a point just beside my head, and I knew he smiled. The firelight cast a red glow down across the right side of his face and body, and his hair was the colour of flame. The heat of the stone ovens made my whole body unbearably hot, and my throat felt suddenly parched.

"I would not have chosen this place to talk," he said quietly, and I was aware of the utter silence in the room, of the women straining to hear what he said. "I would have talked with you privately, but I have much to do, and you are elusive."

"I go out often, lord, hunting with Kallai."

"I have heard that you manage your falcon well," he murmured. "I would have liked to have gone hunting with you, sometime."

He hesitated, and I sensed unease in him. I

wondered why he had come, why he seemed so perturbed. He turned suddenly and made an angry gesture towards the listening women. "Have you all nothing to do?" he cried, and they leapt into action. But they were nowhere near as noisy as before, and they all happened to be working in places nearby that gave them a good view of Amasai's back. I suppose even his back looked fine, straight and lordly as it was. And they could look easily at his hair, rippling long and golden in the fire's light. I had to be content with what the edges of my eyes could see, though he stood within an arm's reach of me, and looked into my face.

"I am going away, Elsha," he said. "Look at me, will you?"

"The women will see," I said.

"Then turn your back to the fire. No — then I cannot see your face. Oh, damn the women!" He looked away, bent his head, and sighed. "I am going to the northern territories," he said, his voice very low. "My high lord has made me commander of his army."

"I didn't know he had an army," I said, surprised. "Does he need one?"

"He has always had an army, to protect our mines and towns against invasion. But more than ever, he needs one now. There are rumours of insurrection in some of the larger mines. The Quelled are becoming restless. I saw that look, Elsha. Joy, was it? By God, you frighten me."

"I hardly have the power for that, my lord."

"You have more power than you know. Are the women watching us?"

I glanced past his shoulder. "Like hawks, lord."

He sighed again, heavily, and glanced down at his hands, clasped on his jewelled leather belt. He dropped his voice so low that I could hardly hear. "Elsha, listen. I will not see you again. That pains me. When — if there is a time when you are no longer his handmaid, will you come to the northern territories, to me?"

"Lord, I thought I am to be his handmaid always, until he dies, or until I displease him. The women said his other handmaid died, and the one before that was — "

"Elsha! Elsha, I did not come to talk women's tattle. We have so little time. Will you promise me this one thing — that when you are released, you will come to me?"

"Why, lord? It is a soldier you want, not a handmaid. I've never held a sword, or shot an arrow, or — "

He groaned, and ran his hand through his hair. The firelight leapt on his face, and I thought I had angered him. When he spoke again, his voice was low and hoarse, his breathing quick and uneven.

"I curse the man who put that brand on you, Elsha! I curse our whole creed, that marks you Quelled and me Chosen. If I could put out my eyes or cut off my hands to wipe your forehead clean, I would. If — " His voice broke, and he turned away from me, towards the smoky kitchen. One of the girls looked up from plucking a hen, saw his face, and looked quickly away.

"Lord," I said, "I promise that if I am ever in the north, I will try to find you. It shouldn't be too difficult, with a whole army for your company."

He turned back to me, and smiled. I looked straight in his face, not caring who saw. I had forgotten how beautiful he was. "I will always count you among my highest friends, my lord," I said.

"Only among them, Elsha? Not highest? Not best?"

"The best can kiss my cheek, my lord, and hold my hand and play his pipes to me."

"And I can only command an army for you," he said, with a sad smile. "Tell me you won't forget me."

"I never forget my friends, lord."

He knelt, suddenly, and touched the stone floor at my feet. When he stood up again, his eyes were wet. "I salute you, Elsha of the Quelled. In my heart I embrace you."

Abruptly, he turned and left.

Shocked silence descended on the kitchen. I felt the women's eyes on me; felt their amazement, their utter disbelief. Then a dog ran in, caused havoc among the hens, and several younger women rushed to put him out. I bent over my vegetables, low, and could hardly see to work.

7

A Friend

The mountain air, misty and edged with snow, cut across my face and crept into my bones. My body ached with cold, and I could no longer feel my feet. My left forearm, heavily gloved and bearing my falcon, was numb with fatigue. Kallai sat hunched, hungry and stiff, his feathers fluffed. I could not fly him in this mist; we would have lost each other in moments. So he had not hunted today, and we both were hungry.

The Firelord was further up the mountain, striding beside his donkey, oblivious of me. We had been travelling nine days now, and I was used to his need for solitude, his strange, quiet way of closing invisible doors between us. Sometimes he walked alone, remote, lost in a distant inner world. Sometimes when we were together, his eyes wore a veiled look, and I knew not to speak to him. But sometimes he was warm and amiable, easy-tempered and talkative. He did not touch me and was not tender, as Amasai had been; but he was gracious without being condescending, and I felt no strain between us. We kept loosely to the Chosen laws, though I stretched my privileges to the limits, and sometimes overstepped them. He did not punish me, and in all his corrections he was not harsh. It was as if with him I was not Quelled. He called me handmaid or Elsha. He no longer called me harsha, or made me feel in any way a lesser human being. For that I loved him.

At night we stayed in tiny caves, each one guarded with his sacred sign. Sometimes in the night I woke, disturbed by the wind or the placid snorting of his donkey, or the howling of wolves on the distant mountain slopes; and always I felt straight away a warm tranquillity, a sense of joy in my high lord's presence. I felt at one with him, at peace.

He stopped walking after a while, and waited for me at a wide part of the icy track. I caught up with him and stopped a little way behind him, to his left. He stood with his back to me, one hand about his silver and wood divining staff, the other holding the short rope about his donkey's neck. Mist clung about him in veils. He wore black edged with scarlet, and his belt was studded with red stones and silver. He wore no hood, even in that biting cold, and his long greying hair flowed down over the black fur of his collar. His robes fell in kingly folds down to his feet, and his boots were red and grey, and the finest I'd seen. He let go his donkey's rope, and beckoned to me.

"There is Talbar," he said. I stood beside him and looked beyond the crumbling cliff at his feet.

Talbar lay below us, wreathed in fog. It was a small mining town in a valley. In spaces between the mist I glimpsed houses of dirty grey, only two or three stories high. In the distance, pale with cloud, were the tattered tents of the Quelled.

The Firelord turned and said: "You are not afraid, Elsha, of a strange town?"

I gave him a grin, my eyes on the dusting of ice on his shoulder. "I'm not afraid, my lord," I said, teeth chattering. "I am so cold, I won't feel it if they kill me."

"I don't think things will come to that," he murmured, smiling. He glanced at his sacred sign, conspicuous and gleaming gold against the heavy black of my cloak. Then he looked again at the town, far below. "This is a mining town, Elsha. The people of Talbar are used to the Quelled. There will be no violence here."

"Then I have no cause to be afraid, my lord."

"Are you ever afraid?"

"Only of myself, lord."

He half turned, and looked sideways at me. I looked at his left shoulder, close to his neck. I had discovered that, because my eyes looked in slightly different directions, I could almost focus on his face while appearing to look at his shoulder. It was a skill I was developing. I saw now that he was thoughtful and grave, though his amber eyes smiled.

"Do you know how old you are, Elsha?"

"Yes, lord. I am sixteen. I was the only harsha at the mine who knew my birth date, because I was born on the day before the Fire Festival began."

He rubbed his beard. "That is strange."

"Not really, lord," I said. "There was no way for us of knowing the days or the passing of the years, apart from the festival. It was the only important day we knew, the only day to measure by. We do not have calendars or water-clocks, such as you Chosen have."

"Not that," he murmured, and he sounded amazed. "Strange, that that was the day you were born. It is also the day I was born. It is one of the qualifications of a Firelord —— to be born on the eve of the festival. That, and to comprehend firestone power, and dreams."

I continued to stare at his shoulder, and hoped he could not read my heart.

He smiled, muttered something to himself, and set off with his donkey down the mountainside. I followed, my beautiful new boots crunching on the frosty ground. I noticed patches of snow in the hollows between the rocks, and on the dim, veiled slopes behind. I could not see the sky at all, for mist.

As we went down into the valley, a cry went

up from the houses of the Chosen. People came out, pointed up at us, and a drum began to beat. I heard bells, the laughter of excited children, shouts, and echoes of song. People gathered on the small open space between us and the town.

The Firelord turned to me. "Move your hood back off your head, Elsha," he commanded.

My face went red in spite of the cold, but I obeyed. I had been hoping they would not find out until later that I was Quelled.

"It is better that they know from the start," he said, and walked on.

What a cheer went up when we arrived! The Chosen rushed to meet him, falling over themselves with joy, laughing and shouting, then remembering to bow, and lifting their heads again, faces shining with welcome and warmth. Then they looked beyond him, and saw me. Some of them didn't see my brand at first, and began to bow. The others dragged them up, pointing at my brand, and murmuring. Silence fell.

"She is my handmaid," announced the Firelord. "She will be treated as the others were, with courtesy and respect."

They bowed then, silently, their smiles frozen on their faces, their eyes carefully off my face. One of the men, our host, went to the Firelord and bowed low before him. "I welcome you with all my heart, my lord," he said fervently. "Long we have awaited your coming. Long we will rejoice in your company. Long we will remember it." He stood again, smiling broadly, and led the Firelord through the cheering crowds down into the marketplace.

I watched from a distance, leaning on his donkey's side, forgotten.

The houses of the Chosen were clustered about a small but busy marketplace at one end of the valley. This was a poor community, and the buildings were not grand. We were guests in the best house, but it was vastly different from the great house at Jinnah where we had stayed. Here only the Firelord was given a bed. I slept in my furs on the wooden floor, next to the fireplace. The house had only two rooms, this lower one for living in, and the upper room where the host and his wife and family slept. The lower floor was kitchen, entertainment hall, living place, and sleeping chamber for the Firelord and me. Outside there was a tiny stable where the Firelord's donkey was housed, and a small yard walled with stones, where pigs and household hens were kept. There was a goat, too, for milk and butter and cheese.

I could stand in our host's door and look straight down the valley to the tents of the Quelled, crowned in mist. It tugged at my heart to see those tents. I stood and looked at them often, and on the second day the Firelord came and stood beside me, leaning on his great divining staff. He had not yet begun to look for firestones;

when he was ready, he would divine. I felt his golden eyes on me, and wondered if he knew my yearning.

"You wish to visit the Quelled?" he asked gently.

"I wish to look upon a friendly face, my lord," I said, "and talk with someone eye to eye."

"Then go," he murmured. "But be discreet. The Chosen here have been most tolerant, but they will not approve of my handmaid visiting the tents."

So I went up into the foothills with Kallai, around the back of the mine, and let him hunt the rooks there; and afterwards I went down to the tents of the Quelled.

A little girl, not branded yet, was playing on the stones outside her tent. She jumped from stone to stone, chanting to herself, swinging a small dead sparrow. She saw the three bloodied rooks I carried, and her eyes went round. Then she noticed Kallai on my other hand, and her mouth fell open.

"Is he alive?" she breathed, dropping the sparrow.

"Yes," I smiled. "See — if you come near, quietly, he'll move his head and look at you. If you move very slowly, he might let you stroke his breast."

She came near and lifted her hand, and Kallai ducked away, beating his great wings. I spoke to him, and he grew calm. But the child had backed away, sucking her thumb, her eyes on Kallai's beak.

"Does he bite?" she asked, still with her thumb in place.

"Only his food," I said. "His name's Kallai. What's yours?"

"Lori." She still looked suspicious.

"Is your caretaker here, Lori?"

Lori nodded, and ran into the tent. She came out with a harsha not much older than myself. I was surprised, as I had never seen a young caretaker before — and never a harsha like her. She had an exceptional face, spirited and fearless and strong. I noticed that her right arm was crooked and paralysed, and she could not work in the mine. She saw my brilliant scarlet dress beneath my black fur, my brand, my Firelord's sacred sign — and her face coloured. She knelt on the ground, and touched her forehead to the dusty stones.

"Welcome, handmaid," she said, her head low, her good arm reaching for the child. "Lori — kneel down! It is the Firelord's handmaid!"

"She's got a bird," said Lori, still sucking her thumb, with no intentions of kneeling. How she reminded me of myself at that age, all yellow hair and grey eyes and wonder and defiance!

"Leave her," I said, putting the rooks on a stone, and reaching out. I touched the harsha's hand. "Stand up, please. I'd like to talk with you."

She stood, and fixed her black eyes on the golden sign around my neck.

"Look at my face," I said. "I am a woman, the same as you."

Her eyes met mine then, and there was a spark between us, an empathy, a kinship.

"My name is Dannii," she said, smiling. "I am caretaker to my brother Ridha's family. Will you honour me by coming to my brother's tent, and sharing my wheat cakes and tea?"

I put Kallai on the ground, out of sight of the rooks, and bound his leash around a rock. Lori stood guard over him, taunting him with her sparrow.

It was cold in the tent, because the firestones were few and of poor quality, the fire small. I realised how close to depletion the mine was, and how urgently my lord's divining skill was needed. I sat on the floor and waited while Dannii spread out our simple meal.

"Why did the Firelord favour you for hand-maid?" she asked, nibbling around the edges of a wheat cake. Her teeth were perfect, and her well-formed mouth had a determined curve to it. Her chin was slightly cleft, her cheekbones high and defined, her face strong yet feminine. Her hair was curling and black, and she had cut it short to her shoulders. It was good to look straight at someone's face again, to watch all the changing expressions instead of imagining them. And Dannii's face was a joy to observe.

"I don't know why he wanted me," I said.

"Though I sometimes think that he tries to make the Chosen see that we Quelled do have intelligence and emotions and feelings, that we're not just animals for the mines. Sometimes when I speak to the Chosen for the first time, they look shocked and astounded, as if they see a talking mule."

Dannii laughed. "And so you change their foolish minds, and show them all how wrong they are."

I shook my head. "I wish I did. I don't impress them, Dannii. I disturb them, tear across the things they've believed for centuries, and they resent me for it."

"Are they cruel to you?"

"Not while I'm with the Firelord. This sacred sign protects me. And the Firelord, if he sees them wronging me, is very hard with them. I cannot defy them, but he defends me, and is my advocate."

"You couldn't ask for a higher one," she said, smiling.

"And what of you, Dannii? Have you a man who protects you?"

She blushed slightly, and looked away, her smile gone. "The Chosen have allocated me to a man, since I am healthy but for my arm, and can bear children for the mine. I go to him if he wants me, so he can't complain to the Chosen, but I will not marry him, and I still live with my brother."

I stared at her, horrified. "Why go to him at

all, if you don't love him? The Chosen can't force you to."

"They can do anything, handmaid. I did refuse at first, and they beat me and broke my arm. So I compromised. I'll bear the four children for them, and then I'll be my own again." She shot me a wide grin, alight with irrepressible humour. "Having an injured arm got me out of the mine, anyway. I love being a caretaker. I can play all day with the children, and climb all over the mountains. Come out with me and see my garden. My cabbages are champions this year."

I didn't see her garden that day; the children saw us and dragged us into their games. The other caretakers were old, and didn't have Dannii's energy. She was the children's favourite. We played games all that afternoon, running in the hills behind the tents, and I hadn't laughed so much in years, nor felt so free.

As I was leaving, Dannii and I embraced. "Come back soon," she said. "Come and share our evening meal with us, and meet my brother and his family. We'll dance, and tell stories around the fire, and old Bior will play his pipes for us."

"It sounds wonderful," I said, and kissed her cheek. I picked up Kallai and the rooks, said goodbye to Lori, and walked back to the houses of the Chosen.

8

Divining

There was a cold wind blowing, the day he went out to divine. The whole town, Quelled and Chosen, went out with us, and the musicians brought their drums, pipes, bells, and flutes. We must have looked a dazzling parade. The Firelord wore all red, and on top of everything he wore a huge flowing cloak with a massive hood that almost hid his face. I, too, wore red, even red boots, and a hood lined with pitch-black fur. My garments, and the Firelord's, had tongues of flame embroidered in gold thread about the hem and sleeves. I had remembered to leave the woman-stone behind, though I felt the loss of it.

I walked behind my high lord, the musicians walked behind me, the Chosen followed them, and last of all came the Quelled. Up into the foothills we went, following the Firelord. The music rang, and the children shouted with excitement. We stopped on a small plateau overlooking the valley. We could see the houses of the Chosen, the tents of the Quelled, and the old depleted mine. Here the wind shrieked down from snowy slopes, and spat ice on our clothes and skin. I wound my scarlet scarf about my lower face, and pulled my hood forward.

The Firelord raised his arms, and the musicians stopped playing. The children fell silent, wrapped for extra warmth in the thick folds of their mothers' skirts. Only a single drum beat now, steady and slow, like a mighty heart. We all stood back, giving the Firelord room on the flat, dusty ground.

He held his divining staff in both hands, and began drawing on the ground. In utter silence we watched, the drumbeat and the wind the only sounds in all that wintry world. In the dust the Firelord drew a large map. He marked the valley, the houses of the Chosen, the dwellings of the Quelled, the mine. He placed stones in the places where rocks and foothills were, and made deep scratches in the earth where there were valleys. When he had finished, there was a replica of the valley and town of Talbar, and the surrounding hills. It was twelve paces long, eight wide, and was so accurate we could see even the plateau where we stood.

It was my turn, then, to play my part. I took five sacred golden urns, placing one on each edge of the map, in the south, north, east, and west; and the fifth in the centre. Into each urn I placed kindling grass and fragments of firestone, and the Firelord lit the five fires. When they blazed, he sat behind the eastern fire, facing west, across the replica of Talbar. I stood behind him, and all the people gathered behind me. It was forbidden to look on the face of the Firelord as he divined.

He lifted his great staff in his hands, placing it just within the place he had made, and bent his head. For a long time he didn't move. We waited, our breath held, our eyes streaming in the bitter wind, our ears filled with the throbbing of the drum. The air was tense, charged with the force of the Firelord's will, his passion for the stones he sought. The whole earth throbbed, caught up in his power, held there while he mastered dust and rock and firestone.

Slowly he stood up. He walked onto the map he had made, and bent for a while over the central fire. He stood side-on to us, though still we could not see his face, lost deep within his hood. I thought sometimes I heard his voice, as though he commanded the fire, but then I thought it was the wind, or the echoes of the drum. The gale tore at the fires, scattering smoke and ash across the small hills and ravines, and across the Firelord's boots. Smoke and dust whirled in his garments, and his cloak billowed scarlet behind him.

He crouched in the northwest section of the map, his staff stretched out across the earth, close to it, trembling with power. Then he moved to the other sections, one at a time, slowly, his staff always close to the ground. In the last sector, the northeastern one, he crouched for a long time. His staff shook in his hands, and seemed to turn of its own volition, twisting his hands, driving the wood and silver across a small ravine not far from the old mine. Suddenly he dropped the staff and it rolled, twisting in the windswept dust, its silver point, filled with firestone dust, forced into the ravine. With a great cry he leapt back, lifted his arms to the skies, and thanked God.

The people cheered, hugged one another, and the musicians all started a crazy anthem that was meant to be reverent, and wasn't. In the midst of the festivities the Firelord turned to me, looked at me over the heads of the children, and smiled. He looked incredibly tired, and older, but there was triumph in his face, and his eyes burned with firestone power. I looked straight into his face, and smiled back.

Then, when the Firelord had erased the map and put out the fires, and I had cleaned the urns and placed them carefully into a woven bag, we headed the procession northeast, into the ravine where the new mine was to be. There, he divined again with his staff, paced out distances, and marked measurements with stones. He told the Quelled where to dig, and how far down the fire-stones were. Then we marched back to the valley, the celebrations already begun, the music frenzied and inspired, the people singing.

I walked at the Firelord's side, as his handmaid, but at a distance from him and the Chosen. Even the children, in all their excitement, remembered not to touch me or look in my face. In the midst of all the joy, all the exultation, all the celebration, I was alone. Only that night, when the Chosen sat feasting around their hearths, I slipped away and joined the Quelled.

Dannii welcomed me warmly, with a kiss on each cheek and a hug, and took me into her brother Ridha's tent. It was crowded. Ridha's wife was there with all her family, and his brothers and their wives and children. And many of their friends were there, celebrating with them the beginning of the new mine. Dannii had told them all of me, I knew; but still they were shy of me at first, not knowing whether to treat me as Quelled or Chosen. I talked with them of my family and Siranjaro mine, and they were at ease then, and told me about their work, and of the dimensions of the new mine marked out that day.

Then the men began to eat, feasting on goats' meat and roasted crows. While they ate I talked with Ridha's wife, Kiran. She was a gentle, smiling woman, and she told me, shyly, proudly, that she was with child again. I watched her with Ridha; there was a bond between them, a unity, that made me ache. I envied her her happiness.

Afterwards I ate with Dannii and the other harsha, laughing, and they told me tales their fathers had told, and they were not so different from the stories my father had told me. The words of our myth-songs, too, were similar, though their tunes were different from our Siranjaro tunes. The similarity between the words surprised me, as there was no communication between the Quelled of different mines. After the feast they asked me to sing one of my home songs. I sang a chanting myth, with the drums only accompanying me; and Dannii said I had a pleasing voice. Lesharo had said a similar thing, though I had thought he liked my voice only because it was mine.

After the feasting we danced, moving in two large circles around the fire, clapping and singing. Their dances were different from Siranjaro dances, and we all laughed at my bungling. One of the young Quelled men partnered me, though he was very shy and barely said a word. After the dancing we relaxed and listened while one of the old caretakers played his pipes. Lori curled on my lap, asleep, her fingers wound with the silken tassles of my dress. I sat with my arms about the child, but my hands held my womanstone, and I listened to the pipes, dreaming. For a blissful, blessed time I saw Lesharo crouching by his fire, his dark head bent, his pipes held to his lips. And I heard his music, finer, sweeter, than any other I had heard, and much more deeply loved.

Dannii, sitting close, bent her head to mine. "What is he like?" she whispered.

I glanced at her, startled, and her lips curved.

"The man who gave you your firestone," she said. "What is he like?"

She read me well, this friend. "He is like myself," I said. "And he plays music sweeter even than this."

She leaned her head against mine and we listened together, and for the first time I thought of Lesharo without grief, but only with joy for all that he was to me.

I wished to stay all night with the Quelled, but knew that the Chosen would have held it against me. So I returned to the house where the Firelord and I stayed. I spent the rest of the night in silence, sitting alone, listening to Chosen laughter and Chosen stories and Chosen music. I sat by a window of the house, the warmth of the fire on my back, the freezing night wind hissing on my face from between the shutters; and I shivered with cold, and longed for the tents of my own people.

I crouched alone in the grey morning shadows outside the house door, and fed Kallai pieces of wings from the ravens he had caught that early dawn. The Firelord came out of the house, and stood a little way in front of me. I stood up, lowering my eyes to the ground.

"I go away today, Elsha," he said, without turning around.

"Away, lord? You said we'd not divine in the next town for a long while, yet."

"And we won't. I will go away alone."

I was appalled, shocked, and immediately guilty. "I have displeased you, lord?" I asked, and dreaded his reply.

"No, Elsha. You have pleased me very well. But I have to go away, and I have to go alone. You will stay here in Talbar, in this house. You will be looked after."

"Can I not come with you, lord?"

"No. But, Elsha — " He turned and looked at me straight, and his eyes were deadly grave. "Wear my sacred sign. Always. Every moment."

"Yes, lord. How long will you be gone?"

"I do not know. Twenty days. Thirty. Maybe more."

My heart sank. All that day it sank further, and by the early afternoon, when he left, I could have cried and held his robes, and implored him to stay. But the Chosen surrounded him, held a farewell ceremony with drums and flutes and singing, and I could not even say goodbye. In the middle of it, the house-owner's wife told me to go and draw some water from the spring, and when I came back, my lord was gone.

9

Earth-Force

The atmosphere of the house changed when the Firelord was gone. There was no laughter, no warmth, no friendliness. I thought at first that they missed his company, and were grieving in some strange way; but then I realised they did not miss his company, but resented mine. They had tolerated me, with him there. But without him, they no longer had to pretend. I was cut off, ostracised. They provided me with space to sleep, and permitted me still to use their vegetables for food; but they would not talk to me, and refused to touch the birds Kallai and I brought in for food. I was resented, ignored, barely tolerated. At first their altered attitude, their hypocrisy, angered me, but after five days it made me depressed.

More than anything, I missed the privacy they had given the Firelord and me. Every morning he and I had been left the lower room completely to ourselves, to heat water and to wash. But now the family was there all the time. Usually the lack of privacy wouldn't have bothered me; having been brought up in a tent with six men, I was not shy of nakedness, mine or anyone else's. Many times I had washed in the Firelord's presence, and he in mine, and never had there been uneasiness or embarrassment between us. Usually he read while I washed, and I doubt he even noticed me. But here, with him gone, the young men of the house had a way of looking at me that made me feel ashamed, and sometimes they whispered things about me and smiled at each other. I would not undress while they were about.

But on the fifth day, I came back from hunting early with Kallai, and longed for a wash. I spoke with the house-owner's wife. She was washing the bowls and cooking utensils after the morning meal, and her daughter-in-law was helping her.

"Woman," I said, standing at a respectful distance behind them, "would it please you to leave me this room to myself sometime today, so that I may wash?"

For a while she ignored me. Then, because I didn't go away, she said coldly: "It would not please me, harsha."

"It pleased you when my lord was here," I said.

"Yes," she hissed, still bending over the washing bowl, with her back to me. "It pleased us all well, when he stayed. It does not please us that he left you here. I have never had a Quelled in my house before. Never has my home been so violated. Nothing about you pleases me, harsha — not your wastefulness, your ignorance, or your presence — and it does not please me to order my household around your worthless needs."

"My high lord said I would be treated well here."

"And so you are, harsha. But for his word, you would have been driven off like a diseased dog."

"I am being driven off in other ways."

She snorted, and handed another bowl to her daughter-in-law to dry. They began to talk together, laughing over some silly thing one of the children had done.

"I would like to wash," I said, furious, interrupting their conversation. Another law broken.

The house-owner's wife turned slowly, and looked above my head. She was white-lipped with fury. "When my lord comes home from supervising the mine," she said, "I will tell him of your insolence."

"And when my lord returns, I'll tell him of your hardness towards me."

"It will be your word against ours, harsha. And your word is worthless."

"My word is not worthless," I said. "I am the

Firelord's handmaid. He will protect me."

"You're not a handmaid!" she spat. "You're not even a woman. You're a sop, a favour to keep the Quelled hordes happy, to keep peace in the mines that threaten revolt. By having a Quelled handmaid, our high lord flatters the slaves, indulges them, soothes them into thinking they have some kind of worth. And we Chosen pay. But for his sake we suffer you. For peace, we suffer — "

"You lie!"

"Oh, do I, harsha? You flatter yourself if you think he protects you. He protects the peace, that's all. He's gone now to send messengers to all the other towns, to all the Chosen, to tell them to be tolerant of you for the sake of peace. He safeguards our Chosen right to own the mines and control the Quelled. He safeguards our power. He does not protect you."

In our rage we looked into each other's eyes. I came close to striking her. Before I did, or said something I would regret, I grabbed my fur cloak and left the house.

I went up the rocky slope behind the houses, past the old stone toilet house, and over a steep ridge to a small valley. A river flowed through the valley, rapid and cold. I went down to the water, stripped, and washed, standing thigh-deep in the icy flow. I was shaking before I started, from outrage and anger; soon I shook from cold as well, and my body went white and numb. I dried myself on the hem of my woollen outer garment, dressed, and pulled my heavy woollen sleeves down over my frozen hands. My fingers were so numb I could hardly lace up the front of my outer dress, and the wind whistled in the gaps and froze my flesh.

I went for a long run, jumping over stones and tussock grass, until feeling crept into my feet again, and my breath made quick mists on the sombre morning air. But I felt no better, and anger still burned in me, about what the woman had said.

Far from the town I sat down on a smooth low rock, took off my sacred sign, and looked at the human eye engraved on it. It symbolised his inner eye, his divining power. The eye glimmered and winked and seemed to mock me, and in sudden anger I picked up a pointed stone and scratched my family sign across it. I made the circle, outside the iris of the eye, and I scratched deeply the waving lines going outwards all around. Somehow the two signs combined, his and mine, made a harmonious design, and defeated my purpose. I put the sign about my neck again, and sat gazing along the valley.

Slowly, peace came. Here I was free, unbound by duties and responsibilities, free of contempt, disapproval, and strife. I was all the earth's, and it was all mine. On an impulse I lay flat on the ground on my front, and listened to the river rush and the wind whisper in the tussock grass.

I stretched out and pressed my palms flat upon the dust, and let the life force of the earth flow into me. I breathed in the clean, wild odour of the soil, and with all my body soaked up the quiet strength of the stones. I felt comforted, cleansed, and renewed. I closed my eyes and thought of firestone power.

I felt a tremor run along the ground, and there seemed to be a movement in the earth, a secret influence deep within, that pulled at me. The feeling shocked me. I knelt up, alarmed, and brushed the dust off my clothes and hands. Then, half afraid and wondering, I put my palms flat on the earth again. The power was there, pulsing beneath my hands, unmistakable. I looked along the valley, estimating where the old mine was. It was westwards, surely, far from here. Yet the power hummed, flowed in the stones and dust, vibrant and alive and strong.

I don't know what made me do what I did next. Curiosity, perhaps, or madness. Or maybe it was destiny. But I decided to follow the power, to trace it to its source. I stood up and took off my boots. I wanted my feet bare on the ground, close to the force and form of earth. My hands shook. A part of me was terrified, guilty that I should even try this thing; but in my heart I was calm, and what I did felt right, very right, and good. So I removed my boots, stood up straight, and looked along the valley.

The power still hummed, moving upwards through my feet, my limbs, up through my body and lungs and heart. It ran through all of me, ringing, and not for all the world could I have stopped it. I started to walk, my eyes almost closed.

Never had I been so conscious of the earth, of the toughness and fragility and flowing life of it. I realised for the first time that the stones were not dead, nor the dust devoid of life, nor the waters vacuous. Our earth lived. It lived and breathed and sang and flowed and ached, in every tiny part. And its singing called to me — whispered, hummed, through the skin of my feet, through my whole self, until with all my being I was attuned to it. I ran then, following the power, ran with joy and a wild, winging certainty, right into the heart of everything I loved. And there was no earth, no cold, no dust nor stones nor water rushing past; but only this joy, this singing, awesome flight straight into the soul of God. Into fire.

I stopped suddenly, dazed. I looked down and saw a darkened place on the ground. It was an abandoned firepit, and the ashes were full of half-burned firestones. Trembling in every part of me, I knelt and pushed my hands into the ash, and lifted out the stones. They still contained unreleased fire, and they hummed in my hands, powerfully.

Laughing, I scooped up handfuls of ash and firestones, and threw them high into the air. I jumped up and did a dance all around the rocks, and sang, and blew kisses to paradise. As in a dream I went back and got my boots, and climbed the ridge again.

Above the town I stopped, turned around, and looked back down the valley. I saw the rushing, bubbling stream, the barren, stony earth, the fierce tussock grasses bending in the wind — and I marvelled that in all that rocky valley, in all that windswept, rugged ground, I had found a tiny pit of firestones. And more than found: I had been led. Drawn. I dared not use that other word. But it blazed along the edges of my mind, and filled me with bewilderment and fear, and the highest ecstasy that I had ever known.

Back at the house, my life carried on as usual. I was shunned and ignored, and left to occupy myself. The women made things as difficult as possible for me: they gave me no privacy, no room around their fire at night so I could cook my food, and banned me from their vegetable gardens. So during the day I lived with the Quelled, and I took to them the rooks and ravens Kallai caught, and we ate well there. I no longer made a secret of my visits to them.

Then one day I lost my woman-stone. I did not know until that night that it was lost. I was spreading out my sleeping mat and furs beside the fire, and I felt in my pocket for my woman-stone, because I always slept with it in my hand. The woman-stone was gone. I went frantic, looking for it. I emptied my bag of belongings all over the floor, searching through clay bowls, cups, and bone spoons. I shook out my creamy underdresses and my bright outer garments, and felt inside the hoods of my fur cloaks. I shook my bag, my sleeping furs, and even looked inside my spare boots. But I did not find the woman-stone.

The house-owner's wife watched as I made chaos all across her floor. In the end I stared at her helplessly, and asked: "Woman, have you seen my firestone?"

She looked disapprovingly at my mess. She was about to go upstairs to bed, and was in no mood for trouble. "If I find rubbish lying around, harsha, I burn it. Especially, I burn firestones."

"You know the one I mean, woman. My special stone. Please. It's the only thing I own."

"Then you should look after it." She turned and went upstairs, leaving me distraught. I looked through all my things again, packed them away, and went to bed. But I knew where the firestone had to be: in the valley, lost the last time I went hunting. And I knew a way it could be found.

Before dawn I woke. I put on my thickest boots and my warmest cloak, and pulled my hood over my head. Outside, it was almost totally dark. I climbed the rocky slope behind the houses, visited the toilet house, then went on up the ridge. I heard noises in the rubbish ravine, and knew the wolves were there. They often came to the town at night, to scavenge for food. Their eyes glowed at me like green fires, but they did not follow me. I went over the ridge and down into the valley on the other side. The sky was a shade lighter now, and I could make out the form of the mountains all around. Mist swirled about me, clinging to my clothes, and settled on my hair and skin like rain. It was freezing. My breath was vaporous, and my boots crunched on the icy soil.

I stood with my hands pushed deep into my sleeves, and faced the length of the valley. I could hear the river on my left, tumbling and gurgling between the rocks, and shrouded with heavy mist. Rocks stood like spectres in the gloom, silent sentinels to the dawn. Our dawns were never lovely, then. They were dull and cold, and grey lightened on grey till it was morning. And all the day was grey, until the blackness of the night.

But this dawn for me was different. This dawn was a beginning, or an end, for me.

Shaking with fear and cold, I bent and unbound my boots. The ground had ice on it, but it seemed important to me to have my skin on stone, my flesh against the earth. I stood up again, straight, and closed my eyes.

Guilt-ridden thoughts clamoured in my head. Who did I think I was — some kind of female diviner? For a few moments I was appalled, horrified at my audacity, my mad arrogance. How dare I trespass on *his* ground, *his* territory? How dare I even think I had the power, let alone the right?

I closed my mind to the voices, to reason and doubt and guilt, and I thought of my woman-stone. I held it there in fiery light in the centre of my mind, felt its texture and form, the warmth and singing power of it. And then I seemed to see, far in a distant place, another image of my stone. But the image was not real; it was more the feeling of an image, the vibration of one. And that other image called to me. And then I knew — I *knew* — where my firestone lay.

But the knowing was a changing thing, strong and sure one moment, then faint the next, and I had to listen, search for it with everything in me. But always it was there. Like the shadow of a flying bird, it passed vivid on the ground one moment, distinct and unmistakable — and then it shrank glimmering and faint, and was almost lost. Then it would flash up again, unerring and swift. And I followed it, running when it ran, walking when it slowed, not looking with my eyes, but with my heart and mind and soul. And then, suddenly, it stopped.

I stood still, breathing hard, disoriented and lost. I was shaking from exhaustion, and felt sweat trickling down inside my clothes. I looked down at my feet. The ground was light now, the mist cleared. I saw only dust and tussock grass, and empty, windswept earth. No woman-stone. Nothing.

I sat down on a rock and stared without seeing at the ground at my feet. Never had I felt so empty inside, so utterly forsaken. Slowly my eyes focussed on a hole, overshadowed by a nearby rock. It was an abandoned rabbit hole, half filled now with dust and grass. My heart started to pound in my ribs, and my eyes blurred. Not daring to breathe, I crouched down and thrust my hand into the hole. My fingers closed around something hard, something that was rounded and smooth and hummed with firestone power.

Marvelling, I drew out my woman-stone, and blew the dust off it. If I could have flown into the air, singing, I would have. Instead, I knelt there on the earth among the tussock grasses, and wept.

The day must have been half gone when I stood up again. My feet were numb, and my whole body shook with cold. Inside, I was on fire. In a daze I went back up the valley, collecting my boots on the way, and on over the ridge to the town. And all the time I was amazed, half fearful of the thing I had done.

10

Visions and Vows

I went to live with the Quelled until my lord came back. Something had changed in me that day I divined, and I could no longer submit to the arrogance and scorn of the Chosen. I do not think I became proud; I simply chose to remove myself from the people who humiliated me. I lived in Ridha's tent, and kept Dannii company during the day, helping her with the children, with gardening and spinning and weaving. Sometimes I borrowed her old clothes and disguised myself as a miner, and worked in the mine a day among the firestones.

I was content and, for the first time in my adult life, happy. Dannii became my dearest friend, a sister, closer to me than anyone had ever been. In personality we were very different:

she was disciplined, resigned, and uncomplaining. She had a serenity that I loved, and she laughed often. In many ways she was like Lesharo.

But in her spirit she matched me. We shared the same dreams, the same vision and hope, the same love of myths, the same pain at being Quelled. There was freedom for me in her company. I could spread my most precious thoughts before her, and know they were safe. There was no scepticism in her, no distrust or judgement or fear. Except in one thing.

I told her I had divined.

Lori had asked me if she could go hunting with Kallai by herself. I would not let her; I was the only human being he answered to. But I offered her my woman-stone to play with, and she skipped off with it, tossing it high in the air, and singing.

"She'll lose it," warned Dannii, looking up from her weaving. We were sitting outside the tent in the morning, watching the children. "She loses things all the time. Tell her to bring it back."

"It can't be lost," I said.

She half smiled, and said jokingly: "Why? Would you divine for it, Elsha?" Then she bent over her loom, struggling one-handedly with a join in the goathair yarn.

"Yes, I would," I said.

She looked up, searching my face for a hint of a smile, her black eyes uncertain and questioning.

I took a deep breath. For some reason, I was afraid of telling her. "I'm not lying, Dannii. I have divined. I have the power."

She put aside the loom, and folded her arm across her knees. She would not look at my face. She trembled slightly, and her jaw had a stubborn line to it.

"I don't believe you, Elsha. I think you are mistaken. No human being on earth has divining power, save the Firelord. No woman has it. And certainly no harsha. Even if she is his handmaid."

"Test me, then," I said. "Hide some firestones somewhere — anywhere — and I'll divine for them."

She gave me a small smile, half amused and half afraid. "Very well," she said quietly, getting up and going into the tent. She came out with a bag of firestones. "These were new from the mine last night. We'll go into that valley where the river runs, and I'll test your power. And if you fail, handmaid, you do all the washing for Ridha's family."

"That sounds fair punishment for fraudulence," I said, smiling. "But what if I succeed?"

"If you succeed, Elsha," she said gravely, "then everything we have ever believed vanishes in smoke."

I sat in a small concealed cave up under a cliff, and covered my head with my arms while Dannii hid the firestones. She was gone a long time, and while I waited I grew more and more tense. My spirit, so certain before, wavered and was afraid. It was one thing to divine alone, with only myself to answer to for failure; but to divine for someone else, to be exposed and answerable to another human being, was to lay my very soul across the ground.

Dannii came back and tapped my shoulder. "It is time, Elsha."

"I would rather you stayed here," I said, standing up. "You might distract me."

"The Firelord had a whole crowd with him, and he was not distracted."

"I'm not the Firelord, Dannii. Did you leave the firestones in the bag, or take them out?"

"It makes no difference whether they are in cloth or rock or water or dust or wind. If you can divine, you'll find them. I'll tell you nothing, Elsha."

"By God, you're tough," I muttered, going out. I heard her footsteps behind me. I went out to the valley, and stopped halfway between the cave and the stream. I knelt down and placed my palms flat on the stones. I bent my head and closed my eyes. It was hard this time, hard to feel the power, the life force running in the ground. I grew hot and panicky. My feelings seemed suffocated, blocked, and did not flow. I stood up again, and walked down by the river. I took off my boots and left them on a stone. The ground was frozen in this place, the rocks still shadowed, dark.

I lay face down on the dust between the clumps

of spiky tussock grass, trembling with cold, my palms and face and all my being pressed against the earth. I began to relax, though the cold shook me. I thought of our Quelled myths about a massive fire that once lit the whole sky and made the earth warm. I imagined lying on a heated earth, with a warm light on my back. Bliss, surely. Slowly I felt the familiar throb and hum of vital energy. The hum went crosswise, at right angles to my body, and I was not in harmony with it.

I moved until I was in line, attuned to it. The hum intensified. I knew then where it came from — from the west, across the river. On my hands and knees I followed it, right down to the water's edge. The power shimmered in the water, vibrated in my hands, surged and rang right through me. I stood up and tore off my outer dress. I dropped it on the rocks, and waded into the stream. The water came only to my thighs, but it was swift, and struck my skin like ice. Within seconds I was numb. But inside — inside I sang and burned with firestone power.

I waded across, my underskirts held high, the frigid water rushing all round; then climbed up on the other side, up across the rocks and dirt and slashing grass, went running, racing, straight to the cleft between the rocks, straight to the hidden firestones. I picked several off the pile and threw them into the air, laughing and yelling.

I heard a splash, and noticed Dannii coming across the stream, unmindful of her clothes. She came running up to me, then slowed as she drew near, her heavy grey skirt dragging at her legs. Her face was white.

"I did it!" I cried, elated, gripping her arms, and kissing both her cheeks. She was shaking all over, and her skin was frozen. She was not smiling. Her look unsettled me, made me afraid. Slowly she knelt and touched the ground at my feet.

"Don't do that, Dannii," I said, crouching in front of her, and taking her hand. "We are equal, you and I."

She shook her head, and I saw that her cheeks were wet. "You are woman, Elsha, high as the high lord, and with a power that equals his."

"Don't," I said, trying to laugh. "If anyone heard you say that, you'd have your tongue torn out."

"For truth?" She stood up. I stood with her, and we stayed there, frozen, shaking with cold and terror, while the wind turned our wet clothes to ice.

"Tell no one of this, Dannii," I said. "Promise me."

She said nothing, but bent and picked up several of the firestones, gathering them into the crook of her crippled arm. She came back and made a small pyramid of the firestones on the ground in front of me. She took a knife from a sheath at her belt, cut off a length of her hair and some of mine, and entwined the dark and the light together. She placed our hair across the firestones, then touched the ground near my feet, and stood up. The act was like a pledge, a promise hallowed and binding. Her solemnity, her almost awe, astounded and humbled me.

"I will never say a word," she said. "But I think the stones themselves will speak, and the earth itself light a triumphal fire for you."

Days passed, and I lost count of them. It seemed as if I had slipped back into my old way: the goatskin tents were my home, and the grey existence of the Quelled had become again my life. Yet all was different. Most of the time I forgot my new-found power, involved as I was with ordinary everyday things; but sometimes the memory would break through like a burst of flamelight in the dark, and I'd stand astounded, surprised and overwhelmed by joy.

And another thing happened while the Firelord was away, to change my life. It happened the day they brought Kiran home early from the mine. Two men carried her, and Ridha ran alongside, wringing his hands and crying, and cursing the Chosen. They carried her into the tent and put her on her sleeping mat beside the fire. She was filthy with dust and sweat and blood, and moaning terribly, and her baby, lifeless, lay cold across her chest. Dannii pushed me outside with Lori, and told me to take the child away for a while. So I did.

When we returned later to the tent, Kiran was

sleeping, and Ridha was sitting by the fire bent over a small bundle tied in a shirt. He was crying, and the sound was terrible to me.

"Kiran's time came early," Dannii whispered to me. "The overseer didn't believe her, and whipped her, and made her carry on. She gave birth at the mouth of the mine, carrying out a basket of firestones. The babe fell on the stones, and died."

Later I took the tiny bundle out to the rubbish pit behind the tents. The Chosen had elaborate funerals for their dead, raising them high on altars and burning them; but the dead of the Quelled were wrapped in rags and thrown into the rubbish pits. But this evening the wolves were already in the rubbish, snarling and snapping over the choicest bits. I carried on past them, went higher up the slopes, and found a crack between two rocks. While I was placing the bundle there, one of the leather thongs tying it broke, and the shirt fell open, exposing a tiny hand. I stared at it, astounded. The hand was exquisite, the fingers slender and softly curled, and with minute shining nails. I took the parcel out, crouched on the icy stones with it, and unfolded it.

The child lay pale in the twilight, perfectly formed, peaceful, unbelievably tiny, and utterly beautiful. The back of its head was cut and bruised, where it had fallen on the stones; otherwise, in every part it was flawless.

Rage swept over me. I stood up. There was no

wind, and the evening was still, still as the child's heart. I could hear sounds from the tents below me; children laughing, and music, and from Ridha's tent the unbearable sound of mourning. I raised my hand in the cold dark, and I made a vow.

"I, Elsha, woman of the Quelled and handmaid to the Firelord, do this night solemnly swear before Eternal God that I will improve the lives of the Quelled, and open the eyes of the Chosen who are blind. I will make new laws, and wipe out injustice. This I swear before God. And nothing will stop me in this purpose, and I shall not rest till it is done."

Then I wrapped the child in the shirt again, tied it with the leather thongs, and hid it deep in the cleft of the rock.

That night I had a dream.

I dreamed that I was in a temple place, and before me was a great golden altar with a brazier burning on it. Carved on the altar in a language I didn't know were several words, but I knew they said: "For the Chosen of God." Beside the altar, dividing it from another part of the room, was a huge curtain. High and black it was, and full of ancient dust. And on the other side of the curtain was a low stone altar, also with a brazier burning on it, and its words were: "For the Quelled."

In my dream I took the curtain in my hands, and pulled it down. I took the brazier from the Quelled altar and placed it on the great golden altar, and the fires of the Chosen and of the Quelled burned side by side, and there was no more a division between them.

Then the dream changed, and I was standing in a high place and tens of thousands of people were gathered before me. I made a speech, announcing new laws and proclaiming a better life for the Quelled. When I had finished, there was great turmoil among the Chosen, though the Quelled rejoiced. But the Chosen dared not touch me, and they dared not defy me. Because in my hand I held the one thing they needed above all else, that no other human being could give them. In my hand I held fire.

One day I was helping Dannii wash clothes in the stream behind the tents, when Lori came leaping and running over the rocks towards us, screaming.

"The Firelord! The Firelord! He's back!" She rushed up, panting, and cried: "We were on the rocks above the town, throwing stones at it, when a man on a donkey went down into the market-place from another way, and all the Chosen rushed up to him, yelling and laughing. It was him, Elsha! Your man!"

I stood up straight, the dripping garments heavy in my hands, and looked at Dannii. There was sudden pain in her, in both of us. I dropped the clothes in a shallow pool, and embraced her.

"We won't leave for days yet, Dannii," I said, and hoped my words were true. "The Chosen will hold a feast for him tonight, and tomorrow they'll show him the progress on the new mine. They'll be days talking and telling stories."

She gave me a small smile, and kissed my cheek. "You must go," she said. "Quickly. The high lord will be looking for you."

I ran off, quickly gathered my things from Ridha's tent, and hurried up the valley to the town. Kallai fluttered on my wrist, disturbed by my haste. I waited a moment or two outside the door of the house where we stayed, trying to calm my thoughts. The door was closed, but I could hear laughter inside, loud talking, and music. I had longed for my lord's return, yet now that he was here, I was terrified. My heart thundered, and guilt and fear tore over me because I had divined. He would know, surely. He would take one look at my eyes, my soul, and he would know.

I took a deep breath, and knocked on the door. The woman of the house answered. She looked beyond me and said: "We told him you had left, harsha, that you deserted this place and returned to your mine."

"Then you lied," I said, going past her into the house. The room was crowded. I could not see my lord, at first. I went to my old corner, dropped my sleeping mat and bag on the floor, and put Kallai on his perch. He was unwilling to leave my fist, and I didn't blame him. I was getting hostile looks already, and someone had spat on me. I realised that maybe they had believed

I had deserted him. Or they wished I had.

I found my lord sitting on a finely carved wooden chair, and I went to him. The men stepped back, muttering, and some of them looked surprised. I dared not look on my lord's face. I knelt before him and touched the floor at his feet. The whole crowd became silent, watching.

"Welcome, my lord," I said, and stood up.

He, too, stood, and in front of all those people he bent and paid homage to me, touching the floor before me. When he rose again, he looked straight into my face, and said: "It is good to see you again, handmaid. I cannot say how good. I was told you had returned to Siranjaro."

I looked directly at his eyes, and smiled. "I will never leave you, lord," I said.

The musicians started playing again, breaking the shocked silence. Our host took my lord a cup of wine, and everyone started talking again. But somehow the laughter seemed forced, the celebration restrained. Excluded, I got myself some wine in my own cup, and sat on a stool in my corner, and held my own private celebration at his return. And sometimes through that long evening I caught his eye, and he smiled at me. Later, when all the guests were gone and the house-owner and his family had gone upstairs to bed, I made up my lord's bed for him, and spread my own sleeping mat and furs out by the fire, and we sat together, he and I, and talked.

There was a peacefulness about him that night.

I had the feeling that, while away, he had done some thing that was deeply important to him, and now his soul rested. I wished mine would. He sensed my unease, and looked at me sideways, with a slow smile. His furs formed soft shadows about his bronze skin, and his own sacred sign glimmered gold on his dark clothes. His eyes were the colour of flame.

"Hold out your hand, Elsha," he said.

I did, palm down, my fingers spread and trembling. He held out his hand palm down, beside mine. His was as steady as a rock, and strong. Our little fingers almost touched. Slowly, to my amazement, he moved his hand over mine and held it. I felt a tingling in my hand, a power, deep and warm and awesome, like a healing. And with it came peace.

"For each of his children God has a dream," he said. "It is the highest dream, the perfect road for us, the purpose for which we were born. And that dream for you was given also to me, Elsha. In a dream I was told of you, and of the place where you lived. It was a vivid image that I had, and it was not wrong. I dreamed of a female of the Quelled who would be high in this land of ours, and who would show all people that the Quelled are not without minds or souls. I dreamed that by her life the Chosen would be made to see a new truth, a new way. I do not know what that way will be. I only know that they see you, and you open their eyes and tear down the walls in their minds. One day perhaps, because of you, the lives of the Quelled will be lifted up and eased. This is your true road, Elsha, your destiny. This, and nothing else."

"And that is why you chose me, lord, for handmaid?"

"That is why."

He smiled, and we said nothing for a while. We sat there a long time, our hands joined. At last I asked, haltingly: "Lord, was there any more in your dream?"

He unlinked our hands, and smiled again, and looked into the fire. "What more could you want, Elsha?" he asked.

I bent my head, and said nothing. But I put my hand in my pocket and drew out my woman-stone. It lay heavy on my palm, and I felt the firestone power humming in my skin, murmuring along my arm and running warm into my heart. And guilt, too, ran warm. Too warm. He knew, and he asked quietly: "What did you do in this place, handmaid, while I was gone?"

I put away the woman-stone, looked into the fire, and swallowed nervously. "I stayed with the Quelled, lord."

"And their tents were more honourable than this house?"

"Yes, lord."

"I am sorry I did not choose wisely for you. I commanded them to treat you well here. I believed they would. The world is more stubborn than I had thought."

"It does not matter, lord. I was happy where I was."

We were silent for a while, and I tried to gather up courage. I glanced at his face again. The firelight leapt across his high forehead, his aquiline nose, and glowed in his black pointed beard. His eyes were shut, though there was a tension about him, as if he waited. He was so fine, so like a king, so worthy of loyalty, of all my honesty.

"Lord," I said, "there is something I must tell you."

"Speak on," he said.

I hesitated. My mouth was dry, and I could feel a pulse throbbing in my throat. "Lord," I said, terrified, "I have divined. I divined for firestone. And I found."

His eyes flew open, held mine, and his face seemed carved of stone. I stared at him, then tore my eyes away and looked into the fire. I felt his eyes on me, tearing, cleaving me open. For a long time he said nothing, and I wished with all my heart I had kept silent.

"You lie, handmaid," he said after a while, with deadly quiet. "You lie to me. No other soul on earth has this power, unless I teach it to him. No woman has the power. No harsha."

I twisted my hands in front of me, and saw that my knuckles were white. "Lord, I divined for my woman-stone when it was lost. And I found it. In that valley behind this town, I found it."

He let out a long breath, and then, to my amazement, he laughed. "Your woman-stone!"

"Yes, lord. My woman-stone. I divined for it. What is funny, lord?"

He was still laughing, chuckling quietly. "Elsha, Elsha, do not alarm me like that! I nearly died of shock. You did not divine for firestone. You divined for your woman-stone. The two things are totally different. Your woman-stone you carry with you always. It is imbued with your feelings, your beliefs, the very smell and sweat of your skin. It is only natural that with the minor intuitive power you have, you knew unconsciously where your woman-stone could be found. But that is not divining, Elsha. That is a very simple use of your natural gift of intuition. You haven't divined for firestones, child. By God, if you divined for *them*, our whole world falls apart!"

He got up, went to the table where the cooking things were kept, and poured himself a cup of warm spiced wine. He brought one back for me as well, and sat with me while we drank. My hands shook, and I spilled my wine all down my dress. I longed, with all my being I longed to tell him all the truth. But I looked at him sitting there in the firelight, shaking his head at me and quietly laughing, and I could not.

Early the next morning we left Talbar. The Chosen wanted him to stay longer, wanted him to see the new mine, and stay and share a celebration feast with them; but he was cool to them, and eager to be gone. The whole town came out to farewell him, but the singing and music were subdued.

I had only a short time — too short — to go and say goodbye to the Quelled, and to Dannii. I came back to the Firelord in tears, and as we climbed the mountain road out of Talbar, rain fell. I walked a little way behind my lord, and noticed that his shoulders were stooped, his walk weary and slow, and he leaned on his donkey for support. He could not ride, with the flowing road so treacherous. Our boots squelched in the yellow mud, and water dripped off our hoods and streamed down our clothes. The way was steep, the rocks rising rugged and watery on either side. The rain stopped after a while, but all around water dripped and trickled, and on the puddles ice formed.

The Firelord walked more and more slowly, and I crossed the rain-washed track between us, and peered anxiously into his face. "Are you well, lord?" I asked. "You seem tired. Worse than tired."

He gave me a faint smile. "You read my soul, handmaid."

I lowered my eyes. "Sorry, lord."

"It matters not, Elsha. I would rather it were read by you than by anyone else." He stopped walking and faced me, his breath white on the chilly air. "The earth grieves, Elsha. The earth grieves, and I grieve, and I am weary of the fight.

For almost all my life the burden of the Quelled has been my burden, and I have fought to lift the prejudices and the hate against them. And the Chosen still won't see, even when I give them you. I grieve that they are so blind. I grieve that it is so hard, and will take so long, to change the laws. I am afraid that when I am gone there will be no one else to carry on the fight."

He started walking again, slipped, and almost fell. I took his arm. "Lord, I will carry on the fight," I said.

He smiled and put his arm across my shoulder, and leaned on me a little, and we went on walking.

"What damaged my sign around your neck?" he asked presently.

"I did. The house-owner's wife told me that you made me your handmaid only to appease the Quelled, and to keep peace in the mines that threaten revolt. For one brainsick moment, I believed her."

He laughed quietly. "For a purpose far greater than that, handmaid, I chose you. Though they believe what they will, for the moment."

I opened my mouth to speak, but he suddenly started singing. A rich, deep, chanting song it was, such as my father used to sing when I was a child. "A Quelled myth!" I cried, amazed, delighted. "You know a Quelled myth, lord!"

He looked at me sideways, smiling. "Tell me one you know, and we'll sing a myth-song together."

I sang one of my favourites, a song of earth and ice and fire. After the first verse, he sang with me. We were still singing as we walked up over the first ridge, and saw the mountains marching on ahead of us, the world frozen, over-shadowed, dark with smoke and cloud.

Then he sang another song, one of the old great Quelled legends, one I had heard long ago from Lesharo and not heard since. It was a song I loved, and it meant all the world to me to hear it from my Firelord's lips.

Let me remember the earthlight,
Let me remember the warm,
Show me again in my dream-sight
The fire at the heart of the dawn.

Show me again ancient shining,
Tell me again what is true,
Fire all the bright world enshrining,
Encircling, life-giving blue.

Help me remember the fullness,
The hills and the harvest between,
Show me in visions the richness,
The gladness and glory of green.

Whisper to me in the dark-time,
Sing me a morning-star song,
Watch with me here till the warm-time,
Wait, while I unmake the wrong.

Oh, remember with me all the earthlight,
Whisper with me of the warm,
Walk with me now in our dream-sight
In the fire at the heart of the dawn.

PART TWO

THE SHINING STAR

11

Siranjaro Fire

The Firelord sat in the centre of the celebrations, his majestic face serene and slightly smiling, his fine dark-skinned hands toying with his silver cup of wine. All around him rang the jubilant noises of feasting, shrill laughter, and talk. The music was spirited, the dancing riotous. Most of the men still sat at the table feasting, but many were at the other end of the great hall, dancing with the women who still waited to eat.

Torches blazed all along the walls, and the fire roared. The din reverberated in the high stone walls, and the wooden floor shook with the wild stamping of the dancers. I stood by the big fireplace at the end of the dining table, and watched.

I could not take part in the festivities. I could not dance, since the Chosen would not touch me;

and the women, when it was finally their turn to eat, ignored me. It was forbidden for me to touch the chairs of the Chosen, so I could not sit at the table; and I could not reach over to get a plate of food without touching an elbow or a shoulder. Had I been better acquainted with these people, I might have risked breaking one of their petty laws; but the Firelord and I had arrived here only this evening, and this was his welcome-feast. I knew by now to treat the Chosen with deference until they were used to me.

The noise was lessening now, and the men stood in groups talking and laughing, while the women ate. It was very late, and the children complained and whined, and the women gave their daughters the finest sweets to keep them quiet. The boys had already eaten with their fathers, but now the younger ones lingered around their mothers for a second picking.

I stood and watched and hungered, and listened to the sounds of eating and talking, and the music. After the fourteen-day trek through the hazy grey of the mountains, the colour and brightness of the hall dazzled me. Firelight poured across the floor, blazed on painted boots, jewelled knives, and polished leather belts. It glowed in fur, on brilliant clothes, gems, and on elated faces.

I pushed my hands up my blue embroidered sleeves, and tried to find my lord. He was talking to the owner of this house, and they were laughing together, the owner pleased and beaming, my lord amused and quiet. Young women went up to him with wine jars and offered to refill his silver cup; but he refused, smiling. I saw their faces blush as he talked to them, and saw them whispering together afterwards, ecstatic, overwhelmed.

Even the men wore that look, when he talked to them. They counted even a word or a glance from him a highest honour, a joy. Never had I seen a soul so utterly adored. I think it was not just his divining power they loved: it was his magnetism, his charisma. Even in a crowded feasting hall, he had that energy, that influence that was like a light on him, and set him apart. He did not even have to speak, and people were drawn to him, impressed and inspired.

But when he did speak, when he spoke as judge and lawgiver, then his word was absolute. I have seen him sit in judgement in the towns we visited, and witnessed the power of his word. Even murderers whom he condemned to death bowed without protest to his authority. In all matters of law and judgement, his word was the last, and people gave him unquestioning obedience.

I was constantly amazed that I could say to him things that others would not even dare to think — and he never chastised me. I said to him once: "Lord, if your word is all-powerful, why do you not ease the lives of the Quelled now, and in one hour change all the laws?"

He gave me a slow, wondering smile, one black eyebrow raised. "Ah — I see a revolutionary," he said.

"It seems a waste, lord, to have that power and not to use it."

His face became grave then, and he sighed. "I hear what you say, Elsha. But the Chosen have spent generations and centuries establishing their order. To break their creed, to alter overnight their beliefs and power, would create chaos. Changes can be made, but they must be made with wisdom, with sensitivity and discretion."

"Sensitivity, or timidity?" I said, and immediately wished I hadn't.

"By God, you push me far," he muttered, and I saw that he was very angry. "Handmaid, by simply having a harsha at my side, I undo a hundred of their laws. You do not appreciate what has already been achieved. You are impatient, impetuous. There are virtues you could learn, Elsha. Patience, long-suffering, humility. Practise them."

I did, for an hour or two. I remembered my dream and my vow to God, and kept my peace. And I saw that the Firelord was not timid, but that he was old and very tired, and the people disillusioned him. I saw that he needed me for a friend, not for a thorn in his side.

I had seen many things, in those seven months that he and I had been travelling, divining in the towns among the mountains. I had seen him celebrate, rejoicing in the Chosen festivals. I had seen him happy with his friends, smiling at their stories, their songs and dramas. I had seen him exhausted on the journeys, worn out by the people's love of him, drained by divining. I had seen him leave a crowded room, and go outside for solitude and prayer. I had seen him adored, seen him celebrated, seen him exulted. And I had seen him smile at me across a quiet fire, and say that above all other things in life, he enjoyed my company.

I watched the Chosen around him now, laughing with him, admiring him, honouring him; and I turned away, warm in my soul, and kept my joy secret.

I went to the door, opened for fresh air, and stood leaning against the edge. Behind me was noise and jubilation and light; before me, the silent dark. I thought of Siranjaro mine, and touched the woman-stone in my pocket. For some inexplicable reason, I felt close to home.

There was a quiet movement behind me, and I realised that someone was standing there, close. Closer than was proper, for a Chosen. I turned. A young man was there. He was about my age, and must have been wealthy, because his fingers holding the wine cup were jewelled, and he wore large precious stones on his clothes. The Chosen wore their wealth. The fur on his quilted scarlet coat was pure white, and rare. His hair was brown and curled, his beard a shade darker. His face was flushed from the fire, or wine. I suspected the latter.

"You wish to see me?" I asked. I called no man lord now, save the highest of all.

He looked at my face, saw that I watched his, and stared down into his wine. "I would like to talk with you," he said. Though he stood with his back to the light, I saw that his flush deepened, and he passed his tongue across his upper lip, nervously. He took a gulp of wine, and glanced again at my face. "They said that you look on men's faces," he remarked, and risked a smile.

"And women's," I said. "You men are not the only ones so honoured."

His smile turned to a frown, though not a serious one. "It is not a sign of honour, hand-maid, for a Quelled to look on the face of a Cho-sen. It is an offence."

"Are you offended?"

He looked straight into my eyes, and blushed furiously. Slowly he smiled again. "No, hand-maid. I am not."

A night wind lifted his hair, and the light from the doorway turned it russet-gold. His eyes were a deep green. He took a long breath and said: "There are rumours that you have strange pow-ers, and that you sometimes bewitch our high lord, and that you and he walk together side by side, touching, like two Chosen."

I made my face expressionless.

He drank some more wine, and licked his lips. He had a handsome mouth, his lips well-defined and almost thin, and sensitive. He had a long straight nose, and his eyes were wide and candid. I loved their colour.

"They say you bow to no one, and that you look in men's eyes straight, and conquer their souls," he said, glancing at me. His eyes lingered just a moment on mine, then he looked at my brand. "I've never spoken with a Quelled before," he added. "Nor seen a brand. It doesn't look so bad. On you it's not a blemish, anyway. I've seen girls with warts worse than that."

I laughed and looked away, out into the night. "Are you always so blunt?" I asked.

He laughed, too, silently, his shoulders shaking. He went outside a short way and stood in the snow, his body half turned towards me. I saw his face in profile, radiant, refined. He was slender, and moved with grace, though he was slightly drunk. He looked at me sideways, thoughtfully, and said: "I think the rumours were right."

I tensed, but kept my face blank.

His green eyes glittered, and he came near to me, unsmiling, almost stern. "I think you break a lot of laws," he murmured. "Nearly all of them. I think you despise our laws, and us."

"I don't despise the Chosen," I said, very quiet. "Only your unenlightened laws."

He looked into his wine cup, tilted it, tipped back his head, and drained the last drops. He tapped my shoulder with the empty cup, earnestly. "Excellent word, 'unenlightened'," he said. "An excellent word, for less than excellent laws. I'm going to get more wine. Don't disappear."

He went away for a short time, then came back with two cups. One he offered to me. As I took it, his fingers touched mine. He dipped his fingertips in his wine, then licked them clean, deliciously. He gave me a slow smile. "Ritual cleansing," he said. "Do you wash, if you touch us?"

I shook my head, and held tight to my cup. He laughed, and drank more wine. I sipped mine, cautiously. I had not eaten since dawn that day. The wine was strong and warm, and heavily spiced.

"They say," he said, standing out of the doorway, but facing me, so the light just fell on him, "they say that the Firelord treats you as a woman highest born, and that he talks to you as if you had a mind that equals his. They say you are a firebrand, that you defy authority and speak treason, and he does not reproach you. They say that he reproaches the Chosen if they chasten you, and that he once Quelled all the people in a town because they tried to poison you. Is that true?"

"In part," I said, feeling over-warm. I went outside and leaned against the old stone wall of the house, facing him. "No one confessed, so he branded all the oldest sons."

He whistled. "You must be a valued woman, to be so powerfully avenged."

I smiled into my wine. Valued woman. The words pleased me.

"Valued harsha, I mean," he added. He shot me another grin. "I forget. You're supposed to have no mind, no emotions, no feelings, no soul. You're not even supposed to be able to talk." He sighed. "Ah, such is the unenlightenment of the Chosen, that we cannot judge aright a simple slave. I'll bet you judge us aright, handmaid. Tell me, what say you of me? As a person. Take away a cup or ten of wine. Would you say I am unenlightened, ignorant, and witless?"

"I'd say your wits are very sharp," I laughed, "to get out 'unenlightenment', without your wine affecting it."

"I wouldn't risk a second try," he said. "By the way, have you a name?"

"My name is Elsha."

"Elsha. Mine is Alejandro. And I did well to get that out, too, through all the wine. But you haven't answered me yet, Elsha. What think you of me? My brain, I mean. My body's excellent, so the girls tell me. But my brain. That's the thing that needs examining."

"I think it is not totally devoid of light," I said.

"Ah, I'm pleased to hear it, Elsha. I worry sometimes, about my brain. I question things, you see: I have to know things, go into them, see them from all sides. I worry me. I worry my parents, too. They say I've got a dangerous soul, for a Chosen. You see — " He leaned towards me, close, his right hand on the stones beside my head, his left spilling wine all down my skirt. "You see, Elsha, I don't believe what I'm told about the Quelled. I think you're humans like us, and not animals at all. You prove it, don't you? You live with the high lord. You're intelligent, well-spoken, fearless, honourable, high-souled, lovely, warm . . . Oh God, Elsha. I'll bet you're warm."

His face was close, very close, to mine, and I smelled the wine spices on his breath. Another move, and we'd be breaking laws. Crucial laws. I ducked under his arm, and he sighed and bent his forehead to the freezing stones.

"That's convenient," he muttered. "Be cool, my fevered brain. And it wouldn't hurt you, body, to take a tumble in the snow." He glanced at me across his scarlet sleeve, and smiled. "Don't tell a soul, will you, Elsha, of this night's talk. They'll kill me or Quell me for what I've said. For what I think I've said."

"I'll tell no one, Alejandro."

"Will I meet you again?"

"I suppose so. My lord said we'd be here awhile. And after that, we go to the sacred mountain, for the great Fire Festival."

"Ah, yes. The Fire Festival. I've got one of those, going on inside of me. I don't think it's sacred, though. Probably profane." He looked into my eyes, and his own blazed like jade on fire. "Definitely profane," he said.

I wished him good night, and fled into the

house. I drank my wine quickly, had a rapid second cup, then escaped to my room. One of the servants had already lit my fire, and torches flared on the walls. Kallai waited restlessly on his perch, missing my company. I talked to him for a while, and stroked his soft breast. Then I took off my heavy outer cloak, my blue dress, and crouched for a while by the fire in my creamy underdress. My room was warm, and was not unlike my room at the great house at Jinnah. This town called Qustra was also prosperous, our host's house grand. The furs of my bed shone faintly red, and the wall hangings and rugs made rich shadows on the polished wood and whitened stone. The ceiling was low, and the huge beams stretched black and ghostlike over my head. For all its splendour, the house overpowered me. I could never relax in crowded houses; I preferred the wind-blown caves in the mountains. And best of all were goatskin tents.

I reached for my blue dress, and took my woman-stone out of the pocket. There was a soft knock on my door. I jumped, startled, and my heart raced. "Who is it?" I called.

"Who are you expecting, Elsha?" called the Firelord's voice, and I breathed a sigh of relief. I put my woman-stone down on the warm hearth, and got up to open the door. But my lord had never come before to my room in these great houses, and I was bewildered, afraid, and befuddled by the wine. My hands shook as I drew back the bolt.

He stood there, smiling. He carried a plate laden with all my favourite food: tiny pies containing berries, smoked hezzin meat, dried fruit from places far beyond our mountains, and fresh vegetables sliced fine and soaked in vinegar.

"I noticed that you did not eat," he said. "May I come in?"

"Of course, lord."

He came in, looked around, and set down the plate on a low table by the fire. His eyes, dark and wise, pierced me to the heart. I swallowed, and looked away. He knew about the young man with the green eyes and beautiful mouth. And why did I feel guilty, I who had done no wrong except drink from a Chosen cup?

"I have something to tell you," he said quietly, crouching down by the fire, and picking up a firestone from the basket on the hearth. He held the black stone out to me, and smiled. "From Siranjaro," he said. "Like your talisman." He placed the fuel on the hearth beside my woman-stone, and warmed his hands by the fire.

"From home?" I asked, surprised, kneeling beside him. "Is Siranjaro close?"

"Close enough to send excess firestone to this town, when it ran low. It is over the ranges east of here, Elsha. Not far, as your Kallai flies. Without wings, a six-day walk."

"Lord, may I go there? Please? My parents, my brothers, all my friends, are in Siranjaro. They have no idea where I am, or what's happened to me. I could go there with a guide, stay a few days, and come back."

"Now is not the time," he said gently. "There is somewhere else I want to go before the Fire Festival. After that, you will renew ties with Siranjaro. I promise."

I looked at the black stone in my hands, and almost cried. Maybe hands I knew had mined this stone, hands I loved. I looked at the fire. "Siranjaro flames," I said. "Out of my home, my mine, my earth."

He gave me a strange, tender look, and a smile lingered about his mouth and in the corners of his eyes. "There is a brighter fire than this, come out of Siranjaro," he said.

For a while we sat there, side by side, the silence easy and warm between us. Slowly he stood up. He seemed suddenly very tired.

"Don't forget your true road, Elsha," he said, and left.

12

Other Fires, and Dreams

I placed the kindling grasses and the firestones in the fifth and final urn, and stepped back. As always, the map of the divining ground was detailed and accurate. The Chosen had cleared away the light snowfall, and out of the frozen ground the Firelord had carved a replica of the place called Qustra. I recognised the great eastern cliff, beneath which nestled the tents of the Quelled. I saw the mountain slope opposite, where the town sprawled across its terraces; and the river valley that divided it from Quelled land. My lord had even placed a trickle of tiny stones across the river, to indicate the rope bridge slung across the waters. I recognised the ground where we stood; a small flat area beside the river on the side of the town.

The Firelord lit the central fire, and from it carried a torch to the four urns I had prepared. Then he, too, stepped back off the replica of Qustra, and for a moment stood by me, close. I felt his sleeve brush mine, and glanced quickly at his face. It was hidden by the red hood of his divining robes, but I felt fatigue in him, and strain.

His room in the house was next to mine, and I had heard him pacing in the night, up and down, the floorboards creaking under his boots. This morning he looked hollow-eyed. I did not know whether he was ill or over-driven. He seldom shared his private feelings. But I felt them strongly, and I always knew what he never told. And I knew now that, for some reason, he was at the limits of his endurance. Even making the replica had taxed him, though I helped; and he had yet to call upon the most exacting powers of all.

He crouched for a while behind the fire on the eastern side of the map, and I could not help looking across him at the mountains, and thinking of Siranjaro beyond. For a longer time than usual he sat there, the edges of his robes in the piled-up snow, his shivering hands gripping the upright divining staff. His hooded head was bent, his forehead resting on the staff. I should have been behind him, but I stood opposite, on the western side of the replica of Qustra, and watched him.

After a long time he stood. He lifted his head,

149

and I saw that he looked skywards, and that his lips moved in prayer. He looked old, so old. It grieved my heart. Slowly, he moved onto the replica, and for a while seemed undecided. The crowds watching grew restless, and people looked at each other, frowning; but no one moved. Even the children were silent, knowing that here something mighty was happening, but not fully understanding it.

The Firelord went to the northeastern sector, beyond a small range behind the cliff, and crouched down. The staff rested horizontally, motionless. His head was bent very low, almost to the soil. I yearned to give him my strength. I would have given half my life to help him. He stood up and moved to the sector in the southeast, and crouched again, moving his staff across the ground. It tremored over a low mountain ridge, and stopped. I watched, engrossed, willing him my strength.

I felt the power of the earth, felt it humming through the soles of my boots, up through my legs and thighs and body, up into my heart and mind. A shudder ran along the soil from the northern sector of the map, on the Chosen side of the river, opposite the Quelled tents and the old mine. Wildly, I looked at the Firelord. He was still facing east, away from it, unaware. I looked at the Chosen. Their eyes were riveted on him, rapt, full of expectation and faith. He lay on the ground now, flat against the earth, still facing east. His staff moved in his hand, towards the south. From the northern mountains behind him the tremor came again, and humming warmth with it. The whole earth seemed to sing, to ring with the silent power of hidden flame. I knelt and touched the ground. It whispered of warmth and strength and living fire. It was more than a whisper. It was a song, a triumphant shout. And could he yet not hear it?

He was standing again, facing the opposite way. I stared at him, frantic. It is there! I wanted to cry. There! Behind you, lord!

He took a step forward, his head lifted, listening.

Behind you, lord! Behind! In the north, behind!

He turned and looked towards me, his face hidden in the darkness of his hood. I was still kneeling on the ground, my palms flat on the earth. I was breathing hard, my thoughts whirled like wild things in my head, my whole body shook and rang with the power I felt. Slowly he turned the other way, towards the firestones, and began to walk to the north.

I bent my head, my spirit spent. Vaguely I heard sounds of celebration, of a great shout ringing in the air, of hundreds of people rejoicing. I saw a great darkness, and a single flame burning. And beyond the flame, as I had seen it many times before, a long high road leading to a temple place. But this time the place became obscured, blacked out with mist and ice and flashing shafts like swords.

When I looked up again, the Firelord and all the crowd were gone. I could see them far in the distance, bright against the rocks and snow. It was the first time in all our divining days that I had not gone on with him to measure out the new mine, and set the exact place. Guilt rushed over me. Had I called aloud? Or only in my soul? And either way, had he heard? Did he know?

Never before had I helped him divine. In the past months I had often felt the power when he divined, but always I had closed my mind to it and shut it out. But today, today when he had laboured and anguished — today I had intervened. And I was terrified. I had overstepped my mark, committed the ultimate trespass, encroached on ground where I had no right to be. I had usurped his power, and had betrayed my lord.

Guilt-ridden, I went back to the town, to the great house where we stayed. I went up to my room and tore off the red divining dress. I put on the least lovely of all the clothes I had been given, the warmest and most practical. It was a dull brown dress woven of sheepswool, and I wore it sometimes on our journeys, when the way was hard and cold. The hem was already worn out from climbing jagged rocks, and there was a tear in one sleeve where Kallai's claw had caught. I did not feel guilty keeping it. Into a large leather drawstring bag I packed two underdresses, a spare dress, an extra cloak, a pair of spare boots, and a towel to dry myself when

I crossed rivers. I packed some flints, a good supply of firestones, and a heavy blanket. If I used his caves on the way, I should have enough provisions to survive. Siranjaro was only six days away.

I took Kallai from his perch, and he sat on the leather glove, alert and energetic, ready for a hunt. Finally, I took off the sacred sign I wore. I had polished it with fine sand, but still it bore the scratches I had made. I wished I could write him a message. Instead, I placed the sign on the floor outside his door, and left. On the way I passed through the kitchens, and took some cold meat and pies and bread left over from last night.

I was barely out of the shadow of the house when I heard someone call my name. I spun around, caught, red with guilt. It was Alejandro. He came sauntering towards me over the uneven ground, smiling, his boots ringing on the stones.

"Greetings, handmaid! Is the divining all finished, over so soon? Why is no one else back yet?"

My head spun. "I left early," I said. "I was not feeling well."

His clothes were all azure blue, and splendid, and I regretted my dusty brown. But he did not notice my dress. His eyes roved over the bulky bag across my shoulder, and on to Kallai on my wrist. "I see. You feel ill, Elsha, so you go out hunting?"

I started walking, to give myself time to think. He followed me, loping in long strides across the ground, groaning. "Not so fast, handmaid! My head has a drum in it today. I've just woke up, and found I missed the fun. But your face is lovelier by far than the Firelord's. Well, not lovely, exactly. Your nose is bent, your mouth is too wide, and your eyes are crossed. But there's something appealing about you."

"Thanks," I said, and couldn't help smiling. I could cope with criticism more easily than compliments from him.

He laughed silently again, his shoulders shaking. "If you're going hunting, let me come with you?" he asked. "I smell dried berry pies in that mighty bag of yours, and cold chicken. I'm starved."

I looked at him sideways, wondering how to get rid of him, and he shot me a devilish grin, and added: "It would also give me untold pleasure to spend time in your company. Those firecrossed eyes of yours have conquered me."

I said, as kindly as I could: "I need time alone, Alejandro."

"A lot of time alone, I'd say," he murmured, looking at my bag again. "Are you sure you're only going hunting, Elsha?"

I was trapped. I hesitated, thinking. "Yes," I said. "And you may come with me, then, but only if you do everything I ask."

"I'll do it with all my heart," he said. "I'm your captive, your bondman, your enchanted slave. Speak the word only, and I'll lay my body on the stones, and make a mat of me for your beloved feet."

"Carry this," I said, giving him my bag, and laughing.

"By God — this is heavy!" he exclaimed, pretending to stagger under the weight. At least, I think he pretended. "What have you got in it — firestones?"

"Some of those. Leave it here, if you like. Somewhere on a high rock, where we can find it later. I don't need all that's in it. Not at the moment."

"I'll get the food out first." Before I could stop him, he was delving deep in the bag. "What's this?" He pulled out one of the underdresses, held it up, and rolled his eyes. "Oh, be still, my beating heart! It is the handmaid's undergarment! Oh, sweet, sweet smell! To conquer a man through his nose, to lead him about — "

I grabbed the dress with my free hand, and stuffed it back into the bag. "It smells of the soap I wash it with, fool!" I cried, furious. I glared at him, my face flaming. "Don't go through my things! Bring the whole bag now, since you can't control yourself. It'll give you a useful occupation. And stop tormenting me."

"I didn't think I was tormenting you, handmaid," he murmured, as we walked on. He carried my bag over his shoulder. "I thought I was amusing you. I had hoped you enjoyed my company. I'm sorry."

I walked on, silent. I had too many things on my mind and in my heart. I wished he was not here. And I was glad he was.

"Elsha, I know something troubles you," he said gently, his sleeve brushing mine as he stumbled on a rock. We were climbing higher, up into the mountains east of the town, away from the divining ground. "I know you were leaving. It's not because of me, is it?"

I stopped walking, and looked at him. His face was earnest, and there were tiny droplets of sweat on his brow and along the dark brown hair on his upper lip. His eyes were golden-green in the daylight, his lashes long and golden-brown. His eyes were full of light. I must have looked confused, because he added, blushing: "They know we drank wine together, last night. My uncle owns the house you stay in. They said my conduct was unacceptable, because I took you wine in one of our cups."

"And the Firelord took me food on one of your plates," I said, tearing my eyes from his. "If he can break laws, so can you."

"But he didn't do it openly. We have to be careful, Elsha."

"Why? We do no wrong."

"You're not leaving because of me, then?"

"No. It's nothing to do with you."

"So you are leaving?"

"Stop it, Alejandro!" I started walking again, quickly, and Kallai clutched harder on my fist, disturbed, sensing what I felt.

156

"Stop what, handmaid? Caring? Being interested? I'd have thought you needed a friend, needed someone to talk with face-to-face, who honoured you. You're in between two worlds, aren't you? You live with the Chosen, yet you're Quelled. Life must be hellish lonely for you at times. I don't blame you for wanting to go home. Even if home is slavery."

"You don't know anything. Not the first thing about me. So stop making judgements. I'm not so lonely that I want to go back to the mine, and I wouldn't waste my spit on your laws. Stop plaguing me. You're like a flea in my sleeping furs."

"I wish I was. No — I'm sorry. Sorry I said that. God, you've got a rage, Elsha. I only came to be your friend. If I fire you up that much, I'll go."

He stopped, and slung my bag to the ground. "I'll see you back at the house. Or maybe I won't. Do you want me to give the high lord a message from you?"

I stood still and stared at him, my heart in pain, and heavy. So heavy. "Yes, please. Tell him I'm sorry. Tell him I need time to think."

He came close to me, and took my shoulders in his hands. "Now let me farewell you properly, like a friend." He kissed my left cheek, and his beard felt rough and warm. He kissed my other cheek, and I felt his breath on my neck, hot and moist. He kissed my mouth, and I was all confusion inside, and chaos, and dark. And out of the darkness I saw the flame I had seen in the vision, and I heard the words my lord had said last night. I fought my way out of the dark, and pushed him away.

I was no longer confused, about Alejandro or my road.

"We'll go hunting after all," I said, smiling, my heart suddenly light. "And tonight I'll cook my lord a raven in his favourite sauce, as a peace offering for him. But there'll be no more kissing between us, Alejandro."

He grinned, and bent and picked up my bag. "It would be sweet, Elsha, to give you covering," he murmured. "But I hear your words, and shall obey. Besides, something tells me that you're on a different road, one to do with fire. And your fire and mine are different."

He slung my bag across his shoulder, smiled, and put his bright arm about my neck. "So we'll hunt, then, Elsha. That poor bird of yours got almost squashed, and tore a hole in my arm. Oh, it's nothing to worry about. I won't bleed to death. I'm the sort who'll die of a broken heart, nothing less."

We did hunt with Kallai. And all the time he flew, Alejandro and I talked. Since I would not talk about myself, he told me all that he believed. I learned that day that the things I believed about the Quelled and Chosen, about equality and truth and myths and humanity, were all shared by a young Chosen man with eyes of green, who looked in my face straight, and had a heart all like my own.

It was dark when we returned to the house. I was too late to cook my lord a raven; the men's meal was already in progress. Just outside the door of the great hall, Alejandro and I parted. In the shadows he took my chin in his hand, and caressed my lips with his thumb, gently. But he did not kiss me. "I have loved this day, Elsha," he said. "Never have I talked like that with anyone. Hold my secrets close, won't you?"

"Have no fear," I said. "It gives me strength, to have a friend."

"You need strength, then?"

I nodded. He smiled, then turned quickly and went inside into the noise and feasting-smells and light. The men had almost finished eating, and I could hear music again. I was glad the Firelord would be occupied and in company. I picked up my bag, went to the kitchens, and left the ravens Kallai had caught. I went up to my room, panting with my heavy bag on all the flights of stairs. I had gone soft since I had left the mine.

The house was silent on the upper floors. I pushed open my heavy door, but before I went in, I glanced at the floor outside my high lord's door. The scratched sign was gone. So he knew. I swore softly, and went into my room. It was in darkness, and smelled faintly of ancient carpets, polished wood, and smoke. I could barely see. I dropped my bag on the wide hearth, and felt in its depths for the flints and firestones. I lit the fire, and knelt in front of it awhile, dreaming of Siranjaro. I tried not to think of Lesharo. I had betrayed more than one man this day.

After a while the fire blazed, and I took a dead torch from its bracket on the wall, dipped it in the flames, and put it up again. The room was warm with fire-glow, and the shadows danced. I heard a soft sound, and looked up. The Firelord stood over by my window. I was shocked, crushed anew by guilt, and could not speak. He came over by the fire, and I saw that he still wore his divining clothes, though the hood was pushed back. His face was tawny and dark, and the firelight flashed in his eyes and turned them coppery. He did not sit, but stood there, silent, overshadowing, and black.

"For the first time, you have displeased me," he said, his voice hollow and deep and almost inaudible. "I ache in my soul, Elsha."

I stared at the fire, hardly breathing, seeing only a man bowed over in divining ground, suffering. "I am sorry, lord," I said.

"Words cannot undo what has been actioned. I had such high dreams for you, Elsha. Fine dreams, dreams I believed you would fulfil. I dreamed of you, knew you before I heard your name, loved you before I ever saw your face. I loved the fire in you. I trusted you. And you have betrayed it all."

"I'm sorry. I could not help it, lord. The power was strong, the song deep."

"That I know. But it must be mastered, Elsha, or all is lost. There is a right time for everything. Have you forgotten what I said last night, about your road? About not losing it?"

"I'm sorry, lord! I went too far. I did not mean you to know. Not yet."

"Know, Elsha? The whole house knows of it! The whole town! It was the major talk at the feast tonight!"

I half rose and looked at him, unbelieving. I couldn't speak, for horror and bewilderment and guilt. He started pacing the floor, furious, his robes swinging as he strode, his shadow raging on the reddened walls.

"Have you no shame, Elsha? No sense at all of what is right? Was it not enough to drink wine with him last night — did you have to come back early today to meet with him, and go creeping off up into the mountains? And in the name of the power, why did you leave your sacred sign behind? So you could do anything, without guilt? So you could throw aside your destiny for a day, forget everything you are, for one brief forbidden ecstasy? And it will be brief, Elsha. He is not on your road. He's a distraction, a momentary madness. He'll finish everything for you."

Shaking all over, I stood up and confronted him. Relief flooded me. I didn't know whether to laugh or weep. "Lord, you talk of nothing!

He's a friend. Only a friend. We did nothing."

"Nothing? Then why did you say you could not help yourself, that the power was strong? How would you know, unless he touched you? And how is it then that you went too far, and did more than you wanted me to know? What are you talking of? I think you lie to me, hand-maid. I feel something in you that is less than all the truth, something veiled. I think you lie."

"I do not lie! Not to you! You know everything, anyway! And even if I did want some brief pleasure, what does it matter? What does it matter if I need human warmth, human closeness, human joy? If you choose to be a priest, untouched and removed from the rest of us, that's a high thing, and I love you for it, and for other reasons. But you have not the right to make me the same as you, to put your restrictions around me, to put your choices and sacrifices on me. I can't live without human love, without a friend to look in my face and touch my hand once in a while. I can't be like you, I can't be the person you expect — "

"You have to be! Elsha, I will not suffer this! Never before in all my life has a woman dared to raise her voice to me! And you are harsha. Without me, you would be nothing."

"I have not changed," I said, "just because I burned my mining clothes and wear your sacred sign. I am still Elsha. Elsha of the Quelled. How can I ever forget it? It's branded on me, burned into me, stamped into my flesh. But it doesn't touch my soul. And my soul is the same, whether I live in a goatskin tent or a grand house, whether I live with a harsha friend, or a Chosen youth, or you. None of you touch me. You don't make me anything. I am me. Myself. Elsha. Woman."

He sighed then, pulled his cloak close about him, and leaned on the wall, away from me. "I cannot fight you," he said hoarsely.

"Then don't, lord. If it is my relationship with Alejandro that troubles you, we did nothing. We talked. And he kissed me, that's all."

I hesitated, and the Firelord turned and leaned with his back against the wall, looking sideways at me, one flamelit eyebrow raised. He smiled faintly. "So, he kissed you, Elsha. And why did you stop there, you whose spirit is all passion and fire? Don't tell me you had a sudden urge to obey the laws."

"I remembered what you said last night, about my road."

He smiled, and rubbed his hand down across his face and beard, and softly laughed. "I think I don't always read you very well, Elsha."

"No, lord. You don't. You're not often wrong, though."

"I am never wrong. It's just that I am not always totally correct. But I can read you well enough, for my purpose." He smiled suddenly, and stood up straight. "I am sorry I did not trust you, handmaid. You know how fine is the line you walk in this Chosen world. You are either worthy and accepted, or you are rejected and de-

163

spised. Remember that it is a wrong for you to touch a Chosen. But for you to receive covering from a Chosen man is a felony they would kill you for, and him."

He came over to me and touched his palm to my cheek, tenderly, and smoothed back my hair from my face. His hand trembled, and his eyes, though they glowed, were very tired. To my amazement he bent and kissed my forehead, on the upper edge of my brand. "Be careful, child," he murmured. "All my hope is in you, my highest dream."

Then he left.

I sank to the floor by the fire, shattered, quaking in every part. Stupidly, I started crying, and couldn't stop. What a day, I thought, sobbing. Conquered by divining power, desertion, fury, kisses, and chaos — and I'd had the gall to say I was untouched.

Liar, Elsha lionheart.

The next three days were busy for the Firelord. He drew up the plans for the new mine, marked the depths and directions of the new firestone seams, and supervised the beginning of the first tunnel.

When I was not with him at the new mine, I was with Alejandro, out hunting with Kallai. We always made a pleasure of the hunts, taking food and wine and scrolled books, so Alejandro could read to me. I cannot say how much I loved his company. With him I laughed, and knew I had not laughed enough before. He was like a medicine for me, a healing, a balm for the world's bitterness.

On my last day in Qustra I went out hunting with Kallai, and Alejandro came with us. After we had hunted, we lay in thick tussock grass on a blanket Alejandro had brought, and he read to me from Chosen myths. I lay crosswise to him, on my back, my head on his chest for a pillow. He had one arm across me, lightly, and with his other hand he held up the scrolled book. Kallai was on a rock nearby, uncomfortable without a proper perch. Alejandro stopped reading after a while, and dropped the book on the blanket beside us. He was laughing in that silent way of his, and I felt his body shake. I laughed, too, at the conceit in the myth he'd read.

"I wish you weren't leaving, Elsha," he said, suddenly grave. "Who will I talk to, when my other self is gone? Who will listen to my inspired madness, and sympathise with my misdirected soul?"

"I don't think it is misdirected," I said, sitting up. "I think your soul is right on the mark. It's the rest of the Chosen race that's errant."

"So half the world is wrong, Elsha?"

"Yes, it is."

He sat up, laughing softly. "Sweet heresies!" he said, and reached for the cloth-wrapped parcel of our meal. He spread it out in front of him. There was a wineskin, too, which he uncorked. He drank deeply, and gave me a scarlet-lipped smile. "I'll miss this good wine, when our high lord goes. They'll put it away until the next important guest arrives, and we'll suffer vinegar again. Do you realise this is our farewell feast, Elsha, since tomorrow you will go?"

"I know it," I said, and waited for him to offer me the wine. He recorked it, and set it down carefully on the ground. He began to eat, hungrily.

This was the third meal we had eaten, just the two of us, out here. Maybe I was crazed to think it, but I had almost hoped that he would let me eat with him. Not afterwards, when he had finished, as tradition dictated — but with him, at the same time. I could have reached out, could have helped myself to a portion of bread and a piece of cheese; but it would have meant more if he had offered it. It would have meant everything.

And it was then, watching him eat before me, that I realised there was inconsistency in him. He said there was no difference between Chosen and Quelled; he said men were not more sacred than women, nor women less than men; he said we were side by side, matched in every way; he *said* all these things — but his life spoke differently. He still ate before me, first, as my lord. And in that simple act, he undid all his words.

I said goodbye to him early the next morning. He told me that his father was sending him to the army in the northern territories, to knock his mad ideas into shape. I told him of Amasai, and asked him to salute that man for me. And I thought to myself that Amasai was not the man for mending mad ideas. Alejandro kissed my cheek and held me close, and said he'd miss me like a kindred soul.

A short time later my lord and I were on a high windy road, our faces set towards the sacred mountain, the site of the great Fire Festival. That mountain I had seen in dreams, and now I knew its name. It was Kasimarra.

But on the way we visited another place, a hidden, nameless place, about which the Firelord swore me to secrecy. And that place, concealed deep within a circle of mountains, and reached only by a secret pass, became for me the most beloved place on earth.

13

The Light in My Dark

The Firelord was ill on our journey to that place. He shook all over, and his long hair was wet with sweat. The beautiful dark sheen was gone from his skin, and he looked almost grey. His eyes were dull, emptied of all passion and power. It grieved my heart to see him this way. Several times he went behind rocks and vomited, and barely had the strength afterwards to climb back on his donkey. I begged him to go back to Qustra, but he said there was a friend he had to see, and he would not be dissuaded from his road.

Thick mist swirled all around, and at times I could see only a step or two ahead. I was afraid of being lost, and only the frequent prayer-stones along our way reassured me. The Firelord was, I thought, beyond knowing where we were. He leaned far forward over his donkey's neck, and at times I was sure his mind and spirit had flown elsewhere. But after a while he turned and waited for me to come alongside, and said: "We are very near now, Elsha. Remember that the place we go to is secret. We will stay here sixteen days, and then we will travel to the sacred mountain, to conduct the Fire Festival. But swear to me again that our time here will be unspoken of for as long as you live."

"I swear, lord."

He went on a short way further, then got off his donkey and began leading it. He turned left, dragging the unwilling beast into a narrow place behind a huge rock. I thought at first he had lost his wits, and was forcing the animal into a place where it would be trapped; but when I followed I saw that the rock concealed a fissure in the cliff.

"Just follow, handmaid," my lord said calmly. "Don't be afraid. I know where I am going."

The crack we entered was narrow and pitch-black. The walls pressed in on either side, close. From far away came the faint hum of firestone power, and a trickling of water. I was at home in the blackness and the rock, but Kallai's talons tightened on my fist, and I felt his fear.

I walked on, blind, following my lord's laboured breathing, and the sound of his weary footsteps dragging in the dust ahead of his donkey's hooves. Suddenly the walls glimmered, and we were out. I stared, dazzled by the sudden light, convinced I was in a dream.

We had come to a place enclosed totally by mountain cliffs, a small interior plain with a high waterfall at one end and a river that vanished into rapids at the base of a cliff. Here there was no mist, no wind. It was like another world.

Around the edges of the plain, in the sheltered places under the towering cliffs, were dwellings built of stone and mud. Some were built into the cliffs, half cave, half house. There were gardens with vegetables and rows of corn, and small herds of goats. There was a mine tunnel going straight into a mountain wall from ground level, with firestone dust blackening the ground around. As I looked, a group of Quelled came out with their full baskets. I looked for an overseer, but saw none. The Quelled walked in a group, laughing and chattering, and one of the women stopped, put down her load, and talked to a small child who ran up to her. No one corrected her; no caretaker came to take the child away. No one supervised. The Quelled took the baskets to different houses, and stayed in them, I assumed to rest, or to talk. I could hardly believe my eyes.

Three of the Quelled men came out again, brushing the dust from their trousers and coats. One of them must have said something witty, because they all laughed loudly, and then walked on, straight and daring, away from the mine. They were not wearing the dull grey garments of the Quelled, and some of their clothes looked colourful and fine under the firestone dust.

Beside me the Firelord laughed quietly, his face

all life again, and urged his donkey on. "Come, handmaid," he said. "I see my friend." He called and waved, and one of the Quelled men turned, and ran towards us.

He was a tall man, well-built, slender, with long dark brown hair and a rich beard. His skin was dark, though not as dark as my lord's. He moved with an easy grace, with energy and strength, though he'd just come from labour in the mine. He reached my lord and they embraced, laughing, and the man kissed both the Firelord's cheeks, and hugged him again. Astounded, I saw that underneath the firestone dust the man had no brand. He was Chosen. And he was young, not more than five-and-twenty. I had expected someone old.

He turned to me, saw the bewilderment on my face, and smiled. He was not a handsome man, but there was something charismatic about him, under all the firestone dust. It was not a physical thing, it was spiritual, and difficult to describe. But I was drawn to him.

The man looked on my face and saw my brand, and he smiled again and welcomed me as he had welcomed my high lord — with a kiss on both my cheeks, and an embrace that made Kallai flutter, and my heart. I was stunned, speechless, undone. All my impressions of the Chosen vanished like smoke before the wind. I heard the Firelord tell the man my name.

"Welcome to my home, Elsha," the man said, taking my free hand. His smile changed, became an almost boyish grin, full of apology and humour. His eyes were the clearest blue, and looked striking against his dark skin. "I've put firestone dust all over you, I'm sorry."

I looked down at my clothes, and thought that I would never wash them again. "It doesn't matter, lord," I said. "I am used to firestone dust. I worked in a mine myself." The admission punished me, but he had to know, and he must have missed my brand.

"So I noticed," he said. "Don't call me lord, Elsha. My name is Teraj."

He released my hand, and we began walking across the dusty plain towards the houses. Teraj walked with his arms about my lord, tenderly, like a loving son with a father. I took the rope about the donkey's neck and walked a little way behind. People came out of the houses or over from the gardens to wave to us and call greetings, and many children appeared and skipped alongside us, enchanted with my bird.

I noticed that most of the people were Quelled, and had been terribly injured. Many of them limped or walked leaning on their friends, or had no arms or hands. I saw a man walking with a stick, tapping it on the ground before him, as though he could not see. One of the children ran over to him and talked excitedly of us, and he looked in our direction, and waved. It suddenly struck me that I had never seen a Quelled before who couldn't work. Dannii was the only one I had ever seen who was too crippled to work in the mine, but she had been able to do caretaker work. Yet many of these people here could not even have been caretakers; they were too crippled, beyond being useful to the Chosen. I marvelled that I had never wondered before what happened to the Quelled too injured or sick to work. I had never seen any. Had the Chosen killed them? Or had they been brought here?

I stopped walking, and stared at a girl with no legs, who moved herself around on a small wheeled platform on the ground, propelling herself along with two pointed sticks. I was shocked, appalled, almost sick. She came close by us, and said something to Teraj, and he pushed her with his foot and sent her racing down a gentle slope. She shrieked with laughter, her sticks waving joyously above her head.

Teraj, seeing my face, my horror, said gently: "I will explain all this later, Elsha."

"But how does she *live*?" I cried, almost in tears. "And that old man over there, with his eyes and half his face gone — where is he from? What happened to them all? What is this place?"

"Later, we'll talk," said Teraj, and took my lord into one of the houses. A boy came and took the donkey from me. I call him a boy, but he was a man. He would have been thirty years old, perhaps, but he was small and squat, and his face was round and childlike. His eyes slanted slightly upwards at the outer corners, his nose was small, his jaw heavy and unbearded. He looked straight into my face, though he was Chosen, and smiled broadly.

"My name's Shimer." His voice was deep and his speech impaired, but I understood.

"My name is Elsha," I said. "I'm the Firelord's handmaid."

"I'm his friend," he said, nodding towards Teraj. "I love him."

I smiled, won by his simplicity, his openness. I had never seen anyone like him before. I followed Teraj and my lord into the house, and stopped in the doorway, surprised and delighted.

The house of Teraj was like none other I had seen. It was one-roomed, large, and built deep into a cliff, part cave, part timbered house, part stone. One of the supporting beams inside was the huge leaning trunk of an ancient tree, its top long lost in soil and stone, but its trunk and roots still strong. I learned that Teraj had carved strange signs on it, and images of birds and unfamiliar animals. The dwelling was a pleasing blend of homely crafts and the richest Chosen furnishings. Tables and chairs were hand-carved and rough, yet stood on finest wooden floors. In other sections the floor was trampled dirt, spread with thick wool weavings more beautiful than any I had seen in wealthy homes. The cave had earthern shelves cut deep into the walls, and filled with unskilled pottery and rough-carved spoons, yet the windows on the timbered side were covered with shutters of outstanding latticework.

Curtains, woven of richest dyed wool, partitioned the house into kitchen, living space, and bedroom. Heavy fabrics blazed on the dark walls, and I glimpsed a magnificent Chosen carved bed laden with wool blankets of scarlet and gold, and rich black furs.

The house enfolded me, welcomed me with the earthy warmth of wool, stone, soil, and wood, and blessed me like an embrace.

It was a blessing, too, just being near Teraj. I watched him take my lord behind the curtains to the bed, heard him talking gently, his voice full of compassion and love, and heard the tranquil sounds of water as he washed the sick man's face and hands. I stood by a window and looked out through the latticework at the peaceful scene outside, encircled and protected by the high mountain walls, and I felt as if I had at last come home.

Teraj went into the kitchen part of the house, and I heard the sound of washing again. He brought me a bowl of warm water and a towel, and I, too, washed. I watched as he set a small meal of bread and cheese on the table, and a bowl of sliced fresh vegetables. He put two plates and two knives on the table. The plates were rough pottery, and I guessed he had made them himself. But the knives had handles of silver, and were ornate. He poured two chalices of wine, and offered one to me. I hesitated. It was a bone and silver chalice, highly valuable, and obviously his own.

"I have my own drinking cup, lord, in a travelling bag," I said. "I'll get it, if you wish."

He smiled, and still held out the chalice. "Why, Elsha? Is my best cup not good enough?"

I blushed, and looked away. "I thought that you, being Chosen, would not share your drinking vessels with a Quelled."

"I see no Quelled," he said.

I looked at his face and saw that his lips were curved, though his eyes were very grave. So blue, his eyes. I took the cup and looked away again.

He went over to the table, drew out two chairs, and invited me to sit with him. I did, though it felt strange sitting on a Chosen chair at a Chosen table, to wait while the man ate. I sipped my wine, and did not look at his face. He picked up a small crusty loaf of bread, and broke it.

"You surprise me, Elsha," he murmured, beginning to eat. "I had heard that you were all arrogance and fire, and that you called men by their names, straight, like their equal. Yet you call me lord, and you won't meet my eyes." There was warmth in his voice, bordering on laughter, rich and enveloping.

So I looked at him over my chalice, while I drank. The wine was warm and smooth, and soothed my heart. In the dimness, he looked kingly, his nose straight and hooked, like the Firelord's, his brow high and clear, his skin glowing and bronze. His mouth was well-formed, expressive and strong, and his eyes — his eyes had blue fire in them. His long curling hair and full beard were dark, with lights like tawny wine. His face was striking, yet had serenity. He had that air of self-command that the Firelord had; detachment mixed with warmth, peace with compassion.

We smiled at each other over the table, and he said: "You asked before about this place, Elsha. It is a sanctuary, a hiding place for the Quelled injured in the mines, or born deformed or mentally sick, whom the Chosen would have killed. They are brought here secretly, and live lives as whole and happy as possible. There are no slaves here, no lords. We all work in the mine if we are able, for as many hours a day as we like, and we share our firestones.

"The Firelord founded this place thirty years ago. There is no name for where we live, and you will find it on no map. If the Chosen knew of it, we would be destroyed. We do not have their laws here, or their creed. We have only the great law of God, which is love; and our creed is that every soul is free to be most truly itself. Aren't you eating, Elsha? I thought you'd be hungry, after your journey."

He broke another loaf, and held half out to me. Astounded, I took it, and for the first time in my life I shared a meal with a man.

We ate awhile in silence, then I asked: "Who heals the injured Quelled brought here? Is there a physician?"

"I heal," he said.

Looking at him, at his gentle strength, I believed him. His very presence healed.

"Is that why my lord came here?" I asked,

glancing back towards the bed. I could hear the Firelord snoring peacefully. "Did he come to you for healing?"

Teraj nodded, and finished his wine. He turned towards the shadows, away from me, and bent his head. I touched his sleeve, and felt a tingling come from him, a vibration not unlike firestone power. I withdrew my hand, disturbed in more ways than one.

"My lord is very ill, isn't he?" I said.

Teraj turned to me again. "He is deadly ill, Elsha. His stomach is destroyed by disease, and it invades his other parts. I will do what I can for him to ease his pain and lend him strength for the Fire Festival, but beyond that I do not know."

Grief and fear washed over me, and I stood up and turned away blindly, lost. Teraj took my cup from my hand, and I felt his arms and the warm firestone dust of his shirt, and the grief and strength of him.

"He does not know how ill he is," he said gently, his hand beneath my chin, lifting it. "Don't tell him, Elsha. He needs all his energy for the festival. Let him think he has a temporary illness that will run its course and go away again."

"What happens if he dies?" I asked faintly, hardly daring to think.

"That is all answered," said Teraj, letting go my face, and smiling. "I hear him waking now. Be brave, Elsha, and let me see that lion's heart of yours."

14

Secret Powers

My lion's heart had never been so sorely tried as it was in the following days. Daily my lord's condition worsened. He vomited constantly, and often it was blood. He was in a great deal of pain, and even in his sleep he moaned and tossed, tormented. Teraj gave him herbal medicines to ease the pain, but the Firelord could not keep them down. His face became an awful grey, and his eyes were hollow and dull. All his years fell on him at once, his hair turned white almost overnight, and he looked, suddenly, incredibly old. He shivered constantly, and his flesh felt like ice.

Teraj made a bed for him on the floor close by the fire, wrapped him in the thickest furs and woollen blankets, and placed warmed stones at his feet. He sat with him nearly all the time, or lay beside him, talking quietly or praying, and always his hands smoothed back the Firelord's hair or massaged his brow, or stroked his wrists. There was so much tenderness in Teraj, it made my heart ache to see it. And healing came from his hands, powerfully. Under his touch my lord's pain eased, his face became, within moments, peaceful and smiling, and he slept like a child.

When Teraj was not with my lord, I was. I sang to him, since that pleased him; and at last I could do what I had always longed to do, and had never dared: I touched his hair and hands, fed him, washed his face for him, and showed him small tokens of my love. He said one day, when he was almost asleep, that my hands had healing in them, and eased his pain as much as Teraj's did. Teraj heard, and smiled. But the Firelord squeezed my fingers, and slept for a long time without pain.

While Teraj and I looked after the Firelord, Shimer cooked our meals and cleaned the house, and did the washing for us. He was a treasure to watch. Even the smallest things he did required the most intense concentration, and he did everything slowly, with great care. If people had not come often to help, it would have taken him a whole day to shake the mats and sweep the floor, and to grind flour for bread. All the time he talked, laughing quietly, sometimes singing. I thought he talked to himself, but I listened one day and realised he was talking to God. And sometimes he lifted his head, intent, listening, as if he heard answers. I mentioned it to Teraj, and Teraj did not think it strange.

"Shimer's soul is all untouched, Elsha, like a child's," he said. "He has never forgotten the God he came from, and he walks every day in paradise. He has the best philosophy of anyone I know, the most wisdom, and the most love. Sometimes he says profound and prophetic things, and they always come to pass."

"I know someone else whose soul is pure," I said.

Teraj smiled, and went on slicing the vegetables. We often prepared them for Shimer, else we would not have eaten our evening meal until midnight, he was so slow. "It is good that you love our Firelord well," Teraj said. "Some of his handmaids used him to further their own ends, and did not love him except for the wealth and position he gave. You stand high above them, Elsha."

"I didn't mean the Firelord's soul," I murmured. "I meant yours."

He looked surprised, then laughed. "You know my soul, Elsha?" he asked, smiling sideways down on me. He was head and shoulders taller than me.

"You wear your soul like a light," I said. "It fills all this place."

"Then tread softly," he said, "you may walk on it." We laughed together, and I threw a piece of parsnip at him. There was a joy in Teraj, a spirit of celebration, that made just being with him a pleasure. We laughed at the simplest things: at faces Shimer pulled; at the absurd, wise talk of children, when they didn't know we listened; at the sight of each other covered in black mud, when we'd worked together in a wet shaft in the mine; and we laughed sometimes at nothing at all, just because we loved each other's company.

We were not often alone. If a woman came to be with the Firelord for a while, and we went for a walk to fly Kallai, or to the mine, or to lie by the waterfall and talk, Shimer always came with us. He adored Teraj. They were always together. Even when we went for walks and Teraj walked close and took my hand, Shimer was always on his other side, talking and laughing to himself in that low, gruff voice. And yet I did not mind his being there; he gave only brightness.

But in the evenings when Shimer was in his narrow bed by the window, and the Firelord snored, Teraj and I sat together by the fire and drank herb tea. He read me the poems he wrote, and sometimes made me laugh, and sometimes cry.

I took the scroll from his hands one night, and looked at it, marvelling at the mysterious patterns of ink on paper. "It is a wonder," I said, "to wrap up joy and grief in signs, for someone else to understand." I traced the forms of the words, and lifted the thick paper and sniffed it.

Teraj grinned. "You won't learn through your nose, Elsha," he said. "But if you want to read, I'll teach you." He got up, lit a candle and placed it on the table. He took some paper and charcoal from a carved wooden box near his bed, and spread them out in the candlelight. He sat down, drew a chair close beside his, and told me to sit. I did, and he started writing on one of the sheets. I watched, conscious of his thigh pressed against mine, and the faint, pleasant smell of the leather vest he wore. His face was golden in the candlelight, his eyes translucent and shining, and calm like still waters. He finished writing, and glanced up at me.

"You're supposed to be looking at the words, not me," he smiled. I blushed and moved my chair away a bit, and studied what he'd done. He explained what the letters were, and the sounds they stood for.

Came the Firelord's voice, across the dark and firelit room: "It's the wrong one, Teraj."

Teraj looked up. "I thought you were asleep, Abishai," he said. It was a word he called the Firelord, but it was not the Firelord's name. I did not know his name, until later. Only Teraj called him Abishai, and I think it was a special term of love between them.

"It's as well I'm not asleep," muttered my lord. "You're teaching my handmaid the wrong language."

Teraj frowned, got up, and went over to the Firelord. I saw him bend over him, stroking his forehead and cheeks, feeling his temperature. "You're cold, Abishai," he said softly. "Would you like me to heat the stones again, near your feet?"

"No. It's more important that Elsha reads. Teach her our high language. Not the common one."

"The high language? It's twice as hard! And she'll never use it. Our common tongue's more like Quelled speech, it'll be easier for her."

My lord sighed and moved restlessly, as if in pain. Teraj stayed with him awhile until he slept, then came back to the table. He gave me a grin, and turned the paper over. "The high language it is," he said, picking up the charcoal. "I have a feeling I'm going to regret this. I hope your brain likes exercise."

"My brain can fly," I said.

His smile grew, and he looked at me straight. "That's good, Elsha. It'll be able to fly all the way to Kasimarra and read the books in the great library there. You'll read all the history of our world, and laugh and weep over the stupidity and glory of the Chosen race."

His face became blurred, and I saw the holy mountain, saw within the mountain, saw vast rooms, and rows and rows of pale scrolls. I saw pages unfurled, saw letters and the shapes of words, and ink, so much ink, heavy and tragic and black. And then, suddenly, an explosion of white light.

I blinked, half blinded by it, and when I looked

again I saw Teraj watching me, his face searching, solemn and alarmed.

"You'd better start teaching me," I said. "There are many books to read."

He said nothing for a while, then slowly he smiled. "So my pupil is a prophetess," he murmured. "I suppose you'll end up living on the holy mountain, being seer and oracle, and setting men's minds right."

"Only if an oracle has the power to change the laws," I said.

His right eyebrow rose. He looked faintly surprised, and amused. "You are an ambitious woman, Elsha."

"I have a vision, that is all. A vision of a better life for the Quelled. And I will win that for them, no matter what the cost."

"If you will be lawmaker, Elsha, you will also need the power to divine. You will need to be Firelord."

"I know."

He shook his head, smiling, not really sure of me. His lips were curved, and very close. "I admire you, woman," he whispered. I closed my eyes. I felt his breath on my face, and his lips brushed my forehead, my cheek. I heard his chair creak as he leaned forward, and felt his hand on the back of my neck, drawing me near, and his mouth moved over mine. Long, long he kissed me, and all the time his hand caressed my neck, my hair, and moved along my throat and down, and left a fire-trail there.

I felt an arm press along my back, and heard a hoarse chortle in my ear. I tore free, and my eyes flew open. Shimer leaned over us, his face a hand's width from ours. He was hugging both of us, beaming, snorting with delight and love.

"I like kissing," he said. "Give me one, Elsha."

I collapsed in my chair, laughing, wanting to weep, to scream, dropped so fast out of tenderness it made me ache.

"Go back to bed, Shimer," said Teraj, chuckling, hugging Shimer's neck, and wrestling with him. "You don't want a kiss from Elsha. Her kisses are horrible."

Shimer stood up, puzzled, only half convinced. "Why did you have one, then?"

"Because suffering is good for me. It shapes my soul, and makes me strong."

"I want to be strong. I want to suffer."

"Not that much, Shimer. Go back to bed and say your prayers, and thank God that she kissed me and not you."

Shimer nodded gravely, shot me a suspicious look, and did as he was told. Teraj gave me a slow and lovely smile, and bent over the papers again. He wrote some more, and I noticed that his hand shook slightly. After a while he gave me the page he'd written, and told me what the letters were. For a long time we worked, and I became engrossed in the strange, beautiful symbols of the high language of the Chosen, and a new world began to be unlocked to me.

We did not notice that the candle burned low

and the fire in the grate was almost out, until we heard the Firelord moan in his sleep, and become fitful. Teraj and I went to him, and I took one of his long, frozen hands in mine, stroking it.

"He's like ice," I murmured. "I cannot feel his pulse, and he hardly breathes." My lord was not awake, but his teeth rattled with cold, and he began to shake violently. Teraj got two more woollen blankets and placed them over him, then poured more firestones on the fire, making it roar. The room leapt with golden light and warmth, but still my lord shivered and moaned.

I got my sleeping mat and rolled it out beside him, close. Teraj brought two cups of warmed wine, and we sat and drank together, quietly, with my lord shivering beside us. In the firelight Teraj's face was infinitely sad, and I dared not ask how grave my lord's condition was. When we had finished our wine, Teraj put our cups away, gave me a brief embrace, and retired to his bed behind the heavy curtains. I heard him undress, and his bed creak as he got in. I heard him murmuring in the high language, and knew he prayed. I sighed heavily, took off my outer garments and my boots, and slipped into my bed.

I put my hand across the gleaming floor, and touched my lord's face. He was cold, locked in lonely cold. I got out of my bed, and slid under the blankets and furs beside him. Even through my woollen underdress, I felt that his skin was chill. He lay there on his back, shivering, and I think he was not even aware that I was there. I lay on my side beside him, my arm across his chest, and held him. He did not move, and his breathing stayed shallow and quick, and he still shook.

I pressed my forehead to his cheek, and passed him thoughts of warmth, of light and ancient skies that glowed, of flame. In my mind I sang him the old Quelled myth we both loved, of the fire at the heart of the dawn, and I gave him my vision of what I believed that to be. Then I dozed, shaking, frozen by his flesh.

Sometime in the night he turned and, twisting my hair about his hands and saying the name Nirala over and over, began kissing my brand, my eyes, my cheek. "I am Elsha, lord!" I whispered fiercely. He drew back, and in the darkness I heard him sigh. Then he pulled me near to him again, and lay very still. I thought he grieved, and I put my arms around him and held him, and he wept silently, his beard soft and rough on my brand. After a while he fell asleep, and so did I. And in the morning when I woke he was still sleeping peacefully, his breathing steady and slow, and he was warm.

All the next day he improved. I overheard him tell Teraj, while Teraj washed him, that last night he had dreamed of the world in Quelled myths, and had never felt so warm, so healed. Teraj, who did not know where I had slept, said that dreams were things of power, and that our own minds held the answers to our pain. "Even warmth is a state of mind," he said to the Fire-lord, and I marvelled that I had known that intuitively.

By mid-afternoon my lord was sitting in a fur-covered chair near the fire, sipping hot broth I had prepared for him, holding the cup in his own hands. Shimer sat at his feet, croaking a Quelled song to him. I shook out his sleeping furs, and was going to put them over a stool by the fire to warm them, when I heard shouts outside, and a woman scream. I dropped the furs, and ran to the door.

Some people had come in through the secret pass, carrying a woman wrapped in a blanket. Teraj was with them. I heard her scream again, and knew she had been injured. I went back inside. I put some water on the fire to heat, and got out his box of cotton bandages and the instruments he used for surgery. He had told me of the things he did to clean up injuries, and though they horrified me, and the instruments he had were terrifying, I knew that it was all for healing, and for good. But as I got them ready for him now, my heart went out to the harsha they were for, and for everything she would suffer before she could be healed.

A man came in, saw that I had prepared Teraj's things, and thanked me. "Teraj said he would like your help," he said. "The woman is badly injured, her abdomen pierced by a fractured beam when the mine collapsed. Teraj wants you to calm her while he operates."

"I can't," I said. "I can't bear to see agony."

"Go, Elsha," said the Firelord, from his chair. "If he needs you, you must go. He does not often ask for help."

Shaking, I followed the man out. The infirmary, where Teraj carried out his surgery, was a small building at the far end of the plain. It was bare, except for a long narrow wooden table, with a smaller table beside it. The floor, roof, and walls were all wood, and scrubbed. The woman was lying on the narrow table, naked but for blankets, and two women were washing her. There was firestone dust and blood everywhere, and I saw that all her abdomen was torn open, her insides exposed. Even the washing was torture, and she moaned and sobbed and begged the women to stop. I turned away, my hand across my mouth.

"Wash your hands, Elsha," said Teraj. "There is a bowl of water just outside, and soap." He was wearing a white apron that covered all his clothes, and was spreading out his instruments on the smaller table, on top of a clean cloth. I didn't move, and he looked at me and frowned. There were four men in the room waiting to help him, and they all looked at me, appraisingly. I felt faint.

"I need your help," said Teraj quietly. "You have some healing ability, I think. It's needed. Don't fail me. Or her."

I went out and washed my hands, watched by the Quelled men who had brought her. I could hear one of them lamenting, and guessed it was her husband. I wished I could encourage him, but my own limbs shook with terror, and my stomach churned. I went back into the infirmary and saw that Teraj was giving the woman some kind of drug to drink. She vomited, and cried with pain. The two women left, and the four men moved close to her, to restrain her.

"Hold her head, Elsha," said Teraj. "Be strong. She must not move. And for God's sake, distract her. Talk to her." He bent over the other table, and picked something up.

The woman groaned and whimpered, and I stood near her head, and stroked her hair. I could not bear to watch Teraj. Never had I felt so outraged, so powerless. One of the men stood opposite me, both his arms clamped hard across the woman's chest. "Hold her shoulders, her head," he said, looking at me. "Hard."

I put my hands on her shoulders, and pressed gently. She looked at me, pleading, terrified. I dug my fingers into her flesh, and we both waited. Suddenly she threw herself upwards, screaming.

"Hold her, Elsha!" shouted Teraj.

So I held her down, hard, but her sobs and appeals were terrible. In the end she screamed for death, to be out of it, and I could bear it no longer. I let her go, and knocked away the men who held her down, and her arms, released, reached out to me. She could no longer speak, and her skin was white like a corpse, and her eyes, imploring, had hell in them. I bent over her and lifted her shoulders and held her, and pressed my face against hers, and wept. I heard Teraj roar and the men shout, and hands pulled at me. I held her more tightly, and screamed silently at God.

"Let her die!" I cried. "You're cruel. Don't you care about our suffering? If you have any mercy, any love, let her die. Or else free her mind, so she doesn't feel." I sobbed and cursed and raged, and the harsha slumped in my arms, inert, and I thought she died. I held her closer still, and took her mind with mine, and we were two birds flying, high, high, beyond the narrow table and the torment. We flew in wind and in the fragile heart of rock; flew in water, ice, and fire. And while we flew, love enfolded us, and we heard voices filled with gentleness, and pipes playing, and the soft laughter of children. We flew beyond the earth, beyond ash and smoke and cloud, and up through a fire so huge it set a universe aflame — and then we were in total light.

I felt hands on my shoulders, and realised my arms and back were aching and strained, and that I had been holding the woman a long time. I let her go, slowly, and laid her down on the wooden boards. Her face was white like bone, and had a strange waxen sheen. She was utterly at peace.

I looked across and saw that Teraj and I were alone with her, and he had put his instruments into a clay bowl to be washed. His apron ran with red. He came over to me and handed me the bowl. He looked at me strangely, as if he were uneasy with me. "Will you wash these for me, Elsha?" he asked, and his voice trembled. "Then it is all finished."

I threw the bowl across the room, and it smashed against the wall. Instruments tumbled across the floor, bending, shattering. "It could have been finished earlier!" I cried, furious. "You're a butcher, Teraj. What you did to her wasn't healing. Couldn't you let her die in peace? Did you have to torture her, have to make her die like that? Everything I've seen of you has been a lie. You're a charlatan, a hypocrite. Oh, you can be gentle with us, so long as we're alive and willing to be healed. But let us choose death, and then you turn that other face of yours, and become brutal and hard. Why, Teraj? Is death the final insult to you, the ultimate proof of your failure? Can't you see what it is to her? It's not failure to her. It's freedom." I pulled the blanket off the woman's body, and stared at the closed wound, smooth, cleansed, beautiful. "You do a lovely job with a corpse," I added bitterly. "I bet you mend your shirts expertly, too."

Before he could reply, I turned and fled back to his house.

The Firelord was not in the house. There was no one there. But his bed was folded back neatly, and the fire blazed, so I presumed the women had carried him out to his favourite place by the waterfall. It was a relief to be alone. I heated some water, stripped, and washed all over. Then I put on clean clothes, combed my hair, and poured myself a cup of strong wine. I sat in the glowing lights and shadows of the firelit house, and tried to soak in its peace. My whole body hummed with a force like firestone power, and when I touched my hands together I saw tiny sparks. I trembled, and felt unaccountably elated, as well as furious.

There was a movement in the doorway, and I stayed sitting where I was, expecting Shimer.

"Woman," said a voice. It was Teraj. I stood up, and put the chalice on the table. My hand shook. I turned slowly, and faced him. He, too, had washed, and the bloodied apron was gone. He crossed the room, and stood before me. I turned my face aside, and would not look at him.

"I will not apologise for what I did," I said. "I cannot agree with your form of healing. I could not stand to see what you did to her while she was fully conscious. If she died because of me, then I am sorry. But I am not sorry that she is free."

I turned and looked at him then, defiantly. To my surprise he smiled slightly, though his eyes were moist. "The woman is not dead, Elsha," he said quietly. "She is well, and asking for you. She said that from the moment you alone held her, she felt no pain." He was silent a few moments, looking at me. "You have a great gift, Elsha. I honour it, and you." And he knelt and touched the floor at my feet. When he stood up again, he was looking at me the way Dannii had, that day I had divined.

Overwhelmed, I leaned against the table, knocking over my cup of wine. The goblet rolled on the smooth wood, and the wine dripped onto the floor. I moved to wipe it up, but Teraj caught my hand and turned me to face him. "You did not know you had this gift?" he asked.

I shook my head. I could not speak. I tried to pull my hand away, but he held it firm. For a long time we were silent, and slowly the storm in me was stilled. Then Teraj smiled, and I felt at peace.

"There is something I want to tell you, Elsha," he said, lifting my chin with his free hand. "I don't want you to say anything, or do anything. But I want you to know what is in my heart, what has been there since the moment I first saw you." He caressed my face a moment, then took both my hands in his. There was power in his hands, too. And in his eyes, with all their blue fire.

"I feel as if I have always known you," he said, "always been close to you, always loved you. Nothing would give me greater joy than to have you stay here, living with me, healing with me, being with me. I believe that together you and I could change the face of human suffering. But I know that you are his handmaid, and I know you have a dream. I want nothing more for you than that you fulfil that dream, and find your own perfect joy. I want you to live the life God dreamed for you — to walk the highest road, do the work you were born to do, and be wholly the person you were born to be. Your fulfilment, your satisfaction, and your happiness mean far more to me than anything I could have for myself. But I love you, Elsha, with a love as powerful almost as my love for God. This love frightens me, it causes me fear and ecstasy and pain and a thousand other things I never knew I could feel. It terrifies me, leaves me wounded and open and vulnerable. But I want you to know it exists. And I want you to know that if there ever comes a day in your life when you want my love, then it is here. I will be here. Always. That is all I want you to know."

He kissed me, gave me a smile, and turned to go.

"Teraj," I said, but he turned back and shook his head.

"Say nothing," he said.

"I have to!" I was laughing, crying, overwhelmed. "Teraj, you can't tell me all that, and then go."

"Why not?"

"Because a love like yours demands an answer."

He came back to me, slowly. "It demands nothing, Elsha. That's what I'm trying to tell you. If I asked you to stay, you'd feel torn between me and the Firelord, between me and your dreams. And a torn person cannot be a whole person." He took my face in his hands, and kissed me again. "If I have you at all, Elsha, it will be in the right time, when you have no other dreams calling you. There may not even be such a time; but if there is, you and I will both know it." He smiled, and added roguishly, "Besides, I'm a fraud and a hypocrite. There's a distinct possibility that you don't even like me."

I opened my mouth to protest, but he laughed softly and kissed me, and went out.

15

My Home,
My Almost-Love

Teraj's home was crowded. Everyone was there, and since there were not chairs enough, we all sat around the edges of the floor on rugs. In the centre of the living space, on the polished wooden floor, people danced, and the musicians were boisterous and bright. We all were boisterous. Quelled and Chosen laughed together, shared wine and bread, and danced. Even the cripples were dancing as best they could, and several times Teraj danced with the young woman with no legs, carrying her in his arms. She clung to his neck, her face shining and full of happiness. She loved him, I think. We all did, men and women. He was equal with the Firelord, with his presence.

The Firelord did not dance, but he moved

around the room, talking with people, smiling often, laughing sometimes. He looked much older, and I still was not used to his hair all white; but his eyes had back their old fire, and his skin was rich and dark again, and glowed. I sat against a wall and sipped my wine, and tried not to be sad. This was the farewell feast for my lord and me. We had been here sixteen days, and they had been the highest and best days of my life.

Teraj came over, sat by me, and handed me a small bowl of dried fruit. "You've hardly eaten all night, Elsha," he said. "You'll need strength for the journey to Kasimarra. It is a long, hard way, and our lord will need all your support. He has made a remarkable recovery, but the illness is still there. This time is only a reprieve."

"We have eight days to get there," I said, picking at the fruit. "We won't need to hurry." I looked across the floor and saw the young woman we had operated on. She was almost better already, walked a few steps every day, and ate small meals. Her husband sat with her, his arms about her, caressing her. He whispered something in her ear, and she gave him a shy, loving look, and smiled.

"They are going to stay here," said Teraj, following my gaze. "Their friends who came with them are returning to the mine."

"If this place is secret," I asked, "how is it that the Quelled all know of it?"

"It is a secret kept only from the Chosen," he replied. "Two or three Quelled in every mine know we exist. And if they leave at night to bring their injured here, and are away only a day or two, they are not missed. Not all the workers are counted, only the troublemakers."

"Careful," I said, smiling, "I was one of those."

He laughed quietly. "I bet you were. The Firelord always did like someone with spark. And you have that, Elsha, and more."

I flushed, and turned the bowl in my hands, admiring it. It was solid silver, inlaid with precious gems. "You have some beautiful things here," I said. "Where do they all come from?"

"The Firelord brings them. Every time he comes, he brings something beautiful." He lowered his voice and added tenderly, "Especially this time."

My flush deepened, and I asked: "Where does he get them from? He has no wealth, and owns only his donkey and the blankets and clothes in his travelling bags."

Teraj laughed. He had a lovely laugh, quiet and deep. "I forget. You haven't been to Kasimarra yet. There, he owns a palace. There are more rooms than you can explore in a month, more treasures, more books, more splendours of the Chosen race than in the rest of the world put together. The Chosen all pay taxes, Elsha. They are tithed a fifth of all their wealth, and it goes to Kasimarra to support the Firelord. They give their best weavings, their best clothes, their best grains and blankets and works of art. And he brings some of it here. He has always called this place home, above Kasimarra. Always, he has loved the Quelled."

"But you're not Quelled, though nearly everyone else here is."

"That's true."

"Then why are you here? Where do you fit into his plan for a refuge for sick slaves? It's not just because you heal, is it? He has a special love for you, Teraj. And you for him. Why?"

"He'll tell you that, in time. Now will you come and dance with me, or shall I ask somebody else?"

"I'll dance. But first, I have something for you." I reached into my pocket and took out a small scrolled page. It was tied with a red silk ribbon and a strand of my hair. I gave it to Teraj. He took it with a smile, and unrolled it. Apprehensively, I watched him while he read. It was something I had written in the high language of the Chosen, something I had made up myself; a poem for him.

He read it through twice, then to my dismay covered his face with his hand. I thought I must have filled it with errors, or made a worse blunder. But when he took his hand down and looked at me, I saw that he wept, and was deeply moved. He said nothing, but softly kissed my mouth, rolled the poem carefully, tied it again, and placed it inside his shirt. Then he took my hand and drew me up to dance with him.

We danced until late, then those of us who

remained sat around the fire and sang, and the Firelord told us stories. But he looked very tired, and soon after, everyone went home. I made up my bed and my lord's, and helped Shimer into his. He was almost asleep on his feet, still singing croakily, and rather worse for wine. While I bent over him, tucking his furs about his short neck, he reached up and hugged me, and said quite plainly: "You'll make the two fires one, won't you, Elsha? You'll pull down the wall, and help the Quelled?"

I was stunned. I remembered what Teraj had said about Shimer sometimes saying prophetic things, and I glanced quickly across the room. Teraj was pouring wine, and had not heard.

Shimer's arms drew me down, and he murmured wetly in my ear: "You will, Fire Woman?"

"Hush," I whispered, and hugged his neck. "Of course I will. But how do you know, Shimer?"

He smiled and rolled his eyes heavenwards, and would not say. I kissed him good night, and he chortled with pleasure, and yelled at Teraj: "Her kisses aren't horrible to *me*!"

When Shimer and the Firelord were asleep, Teraj and I sat by the fire together and shared a last cup of wine. He told me he had something for me, and got up and went into his sleeping place. I heard him open the carved wooden chest beside his bed, and I crossed the room and stood just inside his heavy curtains, watching him, curious. All was in shadow here, and smelled of furs and carved wood, and candle-fire. He closed the chest and came to me, smiling, and gave me a carving slightly smaller than my hand.

I sat on the edge of the bed and turned the carving over and over in my hands, marvelling at it. It was an animal I had never seen before, sleek and curved like a fat fish, but without scales or gills. It had a long slender snout, and a wide mouth that smiled. It was the most joyful-looking creature I had ever seen. "What is it?" I asked, laughing, delighted. "It's beautiful!"

"It's a mythical animal," said Teraj, sitting beside me, smiling at my pleasure. "A dolphin. It's a carving my mother made. There are paintings of them in the books in the library at Kasimarra. My father saw them, and described them to my mother. The dolphins lived in great waters called seas, and were friendly to human beings, so the legends say. They were part of the warm-time."

I stroked the animal with my finger, taking pleasure in its smooth and lovely lines. "Your parents lived in the holy place at Kasimarra?" I asked.

"My father goes there occasionally, though my mother lived here. She carved the dolphin for me ten years ago, just before she died. It is all I have from her."

"It's very precious, then," I said. "Are you sure you want me to have it, Teraj?"

He reached towards me, put his hand behind

my neck and rested his forehead against mine, gently. "I love you, Elsha. If you take my dolphin, then you will carry a part of me with you always."

"I shall always do that," I said, "in my mind and in my heart."

He kissed me tenderly, and then with fervour. He lay me down on his furs, kissed me, caught me in his fire, lifted me up into the awesome dark-light spaces of his love, drew me, moved me, till I was lost, found, sobbing, joying. And his hands, his hands —

"Teraj!" I cried. "Teraj! We cannot do this thing!"

He moved off me and lay beside me on his back, his eyes closed. We were both half undressed, and I don't remember how we got that way. Slowly our breathing grew calm, and he turned to me again and held me quietly, his hand caressing my face. I became aware of the dolphin pressed into my side, and I picked it up and held it before me, and could not see it for tears.

"I'm sorry, Teraj. I have a vow to fulfil in Kasimarra. I can't give you all myself, and then walk away tomorrow. I would never — "

"You don't have to explain, love. I know. I'm sorry for going so far." He kissed my cheek, and his breath was warm and calm. "I've waited all my life for you, Elsha. I can wait again. I'll continue to wait, even knowing that you might not come back. If this time is all I ever have with you, it will be enough."

I tried to smile, and swam the dolphin in the firelit dark above our heads. "I'll come back, Teraj," I said. "But I might be old by then. The world might be warm again, and dolphins might swim in the seas again."

"So I will wait until then."

I sat up, pulled my dress on over my shoulders, and roughly did up the silk ties. He sat up with me, and we stayed there awhile side by side. He held my hand and lightly stroked my inner wrist, and did not kiss me again.

"Teraj," I said, very low, "Teraj, I can't have covering from you, but may I sleep with you tonight?"

He kissed my hand, and nodded. He knelt and unbound my boots and removed them, and then his own. Then he picked me up and placed me in his bed. He came in beside me, and drew the blankets and furs up over us. We lay in the soft dark facing each other, side by side, and he said nothing, but stroked my hair, my brand, my face. Then we lay still, and the only sounds in the night were Kallai restless on his perch, the crackling of the fire, and the Firelord's peaceful breathing.

I slept at last, enfolded in his warmth, more at home here than in any other place on earth. And the wind outside whistled over our mountains, and swept the white road and the high peaks of Kasimarra. And on the cushion near our heads lay the little wooden dolphin, smiling.

16

Gifts

I divided the plucked raven into portions, threaded them onto the sharpened rod, and placed them over the fire. I put some root vegetables on to boil, made a bowl of salad, then two cups of hot herb tea. I took one to my lord, sitting wrapped in furs close to the fire, his face harrowed and grey. His hand shook as he took the cup, and his fingers brushing mine were deathly cold.

"If you wish, lord, I'll make your bed, and you can sleep while our meal cooks."

He shook his head, and smiled faintly through the steam of his cup. "No, Elsha. There are things we have to talk about."

A sudden bitter wind whirled into our cave, scattering smoke and ash, and whipping up the dust. I shivered, took one of my sleeping furs, and wrapped it about me while I sat by my lord and had my drink.

I sat as close to the fire as I dared, without scorching my boots. I had never been so cold as I had been these four days of travelling. We had been through all the worst the weather could give — sleet, ice, wind, storm, and snow. All around us had been the thunder of avalanches, the roar of swollen rivers, the knife-edged relentless wind, and always the cruel unconquerable cold. And inside, my heart was bleaker than the world. Separation from Teraj had torn me in two, left me severed, solitary, disunited from my very soul. I had not known that a human being could feel this, and still live.

The Firelord knew my pain, and I did not know whether empathy with me had made him ill, or whether it was his own sickness inside that ate at him. But he was stricken with cold and suffering, and I ached as much for him as I did for myself.

"Let me take you back to Teraj, lord," I said. "Even if we get to Kasimarra before the Fire Festival, you will be too ill to carry out the rituals."

"We have to be there," he said. "I *am* the festival. There will not be one, without me."

"Then let it be late, this year."

He sighed. "It cannot be late, Elsha. At sunset on the eve of the festival, the two fires in the temple are put out. All night they are out, signifying the darkness that came at the beginning of the world's cold. At dawn I walk the high narrow road to the holy place of the temple, and light the two fires again. Then I light the circle of fires in the topmost tower, and all the people see and know that I have again given heat and light to the world. The fires are kept burning for a whole year, until the eve of the next festival. If I am late, they are out for longer than a night, and great calamity will fall across the world."

"Who says it will?" I asked.

"Elsha, tradition is strong in Kasimarra. Everything is done as it has been done for hundreds of years. I cannot break that tradition, even if to light those fires is the last thing I ever do."

"I think your life is worth more than traditions," I said angrily.

He groaned. "Don't mutiny tonight, please. I cannot bear it. Now listen. You must know your duties at Kasimarra. When we reach the holy mountain, you will see the temple on the highest peak. I will take the high road up. I will be wearing my divining gown, and I am the only person in the world with the right to walk that road. You will enter the temple by the main gate at the mountain base. Wear your divining ritual robes. Inside the temple, in the main great hall, two lines of priests will be waiting to meet you. They will tell you what to do. When I have lit the fires, and as the day grows light, I will walk down the main road going from the temple to the town. You will walk that road with me. It is a very jubilant procession, and the people tend to get carried away. Please keep an eye on me. If I look as if I am going to faint or do anything undignified, you have my permission to take my arm and support me. That will cause mutterings, but nothing like the commotion I'd cause if I fell over." He shot me a pale grin. "I am sorry to be in this state, for your sake as well as mine. Things will be difficult enough for you, without your having to worry about me. After the triumphal walk through the town, we will return to the temple, and I can see the physicians there. If they wish to operate, go and get Teraj. I'll have no one but him slicing me up. Don't send someone else: go yourself."

"Lord, if you are in that much pain now, we are foolish to go on."

"You call your Firelord a fool, handmaid?" He tried to sound angry, but sounded grieved instead. He bent his head in his hands, and sighed.

I turned the raven on the spit, and stirred the vegetables. I felt all his torment like waves over me. I stood up and went to him, crouched at his side, and put my hand on his arm. "Lord, I love you, and your suffering hurts me. Is there any way I can go and light the fires for you, on your behalf?"

He lifted his head and looked at me. His face was grey like stone, and steeled against the pain. Even so, he smiled. "God, Elsha, have you no fear at all? They'd kill you. A Quelled in the holy place is the most foul of all abominations."

"Who says so?"

He chuckled quietly, took my fingers in his, and squeezed them. "Elsha, sometimes you terrify me. I question things, and that is frightening enough — but you cut them open to the core."

"The core's rotten, lord. The Chosen made the laws, the traditions. The Chosen, not God, branded us and made us Quelled. The Chosen made two fires, hung the curtain between, and caused the separation. And that separation is the abomination in the temple, not me."

He looked at me as if I were possessed. "Who told you those things?"

"No one, lord. I just know them. I've known them since I was a child."

"Not the truths, Elsha. The curtain. Who told you about the curtain? No one goes in that room except me once a year, and the old priest who tends the fires. Who told you about it?"

I moved away from him, and sat staring into the fire. "I had a dream," I said. "I dreamed about the two altars and the fires on them, one for the Chosen and one for the Quelled, and with the great black curtain in between. I dreamed that the curtain was torn down, and that both fires burned on the high golden altar, together."

He wiped his hands down over his face, and looked so shaken I thought he was going to pass out. I moved to help him, but he raised his hand. "I am all right, Elsha. But I'm beginning to think I've been mistaken about you. Badly mistaken, about a lot of things."

My heart fell. My whole world fell. I dared not speak, or look at him.

"Elsha, you told me once that you had divined, and I . . . I laughed, as I remember. Tell me again what happened."

So I did, from the losing of the woman-stone to the finding of the firestones Dannii hid to test me. He listened to it all, his eyes closed, his hands folded in front of him. He was so still that I thought he had fallen asleep. But when I stopped talking he lifted his head and looked at me.

"Then I most certainly was wrong," he said quietly. "And I apologise for mocking you. You see, Elsha, I thought I was the one in control. I thought I had called you to be a part of my purpose, my dream. Now I think the dream isn't mine at all, and we're both part of a much bigger one. I thought I saw your road, your destiny. I realise now I haven't seen the half of it. I've been as blind, as mistaken and as prejudiced as the rest of them."

"No, you haven't, lord," I said gently. "You are the wisest, the best person I know. I love you more than anyone else in the . . ." I hesitated, stopped on the edge of a lie. He watched me, half smiling, one eyebrow raised.

"Well, almost," I murmured. "I love you more than anyone, except Teraj."

He laughed softly, put his cup down on the hearthstones, and held his hands out to the flames. Even his hands had aged, these past months he had been ill, and become wrinkled and

211

unsteady. "That much I understand, handmaid. I saw you leave his sleeping place, that last morning. And I saw the kiss he gave you before we left."

"Don't judge me wrong, lord."

"I don't judge you at all. You called me a priest once, Elsha. You said I didn't need human warmth, human love. You were wrong. I have loved."

"I know," I said, and couldn't resist adding quietly: "Her name was Nirala."

He looked startled, and his eyes, narrowed, burned into mine. "So. You read minds, too."

"No," I grinned, "but I slept beside you one night when you were very ill and cold, to warm you. You talked in your sleep."

"You slept with me?" He looked amazed, then he slowly smiled, and an old spark lit his eye. "I'm sorry I missed that, Elsha."

"You didn't miss it entirely, lord. You thought I was Nirala. From the way you spoke her name, I knew you weren't talking about your donkey."

He laughed quietly, then fell silent, thinking; and all the colour was in his face again, at the thought of her, and he looked almost well.

I leaned forward and checked the meat on the spit. It trickled with juices, and smelled delicious. It was almost done. I got up and took two bowls from the saddlebags, and came back to put them by the fire to warm.

"Nirala was harsha," said the Firelord, and I nearly dropped the bowls. I caught them in time, placed them on the hearthstones, and sat down again.

"I was divining in a town," he said. "While I was there, a child was taken injured from the mine, lamed, and the overseer had him killed. The child's mother witnessed it, and attacked the overseer. They were going to put her to death for it, but I intervened. She told me her husband had died in the mine, and that her son had been all she had. I exonerated her, cleared her of all guilt, and swore I'd Quell the first Chosen who tried to punish her. I caused a great deal of ill feeling. My own handmaid walked out on me, and the Chosen in the town were barely hospitable. I knew as soon as I left, they would avenge the overseer and kill the harsha, so I took her with me. I took her to a secret place I had discovered on my travels, that I loved. I made a home for her there. The woman was Nirala. Though I was fifty years old then and she was not much older than you, we grew to love each other, and she became my wife. She taught me Quelled myths and legends, and because of her and the love between us, I began to question everything I had been taught. I began to honour the Quelled, and to seek to make a better life for them.

"I told the Quelled in other mines of the place where Nirala lived, and it became a refuge for the sick and injured. I took one of my own physicians there whom I trusted, and he looked after them. Over the years a community grew up, and the place became home to me, even more than Kasimarra. And Nirala and I had a son."

He hesitated, and I looked into his face and knew. "Teraj," I said.

He smiled, and nodded. "Teraj had inherited my powers, though not for divining, but for healing. My physician taught him everything he knew. The place where my son dwells is the most precious place on earth to me. I grieved only that he was always alone, that he did not find a woman that he loved. Then I saw him with you. You are worthy of each other, Elsha." He smiled, and there was a great love in his eyes. Then he glanced at the fire, at the meat on the spit. "And I suppose you think I'm worthy of that dinner there, burning itself black. Shall we eat it now, or when it's totally ruined?"

I scrambled to rescue it, and as I gave him his, I bent and quickly kissed his cheek. He did not acknowledge it, but lowered his head over his bowl, and ate in silence. Later, when we lay on opposite sides of the fire, wrapped in our sleeping furs, he said: "Elsha, it is a custom among the Chosen, that when a person has a birthday he is given gifts. In four days you will be seventeen. Out of all my wealth, out of all at Kasimarra, what would you want? Name anything."

"Nothing, lord. Thank you."

"Nothing? All my other handmaids asked all the time for gifts — for fine garments, for jewels, for shoes and houses and silverware. In all the year you've been with me, you have never asked me for a single thing. Think, Elsha. There must be something you desire."

"Can I have anything?"

"Anything you want."

"I want the Quelled to work only until morning's end every day, and in the afternoons their time is for themselves, and for rest. I want children under fourteen years forbidden to enter the mines. I want Quelled women to be permitted to choose their own husbands. I want branding abolished."

I stopped for breath, and he asked, sounding amused, "Is that all, Elsha, or are you just warming up?"

"I'm sorry, lord. I thought you were serious."

"And so I was. Consider it all done."

"Thank you, lord. You could do no greater thing for me."

"You'll think of something else, I'm sure."

He laughed softly, and I smiled to myself and rolled onto my side, pulling the furs up over my ears. The wind whistled in our cave entrance, and the smoke swirled. In the back of the cave the donkey stamped, restless, and Kallai hopped sideways on his makeshift perch. I lifted my head and looked through the flames at the Firelord. He lay on his back, peaceful, his pain gone for the moment. His white hair streamed across his dark furs, and shone in the firelight.

"It is your birthday, too, soon," I said. "What would you like me to give you, lord?"

"A smile, Elsha, and a Quelled myth-song."

"Consider that done, also."

"I had not finished, woman. I want you to sing it in the temple at Kasimarra, while we tear down that abominable curtain."

I was silent then, in my joy.

And the night closed in around our cave and the wind subsided; and in the dying fire I saw the flames at Kasimarra, and a better world beginning.

17

Pain, Love, and Destiny

The gale, resurrected in all its ferocity, tore across our path, whipped our clothes, our hair, and made our hands and faces ache. We leaned into it, I supporting the Firelord, he dragging at the donkey. The beast was weary, unwilling, and terrified. Kallai, thrashed by the wind, clung to my gloved fist, his head hunched low. The snow was knee-deep, turning to slush, and our boots and cloaks were wet and freezing. The Firelord fell again, and I struggled to lift him. He rested against the donkey, breathing hard, his eyes closed. His beard and eyebrows were edged with ice, and his skin was grey again.

"Turn back, lord!" I cried, shouting against the gale. "This storm will kill us both!"

He shook his head. "A bridge ahead," he

shouted, hoarsely. "Then a cave, further on. We'll stop there."

To have both my hands free, I tied Kallai to one of the saddlebags for a perch, though he fought me over it. Then together my lord and I forced the donkey on, pushing, dragging it up the treacherous path. At times we passed between steep cliffs, and there was blessed calm from the wind. Then we were up on a ridge again, buffeted, reeling under the fury of the elements.

We came to the edge of a ravine, so deep and vast that the river below was a distant thunder, its turbulence lost in haze and the white rage of the wind. There were strange booming echoes in the depths, sounds strangled by the wind, cries and voices and distant, wasted howls. And across the abyss, tapering to nothing on the remote cliff, a narrow rope bridge, age-old and damaged, swinging crazily.

"We can't cross that!" I cried, clutching my lord's arm, terrified. "We'll be killed!"

"I've crossed it many times!" he shouted back, stooping to check the straps holding the saddlebags, and checking the donkey's halter. "We must cross, Elsha. There is no other way."

I stared across the chasm, an awful fear sweeping over me. I backed down the path, away from the edge, the bridge, the howling, yawning gulf. The Firelord came back to me, and put both his hands on my shoulders. He shouted, and I could hardly hear above the wind. "Elsha, we have no choice! You go first, alone, then I will follow with the donkey. Hold tight to the handropes on either side, and walk slow and steady on the wooden boards. Where they are missing, cross the gaps slowly, your eyes straight ahead. If the bridge swings, keep as still as you can until it stops. Never look below. Keep calm. You'll get safely across, I swear."

"Cross with me!" I cried. "I can't do it alone!"

"You have to! It won't hold us both and the beast. And I'm letting the falcon go, Elsha. The donkey must not be distracted by him." He went back to the petrified donkey, and I saw him take out his knife and slice through my bird's leash. Kallai took flight, battling the gale, vanishing in the mist. I knew it was the last I'd ever see of him.

Through a blur I saw the Firelord take something out of one of the saddlebags, something scarlet and heavy. He brought it back to me, with a rope, and tied the bundle across my back. It was his divining robe. I thought it was a strange thing for him to give me to carry. "It'll ease the weight on the beast," he shouted. He tied the rope at my waist, and must have felt me shaking, because he looked into my eyes and smiled. "Go, handmaid," he said. "I'll see you on the other side."

I shook my head.

"It is a command!"

"No, lord."

He took my arm, and forced me to the edge of the abyss, to the beginning of the bridge. It snaked across the white depths, a line of flimsy rope across a frozen hell.

"Go!" he shouted, from behind. He put my hands on the ropes, and pushed me. I felt his arm press about my back, his beard rough against my cheek. "Go, woman. There is no other way."

I turned my head. He was weeping, I think, or else the wind made his eyes moist. And his eyes held pain in them, and love, and other things I couldn't read, but which frightened me.

"Lord — "

"Go!"

I went, one foot after another on those broken, ancient boards, my hands gripping the worn ropes at my sides, the wind whipping me, tossing the bridge; and all around was wild white. I was between heaven and earth, life and death only a slip of the foot apart. I dared not look back or below, but only looked along those narrow wooden boards, those frail ropes, as I went on, creeping, helpless in the gale.

I went on forever, it seemed, suspended on those threads. At times the wind threw me about so violently, I shut my eyes and clung with all my strength, and thought my time had come to die. I shook so much I could hardly hold on. And all the time my heart thundered, and the sweat of fear trickled down inside my clothes.

At last I saw the cliff and the rocky path on the other side, and the ends of the bridge tied to the upright poles. The bridge was badly damaged at this end, the ropes torn and frayed by the wind.

As I stepped off, I heard small threads snapping. I clung to the rocks at the side of the path, trembling, feeling sick, inexpressibly relieved to be on solid earth again.

I looked back along the bridge, but could see little. Mist, shredded by the gale, raced across the chasm, and I was aware again of the echoes, the weird sounds made by the wind in the ravine far below. I saw the bridge quiver and tighten, and knew that the donkey and my lord stepped on the other side. I gripped the rocks, ice forming on my hair and hands, and waited for him. A thousand years I waited. I cursed the mist. I could see nothing, nothing but white. Then I thought I heard a sound, a shout, and a hoof striking wood. The bridge swayed, and was still again.

"Can you hear me, lord?" I called.

His voice came back, wraithlike in the wind; I could not make out his words.

"The bridge is damaged!" I called. "Leave the donkey. Come on alone."

I waited again, hardly breathing, terrified. I saw the ropes of the bridge go tense, and threads break. There was a creaking, snapping sound, and a great and awful cry; I saw the ropes part, tearing, separating, threads flying in the wind, rope and wood and life hanging, falling, gone.

Then there was silence, but for the storm. And nothing. Nothing across all that abyss but mist and ice and wind.

I stared at it, unbelieving, half expecting the ropes and wood to materialize, to form again with my Firelord there, smiling, and laughing in that quiet way of his. But the ropes did not come back, no matter how hard I stared and hoped and prayed, and after a while I knew they never would. And I knew I'd never see the Firelord again, or hear his voice, or know the great and gentle way of him.

There are no words in our language to describe where I went that day. I don't remember what happened to me, physically. I know only that my spirit went to some terrible place, some place desolate and full of pain. Somehow I came back from it. Cold brought me back, I think; my body shivering reminded me it was still alive and needful of my care.

I was covered with snow, my feet and face were numb, and my hands were bruised and bleeding. With great difficulty I untied the knots of the rope binding his robe to me, shook the robe free, knocked the ice and snow out of it, and put it on. It dragged on the ground, but warmed me a little. A strange sense of unreality settled over me. The Firelord's presence had filled my thoughts, my days, and all my road ahead. I felt now as if a part of my own self had been cut off. In disbelief I clambered up and down the treacherous edges of the ravine, calling to him, twice nearly falling, and missing death by wild seconds. In the end reason prevailed, and I struggled along the road away from the ravine.

I was so cold, my fingertips were black and

tipped with white, and I could feel nothing. At some time I sat in the snow and took off my boots, and found that my feet were black. I put my boots back on, but could not bind the leather thongs. I tramped on, talking to myself, sobbing, laughing sometimes, on the edge of madness. I looked for the Firelord often, positive I would find him; at times I ran on, stumbling, convinced I'd see him tall and kingly on the way ahead. Then grief would hit me, sharp and cutting deep, deep. I cried helplessly, and my tears turned to burning ice on my cheeks.

I came to a cave, and saluted the Firelord's sign on the entrance. Inside, I searched the shelves for firestones, for flints. There were none. Neither were there blankets, and the wine vessels all were empty, some broken on the floor. The cave had been ransacked.

I laughed hysterically when I realised it. The only cave of his I had ever seen robbed, and it had to be this. I had no firestones, no flints, no fire to sustain my life. Without food I could live for forty days. But without fire I would not survive the four days left to Kasimarra.

I sat in the dirt at the edge of the frosty firepit, and pulled his divining robe closer about me. Night fell. The wind shifted and drove snow far into the cave, and the cold disturbed my mind. I found myself at some time in the night wandering outside in a blizzard, singing Quelled myths. Teraj stood in the snow holding a blazing torch and a scrolled book, but when I ran towards him he smiled and vanished. I heard Lesharo's pipes, and followed them, almost falling into a crevasse. I could see nothing except visions that taunted me, and were lies.

Sometimes a terrible guilt flooded over me, for not going further to help my lord, and I tried to go back to the ravine, back to where he lay hurt and helpless, calling for me. I felt guilty for failing him, guilty for walking away, guilty for being alive. I heard voices, terrible accusing voices, and people came and looked on my despair, and spat, and said I caused his death. I crawled in the frozen dawn, through snow and ice and on the edges of ravines, crying out for help. The snow was piled high all around, and I could not walk. My clothes were soaking wet, and hard with ice. I was in agony with cold. My fingers were black, and somewhere I had lost one of my boots. My exposed foot and ankle were black and numb, and my limbs were like a stranger's limbs, not mine. Even my spirit felt strange, almost separated from me. I felt near to death.

I curled up in the snow. I heard voices again, and half sat up, thinking rescue had come. I tried to call out, but ice cracked my lips and made them bleed, and my voice was lost in the wind. I saw Teraj again, not smiling this time, but bent over by his bed, anguished, crying out in prayer. I heard my name often, and wanted to call to him, but could not. In the dull daylight came snow and wind again, shadowed ghostly forms, and music and voices. I wanted them to go away so

I could sleep. Weariness weighed on me, heavily.

"Stand up, woman," said a voice, and I lifted my head. Snow and sleet drove hard into my face, and I dashed my hands across my eyes, clearing them. I thought I saw a man, tall and firelit in the grey, walking towards me. "Stand up, woman," he said again.

I struggled to my feet, fell, and stood again. The man was still there, half hidden by the storm. Incredibly, he wore no cloak in all that cold, and his robes were thin and woven fine. His hair was free of sleet, and shining in the firelight. He came closer, and I saw that he was smiling. I thought he was Amasai, and spoke that man's name, and tried to run forward. But the wind and deep snow prevented me, so I stood, shaking with cold, and looked at him.

It was not Amasai. It was a man I had never seen before. And he did not carry a torch, yet I could have sworn it was firelight on him. The storm abated, and in the calm I examined his face. Powerful it was, strong and compassionate, and not unlike Amasai's. This man, too, was beautiful. Yet it was not his face that arrested me, made me stand straight and tall, unmindful of tiredness or pain; it was the joy that came from him. It was so great, I could have sworn the air was filled with his laughter; yet there was only the wind. He looked on me with so much gladness, so much love; it was as if he had known me all my life, and all that time had longed for this moment, this meeting place with me, and seeing me gave him the greatest pleasure. There were six or seven paces between us, yet I felt totally encompassed by his delight in me. I felt elated, embraced.

"Are you Quelled, lord?" I asked, shivering. "You have scars on your forehead, though different from my brand."

"There are no Quelled," he said. Still he smiled; still that jubilation came from him, that amazing joy. His eyes never left my face.

"Do I know you from somewhere?" I asked, smiling, mystified.

The wind tore across the snowy waste between us, and I lost his answer. I shivered and pushed my frozen hands high into my sleeves. I was unbearably tired, and my body felt like stone. My mind began to wander again, and other voices called in the gale. I wanted to fall into the snow, and sleep.

"Warmth is a state of mind, Elsha," he said.

"I know," I said, yawning. "I heard Teraj tell the Firelord. My lord was his father. They looked alike, come to think of it."

"Warmth is a state of mind."

"I know. I warmed the Firelord when he was cold."

"A state of mind."

It struck me, then. It was so simple, so clear, I laughed. The shock of my laugh jerked me back into awareness. "Are you saying," I said, "that if I think about it hard enough, I can make myself warm?"

He did not answer, and at that moment a snowy squall hit us, and the force of it knocked me over. When I recovered, the vision had gone. I stumbled forward through the snow, and looked all around for his footprints. There were none. But his presence remained, and his words.

I closed my eyes and sang the Quelled myth about the fire at the heart of the dawn. I imagined fire, a sky full of fire, and the air warm. I imagined the fire inside myself, flowing in my heart, my veins, my lungs and body and limbs. I thought of firestone power, racing and warm within, ringing, singing, blazing in me, flaming in me. I though of Teraj, of all his love lifting me, setting me alight.

I opened my eyes and looked down at my hands, and saw that the black was changing, and in parts my skin was almost pink again. I laughed, and lifted my arms, and saw steam rising from my wet sleeves. I looked down, and saw that the snow had melted about my feet, and my foot without its boot was almost the normal colour. And all my body was warm, warm, as if I had a fire inside.

I shook my head, thinking I was seeing visions again, and walked on through the snow. I came to a flat place, all white, and brushed the snow off the stones on the side of it. I discovered that they were carved with travellers' prayers, and knew that I had found the road again.

A long, hard road it was, but I was warm inside and out, and the terrible weariness and despair that had crushed me before were gone now. Gone, too, was the blackness in my hands and feet, and strangely it did not return. I thought of the man I had seen, and the memory gave me peace. With the peace came a purpose.

I knew I had to go to Kasimarra and tell the people there that their Firelord was dead. It was a goal, and I needed one right now; but it was a sorrowful goal. I, who had wanted only to bring good news to the Quelled, would give instead to the whole world the most terrible news of all. No Firelord, no divining power, no firestones, no fire, no . . .

A memory glowed like a spark on the edges of my mind, flared into a tiny flame, and ignited. I thought of conversations with Teraj, of fantasies that had bemused us, blown our world away. I saw a dream I'd had, of hands tearing down a curtain and combining on one altar two separate fires. I saw those same hands holding fire, fire for all the world, all people. My hands. My fire.

A vision huge, stupendous, began to form. I shook my head, denying it. They'd never allow it. They'd kill me first. Or would they? *Could* they, if I were the only soul on earth with divining power? If they rejected me, if they killed me, they'd lose their only life-link to the warm. They had to accept me. They had no choice.

I stopped walking and leaned against the prayer-stones for support, overcome by the thoughts. They crashed down on me, ringing like a song, like stones of a tremendous mosaic all falling into place, like threads of a tapestry moving into a vast design. Everything fell into place, all my childhood dreams, my divining power, my hopes for the Quelled, the Firelord's death, my life. It was all there, mapped out like a road in front of me. All I needed was courage. Courage to do it alone, without the Firelord. Courage to *be* the Firelord.

I stood up. I pulled the divining robe higher on my shoulders, feeling the richness of the fur, the warmth, the weight of it; and I started on the road again, to Kasimarra.

18

High Road to Kasimarra

The next two nights I stayed in the Firelord's caves, both plentifully supplied. A thousand times I blessed Amasai for all his care; in one of the caves there were even clean clothes, including a handmaid's dress and underdress, and boots. There were clothes for the Firelord, too, that sharpened afresh my sorrow.

From the last cave I took a long-bladed knife, flints, and a wooden torch to light. Then I went back up on the road again, with the Firelord's gown rolled under my arm. My hood I pulled well down over my head, hiding my brand.

It had stopped snowing. The road was slippery with ice and melted snow, and the rivers boomed all around, but the air was clear and crisp. I missed Kallai's presence on my wrist, and mourned again for him. It was strange to walk totally alone. Yet there were many travellers on the road, going to Kasimarra. They were all Chosen, and though many of them greeted me, looking curiously into my face and wondering why a woman travelled alone, I avoided talking much to them. One child I asked, as he ran ahead of his family: "It is the eve of the Fire Festival, isn't it, today?" He looked at me, laughing, and said everyone in the world knew that. So I walked on, sure, resolved in all my purposes.

By evening there was a great crowd on the road, enlarged by pilgrims from all the villages and towns around Kasimarra. Many of the Chosen rode donkeys, or walked in large groups, colourful and bright, and singing Chosen songs. There was excitement in the air, a feeling of festivity and anticipation. It was misty now, the air growing dark, and many of the travellers carried burning torches. The light glittered on their jewels and on the embroidery on their robes. Children grew tired and were carried on their fathers' backs, and lovers walked hand in hand, talking quietly and laughing.

I wished I could have walked alone; I knew we neared the holy mountain, and I wanted to be alone for my first sight of it, to hold it forever in my memory as a sacred moment. Instead, I came upon it suddenly, jostled around a corner with a crowd of jubilant pilgrims, and my private joy was picked up and spun into the evening by their cheer, and for once in my life I joined the Chosen in their celebration.

And Kasimarra, centre of their world and mine, towered beyond the mists, shining, aflame with light. Like a rising dream it was, a mountain pinnacle turned temple, a holy place of stone and ice and fire. I could not tell where mountain rock ended and temple began; it sprang from the mountain itself, and was all stairways, lofty roads, terraces, walls, steep roofs, and towers lost in mist. From every window poured the light of fires, and the radiance danced on walls and turned the mists to gold. It was luminous against the night, and the gold gave it holiness. It was exactly as I had dreamed it.

At its base, the town sprawled. Beyond the town, half hidden in the mist, I saw another road. Elevated, winding upwards on a narrow ridge, it led to the very heights of the temple. It was the high path to Kasimarra. The road I was to walk.

I saw where it branched off to the left, not far ahead from where we were. I went with the pilgrims down to the crossroads, and they all went on down the wide access towards the town, and I sat on a prayer-stone at the side of the road, and waited.

It was almost dark when all the people were gone, and I lit my torch and went up the high road on the ridge. The road was only a track, narrow, very steep, and lined thickly with prayer-stones. There were signs at the beginning of it, large messages written on flat stones. They were written in the high language of the Chosen, and some of the words I could read. They were warnings that this road was the Firelord's road, and everyone else was strictly forbidden. There were prayer-flags hung across the road, and more warnings. I went higher, clutching the torch, and his robe. The last sign of all, as I understood it, said: "He who reads has entered holy ground, and stands in temple precincts. If you are the Firelord, you are blessed. If you are not, you enter under pain of death."

I walked on. After a while I put on the Firelord's robe, for warmth and protection. If anyone was watching from a distance, they could possibly see me in the torchlight. I pulled the hood up over my own, and made sure all my hair was well concealed. I wished I was taller.

The night deepened, became pitch-black, and a strong wind blew. I could see nothing but the steep road ahead, rugged rocks, and at times, across the misty valleys on my right, the fires of Kasimarra. I noticed that in the temple summit the light had all gone out, and I realised that was where I'd light the fires to show that the Firelord had returned.

I came to a cave, and noticed the Firelord's sign scratched above it. It was a small cave, with room barely to stand, but it looked homely, and gave a good view of Kasimarra, the temple, and the eastern skies beyond. I realised, with a rush of gratitude, that this was where the Firelord had waited on his long watches for the dawn. Knowing that he had been here, that he, too, had waited and watched, comforted me and gave me strength. So I waited there, singing Quelled myths when panic threatened. After a while I opened a small parcel of food I had brought from the last cave. It was dried fruit from some far exotic place, some slightly mouldy hezzin meat, and some grains. I had brought a small wineskin as well, though I drank the wine sparingly. I had no intentions of staggering into the temple at dawn, or of missing the dawn altogether. But I took a mouthful or two to celebrate, remembering that this night I was seventeen. Then, fortified, I sang again, and watched.

At last the skies began to lighten behind Kasimarra. I got up, took the torch, and hurried along the ascent. The way became very steep, the ridge turned suddenly to the right, and Kasimarra and the temple place were directly in front of me. Below, the town already showed signs of life; torches moved along the roads, and the lower door to the temple blazed suddenly with light. Above me, at the end of my road, the temple waited, silent and serene.

My torchlight showed that the ridge had become narrow with near-vertical sides, in places no wider than the path itself. I felt as if I walked a knife's edge. The wind was very strong, and whistled across my path and tore at the flames in my torch. I held my hood down low over my brand, and walked on. I was close to the temple now, and could see the Firelord's door. I hesitated a moment, swept by the wind, by fear of the dizzy height, by terror of the enormity of what I was about to do. I said a prayer, took a deep breath, and entered the temple.

I had expected a grand entrance, but my torch-light showed a tunnel. Shaking with fear, I pulled the Firelord's hood low over my face, drew the sleeves down over my hands, gripped the torch and the knife in its scabbard on my waist, and went in. The tunnel was not long, but smelled damp, and the air was stale. I remembered that it was used only by the Firelord once a year.

Guards stood at the end of the tunnel, barring it with swords crossed. As I drew near, the swords parted, were lifted upright. I gripped my knife, futile against those blades, and went in. The temple was vast, and dim with candlelight and shad-ows. I dared not look at the guards. I bent my head low, feeling the heavy hood covering my face, my pale hair, and went straight on past, across polished firelit floors, crimson carpets, and on until I came to two doors. They were pure gold, and beaten into beautiful designs of strange birds and beasts, wide wilderness places, and for-eign cities. In the centre of the doors, divided by their opening, was the Firelord's sacred sign: the diviner's eye.

I pushed open the doors and went in, and they swung closed behind me, silently. The room was not large, but it was extremely high. I was glad I had my torch. There was no light here except a pale grey dome in the roof. Immediately in front of me, glimmering in the torch flames, was a golden altar. It was not large — about as high as my waist — and had nothing on it except an iron brazier for fire, black and unlit, and the words inscribed on the altar's edge: "For the Chosen of God." They were written in the high language. The brazier was filled with fresh fire-stones sprinkled with kindling grass.

Beyond the altar hung a huge black curtain, high almost as a two-storied tower, its top lost in the shadowy heights. It hung across the entire width of the room, its folds ghostly in the torch-light, glimmering with dust and ice. I went behind the curtain and saw the second altar. It was stone, and inscribed with the words: "For the Quelled." Its brazier, too, was waiting for fire.

I placed my torch across the stone altar, and stood for a while in the darkness, listening to the silence. There was a wondrous peace in this place. A living peace. I remembered that I stood in the most holy place, and knelt and touched the polished floor. Then I stood and picked the brazier up. It was heavier than I expected, and still warm from yesterday's fire. I carried it around the curtain, and placed it on the golden altar beside the brazier of the Chosen. Then I took the great curtain in my hands. I started to sing a Quelled myth, as my lord had asked me to; but I was too choked with emotion and dust. I dragged on the curtain, heard it tear, and clouds of dust fell out of it. It was so ancient, I was afraid it would tear to shreds in my hands, and that only the hem would come down. I gathered it in my arms, swung on it with all my weight, heard it ripping free of the high hooks that held it — and tore it down at last. It fell in massive folds behind the golden altar; a pile of ancient weaving, fragments of rotten cloth, and the dirt and prejudice of centuries. I walked over it, picked up the torch, and lit the two fires on the altar, the Quelled fire first. I did sing the Quelled myth-song then, haltingly, overcome with feelings, and wishing with all my heart that my high lord was with me. Perhaps he was.

I knelt on the icy stones before the two fires, and offered God my thanks. It was more a cry of triumph than a prayer; but I think it pleased him. Then I went out again, and saw that the two guards were gone. I found some stairs going up to a higher place, and a circular room with huge windows all around and other braziers waiting to be lit. So I lit them all from my torch, singing my Quelled song, and all of Kasimarra knew that the Firelord had returned.

Then I steeled myself for the hardest challenge of all: my meeting with the priests. I shook the curtain's dust from my garments, wishing I looked more glorious, and began descending the stairs to the lowest temple floor. Hundreds of stairs there were, and countless passages. Sometimes I passed unshuttered windows, and looking down saw the town far below. The main road to the temple was teeming with people, all shouting and cheering. As I descended, the cheering grew louder, more frenzied and tumultuous. I ran faster, my heart hammering. I came to a pair of massive wooden doors, richly carved. I threw them open and ran through.

The room was vast, more a courtyard than a room, and it had no furniture save a raised throne at one end, and hundreds of torches blazing on the walls. A thousand men stood lined up on either side of me, and they barely covered any floor in all that place. Their priestly robes fell in stately scarlet to their golden boots, their oiled hair shone, and their faces, ritually washed, were aglow with torchlight. We stared at each other, unspeaking, and I don't know who was more shocked, them or me. I took a deep breath and brushed my grimy hair out of my eyes. I pushed back the dusty hood, and knocked the remains of cloth and dust from my crimson robes. The flames, embroidered gold across the sleeves and hem, were dull with dust. For one terrible moment I thought I had done it all wrong. I was ashamed of my dirt, for being unprepared. But then I remembered that my dust was from a holy work, and that I was prepared — more prepared and qualified than anyone else on earth.

I said to the priests: "I am Elsha of the Quelled. I was the Firelord's handmaid." I hesitated, fighting a fresh onslaught of grief. My voice sounded strange in that huge, echoing place. "I bring news of him. Heavy news. He died on the road between Qustra and here, on the last bridge."

They stared at me, their faces white, and I could not tell what they felt. I wondered whether they were deaf, they were so still, so silent. Then one of them broke ranks and stepped forward. He was an old man, tall and straight and with a face like stone, cold and relentless. He would not look at my face, but looked beyond me, at the air above my head. I looked straight at his, and saw that his mouth had a twisted, brutal look about it. When he spoke, his lips hardly moved.

"We know who you are, handmaid," he said. "We have heard reports of you, and know that you speak fluently and have some measure of intelligence. We know that the high lord was pleased with you, for reasons we do not comprehend. We were expecting you, though not in this manner of arrival, nor wearing his robes. How did you come in?"

"Through the door at the top of the high road."

There was murmuring again.

"That was a holy road, harsha, that you had no right to walk. And you have no right to wear those robes. We will make an announcement to the people of the Firelord, and then we will do what must be done."

"You cannot put me to death," I said, "without condemning every person needing fire. I came by the high road, and I wear this gown because I can divine and I am your new Firelord. He gave me this gown, and I believe I have his blessing."

The priest spoke a word I did not understand — a word strong like an oath. The other priests murmured among themselves, shocked, then were silent again. From outside came the tumult of the crowds clamouring for the Firelord. I turned to go out and confront them, but there was a hiss of a sword whipped from its scabbard, and steel flashed in front of me. The priest pressed the blade flat against my chest, and forced me back.

"You do not understand, handmaid," he said, still not meeting my eyes, his face set and inexorable. "I am Maelmor, the high priest. In these temple precincts, my word is law. Your word is not worth the breath you spend on it. The news you bring will have to be confirmed. And you will be tried, your divining ability tested to the furthest degree. Pray that we are satisfied."

He sheathed his sword, strode down the long lines of priests to the temple doors, and opened them. I glimpsed the crowd beyond. It was overwhelming. People lined the road, the walls on either side, the terraces and rocks beyond, the valleys, the stones, the paths. They clambered on the roofs of the houses, out of windows, and hung from balconies and towers and every high place, to get a glimpse of the Firelord. The tumult was deafening. Trumpets blared, cymbals crashed, and drums throbbed. People screamed, cheered, applauded, and sang. When they saw that it was the high priest and not the Firelord, they fell utterly silent. He closed the doors behind him, and we heard his voice raised, powerful, but his words were muffled. Then there was another sound, anguished and terrible. It was the people wailing for their diviner.

I lifted my head and stared at the rows of priests. Some of them were weeping silently, tears coursing down their still faces. But some, dry-eyed, were looking at me, and their look was worse than grief. It was the look of deepest hate.

19

The Test

They let me stay in a lower temple room that night, on a mat with one blanket and no fire; and the next morning they took me outside. Two hundred priests were to test my divining power. Maelmor was one of them. They took me to the mountainous area beyond the city. A bitter wind was blowing, and ice made the ground treacherous. The very air was treacherous. They blindfolded me when they took me out, and made me walk a long way over stony places and up and down steep valleys where the wind howled and the force of it nearly knocked me over. The blindfold did not trouble me; eleven years in the mine had taught my feet discernment, and though I stumbled sometimes, I did not fall.

I felt unnerved and on the edge of chaos. All

night I had stayed awake, meditating, reasoning myself into a state of calm. I had almost managed it. But this morning the hostility of the priests clashed with my fragile peace, and jarred my feelings. I felt out of harmony with myself and with the earth. It was a feeling incompatible with divining.

At last we stopped, and I heard the crunch of stones as the priests gathered behind me. I felt someone move close, and my tension grew. I sensed evil in the air, and remembered the blindfold put on me when I was a child, and the branding.

"You will divine," said a voice, close. Maelmor's. "You have until evening. I decide when the test is finished. If you find firestones, you will live. If you do not, you will die. This is the only test. There is no second chance. You may begin."

I turned my back on him, and faced the open spaces where the wind blew clean and strong. I walked away from the priests, then crouched down and removed my boots. I touched my palms to the earth; then lay full length across it. I could feel nothing. Not daunted yet, I stood up and walked slowly across the stones, slipping sometimes in the ice, my feet frozen and numb. For a long time I walked, my eyes closed beneath the black cloth. My whole mind and body were aware of the earth around, conscious of the wind and rock and hidden inner forces. I felt a strange liquid running through my bones, and realised, with wonder, that I crossed an underground stream. I walked on slowly, calm now, sure in my purpose. There were no firestones.

I lay down full-length on the ground, my forehead pressed into the dust, my arms spread out, my hands flat against the earth. In my mind I became a shadow of myself, an echo, a shaft of energy racing deep within the rock, seeking, knowing, alive to all that lay below. I saw gold glimmering, and primeval bones. Darkness was everywhere, the shifting, living dark of rock and crystal and ancient seeds. There were no firestones.

I walked for hours, feeling out valleys, hills, and plains of tussock grass. I climbed outcrops of jagged rock, scaled a craggy ridge, and negotiated freezing streams. Again and again I walked and lay down, and again and again I found no firestone power. I began to tire, physically and mentally. I thirsted, and my body was in pain with the cold. I could no longer feel my feet, let alone the earth-force under them. I began to despair. Never before had it taken me so long to divine. Never before had there been such a total absence of firestone power. There was not even a remote humming of the power from seams far too deep to be mined; there was no shadow of firestone ash, or the remains of long-ago fires. Nothing. Nothing under the earth or on the surface of it. Nothing but hostile priests waiting.

Priests. I could still feel them, sense their malice, their dangerous animosity. And there was something else, something dark and slippery that ran along the edges of their hate, and caused new fear in me.

I stood up and walked back to them. I shook from weariness, cold, and dread. My lips, cracked from the icy wind, were caked with dust. I took off the blindfold. To my amazement I saw that the skies were already darkening towards evening. The priests were in the distance, standing in a long line on a ridge. Behind them the towers of Kasimarra rose in mist. The priests were in black, and blackness hung like evil over them. They all wore swords. I strode across the ground between us, climbed the ridge, and threw the blindfold at Maelmor's feet. I was breathing hard, my throat hurt, and sweat ran down inside my clothes.

"You lied," I said. "There are no firestones."

He gave me a strange look, a twisted smile, half victorious. But he said nothing. A fury hit me, so great I could have struck him. For a long time we looked at each other, eye to eye, unflinching; and while I looked at him I saw again that other thing, that slippery, insidious, secret thing. I looked at the priests standing alongside him. They wore the same look. I knew then.

"As God is my witness," I said, "I am a true diviner. But you are liars and deceivers, and not even true priests." Then I turned and started walking towards the city. I had to pass their ranks, and as I passed each priest, I knew I passed the possibility of death. I wondered when they would strike, here or at Kasimarra. And yet a strange peace came over me, an unaccountable certainty that all was well. And through that peace — because of it, perhaps — as I passed the final priests in the line I was aware of a faint vibration. I stopped, transfixed. It was small, a shadow, a merest whisper. But it was there.

I walked back the way I had come, slowly. The hum grew stronger, called to me, drew me. I stopped in front of one of the younger priests. He met my gaze, his face flushed and apprehensive.

"You have a firestone," I said.

He glanced past the line towards Maelmor. The high priest came towards us, quickly. His face was inscrutable, but he nodded at the priest. The priest slowly put his hand in a pocket and drew out a small object wrapped in scarlet silk. It was bound tightly, and tied with gold thread.

Maelmor stood behind me. He gave an order in the high language, and every priest reached into his pocket and took something out. There before me, bright as fire against the black robes, were two hundred scarlet packages, all identical. I stared at Maelmor, not understanding. He gave me that odd smile again.

"You said there were no firestones, handmaid," he said. "You see, there are two hundred of them."

I still smelled trickery.

"No," I said. "There is only one firestone. This one."

I took the package from the young priest's hand, and untied it. It was a firestone.

The priests all unwrapped their packages and threw the contents on the ground. Theirs were all stones, ordinary stones. I alone held firestone.

Victory soared in me. Then I saw Maelmor's face, and knew my battle was hardly begun.

"So you can divine, handmaid," he said, through clenched teeth. "We each carried a stone, but we did not know who held the firestone. Diviners sometimes read men's minds, and our own thoughts could have given you a sign. It was the hardest test I could devise. You passed. I will await confirmation of the Firelord's death. An envoy has been already sent to the bridge you told us of. When his death is confirmed we will hold his funeral feast. Twenty days after that we will hold the ordination of the new diviner."

"I will stay here at Kasimarra until then," I said. "There is much I want to do. I have heard of your great libraries here. I will require — "

"The libraries are forbidden to you," he said. "You will be permitted to stay in the diviner's apartments. You will hold no authority anywhere in the temple."

"I will go where I like," I said. "I am Fire Woman."

"You're not Fire Woman yet, harsha. Even if the Firelord's death is verified, there are still twenty days until the inauguration of the new Firelord. A lot can happen in twenty days."

He shouted an order then, and all the priests

turned and began walking back to Kasimarra. I was abandoned there, with only the wail of the wind and encroaching dark for company.

I lived in relative peace at Kasimarra. To occupy myself I explored the vast temple complex, roamed in the dim and deserted corridors and halls, lost myself in the maze of passages, tunnels, and cellars, and climbed the towers and the windswept balconies. I discovered huge hanging terraces that jutted far out from the temple walls, suspended somehow in the howling spaces high above the ravines, their wind-worn stones filled with dirt and ancient roots of plants. They intrigued me, those great abandoned terraces; I could not guess the purpose of them, or how the soil and remains of bygone plants had ever been carried so high on the gales.

I stood in the doorways of the sanctuaries where the people worshipped daily and took part in the elaborate temple rituals; and I decided that their religion was to do more with the prestige and power of the priests than with the love of God. I came across the treasuries filled with precious gems, fine garments, jars of gold, and priceless works of art.

I went for walks in the mountains around Kasimarra, watched the men racing the horses from the Firelord's stables, and the falconers hunting. I went out to the shooting-ground and watched the archers practising, and witnessed tournaments and games. In the long evenings I haunted the solitary places, restless and yearning, and thinking of Teraj.

More than anywhere else, I haunted the corridors around the great libraries. I remembered the vision I had seen of the thousands of scrolls, the secrets centuries old and shrouded in ink. But the doors to the libraries were guarded, the truths hidden, safe behind swords and the commands of Maelmor. I longed to know what it was they were hiding.

I began to feel lonely and isolated. I craved company, and thought of Dannii. But I dared not bring her here to Kasimarra. Her time would come when I was Fire Woman, and she would be — if she wished it — my handmaid and my friend. But for now there was only one person in my life who would look on my face and talk to me. She was an old servant who had been the Firelord's personal waiting woman, when he stayed at Kasimarra. Our friendship had a strange beginning. She found me one day grieving for the Firelord, and came and talked to me. She would not sit by me, as I was harsha, but she stood near, and when she spoke her voice was soft and comforting.

"I loved him well, too," she said. "He was the kind of man who commanded love. Still, he was a solitary soul. He asked me many times to sit with him in his library in the evenings, and talk with him. I think he was desperate for a friend. A firelord's road is not an easy one."

She said no more that time, but her words

comforted me. And they disturbed me.

The next day she brought me my clean robes, and I noticed that she had placed sweet-smelling herbs in them. I thanked her, and she looked at my right shoulder, almost at my face. "I served him well, for forty years," she said. "If your company was good enough for him — " She did not finish.

We talked several times after that, and I think we came to admire one another. She was a tall, stately woman, and could be arrogant at times. But there was wit in her, too, and insight. Her name was Laken. Though we had no long conversations, our shared grief for our lord was a strange bond between us. She helped me more than she knew, in those early days at Kasimarra.

In the evening of my fifth day there, the priests arrived from visiting the place where my lord had disappeared. They informed Maelmor that they had seen his body, but had not brought it back; it had been inaccessible. They said that he was dead, beyond doubt.

That night Maelmor lit the great torches on the walls outside the lower temple door, and called an assembly of all the people. In a huge dark silence he made this announcement: "It has been verified that our Firelord, the high diviner Xavier the Fourth, is dead. Tonight there will be a funeral feast in his memory. A possible aspirant for future diviner, Elsha of the Quelled, is this day in residence in Kasimarra."

There was a moment of stunned silence; then

murmurings and cries of outrage. Soon the crowd was frenzied, roaring with disbelief and horror. Maelmor raised his arms, but it was a long time before the people were quiet again. Then he said: "She is not yet designated to be the new diviner. The choice is not certain. The appointment will be made in twenty days."

So said Maelmor.

The Firelord's funeral was the most lavish Chosen feast I had ever witnessed. I was supposed to have been a major part of it, but I was in an awkward position. As possible future diviner, I should have been seated at the high table, in the place of greatest honour; but as a Quelled, I was not permitted near the table. Maelmor was in a predicament, and it did not improve his humour. In the end he had three tables set, two long ones on either side of a small one, with short distances between; mine was the small one in the middle. So I ate with the priests, but apart from them. And even eating with them broke vital laws. My very existence in the temple broke ancient traditions, and caused conflict and bitterness. Maelmor sat to my left, in the second most honoured place; and I was keenly aware of his fury and helpless hate.

Halfway through the feast I said to him: "High priest, this is as difficult for me as it is for you. But we have a long way to go together. Please let there be cooperation between us. I offer you a cup of wine, in the name of peace." And I held out the Firelord's cup, encrusted with jewels, and priceless. I had not yet drunk from it; it was, according to their laws, still clean.

But he dashed it from my hand as if it were the vilest thing, and the whole room fell silent, watching us.

"I will never drink a cup from a harsha's hand," he said, in a low shaking voice, "though the cup be the Firelord's, and the harsha be future high lord. God has deserted us, and evil mocks us in his place. Your hand holds fire, and that we must have; but the rest of you remains less than animal, and abhorrent. I do not make peace with what I loathe."

Long years of silent submission in the mines had trained me well. I got up calmly, and picked the cup from the floor and placed it back on my table. I washed my hands in the golden bowl placed there for the conclusion of the meal, and dried them on the towel provided. I turned to Maelmor, and bowed low. When I stood, I raised my head high, and looked straight into his face. He flushed with rage.

"You have the truth all twisted, Maelmor," I said. "God has not forsaken the Chosen. He has remembered the Quelled."

We came to a satisfactory agreement, the priests and I: we ignored each other. Though I lived in the Firelord's apartments, I received no honour, no recognition. I suspected they were hoping for a miracle, another diviner; Chosen of course, and male.

And while they hoped, I planned my victory. In my mind I wrote the new laws that would transform my world; I went over them again and again, refining them, perfecting them, praying them through to flawlessness. All my power, all my intent, lay in those laws. I planned how they would be recorded, given out, and enforced. I chose the people who would be my advocates in this huge undertaking; and I raided the Firelord's private treasuries, and bribed menservants to carry messages for me. One I sent to Lesharo. The other I sent by horse, urgently, to the northern territories to Amasai.

20

The Myth

My inauguration morning would fall on the seventh day of the Chosen month of Sabiya. It was now only ten days away.

I went to the topmost pinnacle of the temple, searching for the first sign of an approaching army. I saw only two horsemen riding towards Kasimarra, a trail of dust streaming behind them.

That evening when I was alone in my apartments, Laken came to announce that a Quelled man had arrived. I asked her to take him to the small but beautiful library next to my room, where the Firelord had entertained his guests, and which was filled with his personal treasures. There were statues, paintings, and cabinets full of his favourite books. The room was not ornate — it was very plain, compared with others in the place — but its walls were hung with magnificent tapestries, and there were old carvings of animals I had never seen before. Some of its furnishings were rustic, and there were pieces of pottery and weavings that were rough and not made by craftsmen. It reminded me in many ways of Teraj's home. There was even a bronze image of a dolphin on one of the hand-carved tables, and a mural of a vast turquoise place with dolphins leaping in it.

The Firelord's library was tranquil, and I loved it best of all the rooms at Kasimarra. But tonight when I went there to meet Lesharo, my heart was banging like a drum, and my right hand was deep in my pocket, clutching the woman-stone.

When I entered the library, he was standing with the bronze dolphin in his hands, and he did not notice me at first. Then I spoke his name, and he put the dolphin down and faced me. For a long time we looked at one another without speaking. He had not altered, except that his hair was more grey above his brand. He seemed confused and deeply moved, his face intense, his blue eye burning and full of feeling.

At last he came forward, knelt, and touched the carpet at my feet. I took his hands, and made him stand. His hands were rough, still black-stained from the mine. His ragged clothes were thick with firestone dust and the dirt from his long journey, and his boots had left mud tracks on the floor. Yet he was noble and excellent to me, my soul's kinsman, my oldest, almost dearest friend.

"Welcome to Kasimarra," I said. "Oh, Lesharo, it seems an age since last I saw your face."

"It is only a year," he replied, withdrawing his hands. For the first time in our lives I felt a wall between us, an awkwardness. I wondered whether it was because I was almost High Diviner now, or whether it was Kasimarra that disturbed him.

"Please sit down," I said, indicating a chair. I noticed that Laken had lit the fire in here, and was glad. We sat on either side of it, though he was at an angle to me, his blind eye on my side. He sat rigidly in his chair, looking into the flames.

"Tell me of home," I said.

"Your family is well," he replied, turning to face me. "Your oldest brother is married now. Your mother is a caretaker, and is fine. Your father . . . he has aged. Your disappearance was hard for them. And for me." The words were spoken softly, yet they held a year of hurt.

"I did not choose to leave," I said. "I was called. I asked if I might go back and say goodbye, especially to you; but I was denied. The parting was painful for me, too."

For a long time he studied my face; then he slightly smiled, and looked into the flames again. "We heard that you were the Firelord's handmaid," he said. "They've made up songs about you, in Siranjaro. The songs were a little too inspiring, perhaps; some of the miners became insubordinate, and rose against the overseers. The army's been twice to put down rebellions. I have heard that it is the same in other places."

"It may get worse," I said. "It is ten days to my inauguration, and I had hoped the army would be here by now. I am going to exercise the Firelord's right to change the laws. The Chosen will fight me every step of the way."

"That they will. There'll be civil war, Elsha."

"Then I hope to God that what I do is right."

He looked full in my face then, and his smile was the old smile I loved, serene and warm and encouraging. "You are right, lionheart. Never doubt it."

"You've changed your tune," I said. "You told me once that defiance was not worth its price."

"That was the only foolish thing I ever said. Since you walked with the Firelord, I have seen the Quelled stand singing, filled with inspiration and hope. Long we have dreamed of revolt, but always our defiance has been ineffective, stamped out before it was hardly begun. We were scattered, like sheep without a shepherd. Now we have a champion. You'll give us our revolution — and you'll give us power behind it, a Firelord on our side, and laws to back us up. You will achieve in your lifetime what we might otherwise have done in centuries. I cannot tell you what you mean to us. To all the Quelled. To me. I honour you, Elsha. I love you well. All the Quelled love you."

For a while we sat there looking at one another, hesitant, overwhelmed. Then suddenly I found myself in his embrace, and the feel and smell and touch of him was like a homecoming to me, and I felt again all the passion and pain and hope and wild dreaming of a child in Siranjaro.

And it was good.

Two more days passed, and still there was no sign of Amasai and his army, nor any word from him. I began to fear that the messenger had taken his gold and deserted me. I went three times a day to the towers, and looked out across the mountains and valleys for a sign of an army on the march. Without Amasai, my cause was lost. As Fire Woman I could write new laws, I could rewrite the entire social structure of my world — but without supporters to issue and enforce the laws, I could achieve nothing. Amasai was vital to me.

Lesharo knew my inner fears, and his serenity was my strength. To him I told my new laws, and my plans for establishing them.

"There'll be a new order," I said, "founded on the dignity of the Quelled and their equality with the Chosen. Envoys will go to every mine to instruct the overseers and to ensure that the new laws are adhered to. Branding will be abolished. There will be hospitals for the miners, schools, and time to rest. Women will choose their own husbands, and children under fourteen will be forbidden to work. Overseers will carry no whips, and disputes will be settled between the chief overseer and representatives from the mine. The Quelled will have a voice, Lesharo. A life."

"But how will you know that the overseers keep to the new laws?" he asked. "Once the envoys leave, anything could happen in the mines. The Quelled could be worse off than ever."

"That is why I need you, Lesharo. You have a way with people, and can reassure, organise, and lead them. I want you to travel to every mine and talk to the Quelled. I want each mine to choose an ambassador who will report to me in Kasimarra three times a year. The ambassadors must be trusted delegates, whom the Chosen can't intimidate or bribe. They'll give me true reports. And I'll visit the mines myself, if I suspect disorder. Will you do this thing for me, Lesharo? I will give you everything you need; a horse, clothes, gold, guards to protect you on your journeys — "

He leaned close, and pressed a finger to my lips. "I don't need persuading, Elsha. I will do anything I can for you. And I think I'd rather walk than ride. Horses are irksome things if you're not used to them. I'm still raw in places, from the ride here."

We laughed together, and he reached across the table to a piece of fruit. He sliced some for me. We were having our evening meal, and I still was not used to eating with him. Being with Lesharo, seeing his slow smile and his gentle ways and beautiful hands, reminded me piercingly of Teraj.

My heart and mind were with Teraj every moment, and I longed for his company. He had sent me one treasured letter, and I kept it on me always, bound about the dolphin with a strand of his dark hair and a scarlet cord. I dared not send a letter back to him, for fear of Maelmor's spies.

And Lesharo too had his yearnings. He had a wife now, delegated to him not long after I had left Siranjaro. He said he had grown to love her, and they had a son. Strangely, our other loves touched not the bond between Lesharo and me; we were kindred souls together, like brother and sister. There was still that easiness between us, and nothing had changed with us since Siranjaro.

Laken hovered about us like a mother hen every moment we were together. She sat in a corner of the room now while we ate, and made a tapestry. I offered her a cup of wine, but she would not drink with us. She was a strange mixture, upholding lesser Chosen traditions, and breaking greater ones.

She measured me for new robes, and spent hours explaining the complex rites connected with the Firelord's inauguration. She listened critically to the speech I would make, and helped me record the new laws. And another thing she did, which meant more to me than all her other encouragements.

I asked her the next day, when we were alone together, why the libraries were guarded. Her face became intent, disquieted, as if something weighed heavy on her mind.

"It is worth more than my life to tell you," she said.

"The Firelord had a son," I said, "and he started to teach me the high language of the Chosen, so that I could read what is in those libraries."

If my news shocked Laken, she did not show it. But she looked at me for a long time, and I had the feeling she was weighing me up, judging my intellect, my soul. Then very quietly she said: "In the third hour after nightfall, meet me in the infirmary. If you are questioned, say you are not well, and have sent for me. I will come, and we will wait till it is safe. There is a door between the infirmary and a library room where the medical books are held. From there the libraries are ours. And, woman — don't tell a soul, not even your Quelled friend."

It was freezing in the corridors at night, and the wooden floors had ice on them. I took a torch with me, and the flamelight glimmered on the old stone walls as I hurried past. I had been to the infirmary before, when I had a headache and needed herbal medicines; so I knew where to go. The infirmary was huge and dimly lit. There were about fifty beds here, though only three were occupied. The patients slept; a physician dozed in a chair by the fire at the far end. The wall to my left was full of cupboards and shelves, and my torchlight flickered across thick glass bottles, ancient dried plants, and metal instruments. I thought again of Teraj, and longing swept over me.

I felt a hand brush my arm, and jumped. It was Laken. She held a finger to her lips, and signalled me to follow her. We passed the wall of shelves, the antiquated cupboards, and went on past half-open doors. Our torches briefly lit up tables inside, narrow and bare and scrubbed. We came to the final door. It was closed and bolted, but not locked. Laken glanced behind her at the physician. He still dozed. Soundlessly, she drew the bolt. She pushed open the door; heated air and the smell of parchment breathed over us. We went through; she closed it behind us, and it grated on the stone surrounds. We waited, not breathing. She gave me a tense smile, witchlike near the flames, and drew me after her into the room.

A brazier burned here to keep the medical parchments from becoming mildewed. The room was warm, and gleamed with shelves of rolled books. Charts hung on the walls, showing gruesome pictures of people without skin, some with all their organs exposed. I stared at them, fascinated and appalled. Laken took my sleeve and pulled me into another room beyond, a smaller room, unheated. Here were kept jars of human remains, diseased organs, and unspeakable things. I covered my mouth with my hand, and Laken hurried me past.

We went down a narrow stone passage and came to a heavy door. Laken leaned on it, opened it a crack. She pressed her face to the gap, and I could hear her breathing quick and tense. At last, satisfied that the room was vacant, she swung the door open.

Kasimarra's libraries stretched before us, luminous with torches, braziers, and candle-fire. Huge they were; high glowing rooms with massive archways between; wooden floors shining and rich with rugs; and scrolls. Tens of thousands of scrolls, all neatly shelved and labelled, and holding the Chosen wisdom of centuries.

I walked between the shelves, overwhelmed. I felt Laken take the torch from my hand, and heard her place it in a bracket in a wall. "There is only one scroll you need to see," she said.

I followed her to a section of the library slightly apart from all the rest, heavily curtained and concealed. Here the books were in ornate cabinets. Oil lamps hung from the ceiling, and the room was splendid with tapestries and painted walls. I looked at the things they depicted: another world, a world of alien blue skies, strange animals, and an emerald earth. And in the sky, painted in metallic gold that shone, was my family sign.

Laken pushed a scroll into my hands, but my eyes were on the painted wall.

"Laken," I said, "why is the sign of the lion on the wall?"

"It isn't a lion," she said, and her voice sounded high and apprehensive. "Read the scroll, Elsha. We haven't all night. If we're found here, I'll lose my life. God knows what they'll do to you."

I tore my eyes off my family sign, and looked at the scroll in my hands. Carefully, for the parchment was brittle with age, I unrolled it. The scroll was edged with borders of flowers and plants delicately painted, and was beautifully lettered. The script had turned brown, and was difficult to read. There was a date scratched on the ancient wood of the scroll, but I couldn't decipher it.

I looked at Laken. Her face was fervent, white. "I can't read it," I said. "It's in the high language. I don't know enough of it."

She took the scroll from me, and I saw that her hands shook. "It was written five centuries ago," she said, her voice quavering. "The Firelord told me of it. I think not many people know it exists." She drew a deep breath, and read it to me.

These are the first words of the people calling themselves Chosen, written by the prophet Hamash: This is what occurred in the days following the time of the shaking, when stars fell and meteorites struck the earth, when the dust covered the sun and the world shifted on its axis and the cold age began. In those first days the people who were left, whose lands were de-

stroyed, travelled to find another place less devastated. They found it in the mountains of Galenia, where there dwelled a peaceful and prosperous race. This race lived in grand homes built on the mountainsides, homes of wood and stone and fine furniture. They had a city called Kasimarra, with a palace where their king lived. The palace was reached by a high road, and was at that time undefended, as the king was a man of peace who had no army. He and his people were easily defeated, and their homes taken over by the stronger nation.

At that time the cold would kill a man within half a day if he was unprotected from it, and the new race needed fuel for fires, and fuel in plentiful and constant supply. All the trees were cut down and burned; then a new fuel was needed. Such fuel was hidden in countless seams in the mountains of Galenia, but was obtained only by long and hard labour. So the conquered people were enslaved, and by their labour the fuel was procured. But the slaves rebelled, and many escaped, and the master race devised a way to suppress them totally.

A new religion was written, in which the master race proclaimed that God himself chose them above all others, and gave them special power and wisdom to redeem the world from the cold. These new teachings were designed to justify the enslavement of the weaker race.

The slaves were branded, their language obliterated, their religion erased, their rights as human beings abolished. Succeeding generations of the master race were taught that the quelled race was subhuman, of low intelligence and no feeling. The slaves were bred for the purpose of mining only, and were given the status of beasts.

Over a period of time, the quelled themselves were deceived, believing themselves to have no souls or minds, and to be totally inferior to their masters. The deception was so cunning, so complete, that later generations of both races believed it to be a truth. Therefore there was no conflict; the Chosen became absolute lords, and the Quelled became what they believed they were — voiceless slaves with no capacity to fight.

By this means, the world was kept alive by fire, and the fuel supplies maintained.

These words are true, and are to be kept concealed in the library in the palace of the Quelled king at Kasimarra, which is now the temple for the new religion of the Chosen. They are written in the tenth year after the end of the old world and the beginning of the cold age.

I heard her roll the parchment again, carefully; heard her replace it in the cabinet and close the door. But I did not see the room, or her. I saw countless generations of Quelled all rising to their feet, exalted in the light of truth. I saw the golden sign blazing on the wall, that once a king had seen. A king, my ancestor. Father of my race. My royal race.

My mind could hardly take it in. Joy swept

me first, and wonder that all my life I had been right. I thought of the other revelations in the scroll: of the former world, warm and green and blue; of the beginning of the cold age, the shaking of the earth and the blanketing of dust; and of our being suppressed. We sang of it all, in our myths. We Quelled had been right, right for centuries.

And the Chosen — the Chosen had built their religion, their entire civilisation, on a monstrous lie. Anger flooded me, a terrible hating rage against the Chosen for inventing the lie, and anger at us for so long believing it.

Then came the grief.

And while I cried, sobbing for the humiliation and poverty and pain of all my race, old Laken cried and rocked me in her arms, and murmured love to me.

I could not have slept afterwards. I did not return to my room, but wandered through the dark corridors, stood in stately rooms filled with magnificent treasures, and touched age-old furniture and works of art. I went out to the great abandoned terraces, and stood there with the wind whipping my clothes. I saw the soil in the cracks between the ancient stones, and the twisted roots of bygone plants; and I remembered the myths my father had told me, of a time when we Quelled were lords and lived in great dwellings high in the mountains, with vast gardens that hung there in the shining light. And I longed to see Lesharo in the morning, and hear him sing the songs that were no longer myths, but our true glorious history.

It must have been near dawn when I went back to my room. To my surprise, a servant waited there, looking angry and nervous. She noticed that I was fully dressed, and frowned. "So you already know," she said.

"Know what?" I asked. "I could not sleep; I've been walking on the terraces."

Her eyebrows rose, and she said arrogantly: "You have a visitor. He's been travelling a long time, on foot. He demands to see you. He says the matter is extremely urgent. He will tell no one what he wants. He must speak with you. He is in the great hall on the ground floor. He waits now."

Deeply apprehensive, I went downstairs and entered the great hall. It was the same hall in which I had first confronted Maelmor and the priests. I closed the huge wooden doors behind me, and faced the man.

He was about my age, and had long dark hair, a sable beard, and dark flashing eyes. He was standing by a wall torch, and the light glinted on the jewel fixed to his black cloak, and on his leather belt and sword hilt. His clothes were grey and ragged. A servant had given him a silver goblet of wine, and when he saw me he took a slow sip of it, and gave me a long appraising stare. He was all defiance and anger, and the very air about him was tense.

"Elsha of the Quelled," he said, with venom. "Seven days I've walked to see you."

He came over to me, his eyes flickering across my clothes, my hair, my face. He half laughed, and gazed in my eyes with scorn, straight, as if I were not Quelled. "So. My great adversary. Greetings."

"This is hardly an acceptable hour for visiting," I said, "and I am cold and tired. State your business, and go."

"My business, harsha? My business is the business of divining. I have come to take my place. The former Firelord trained me in the laws, and in the diviner's powers. He had designated me to replace him. I am Zune, the new Firelord."

I closed my eyes and tried to stop the awful wheeling of the earth.

"You joke, surely," I said. "He said nothing of you, or of training someone else."

"Why should he? It was nothing to do with you. But when he left you at Talbar, he visited me and completed my training. He suggested that I ask you to be my handmaid. I know that he was well pleased with you. But your work is done. You are free to return to Siranjaro."

"My work is hardly begun. I will not leave, Zune. I am here as future diviner. I have passed the test, my divining power is proved. Ask the priests. They will confirm that."

He sighed, and swore under his breath. "I do not question your power to divine," he said, turning side on to me, his jaw setting in a hard, determined line. "I question your right to be here. You are female. Quelled. The Chosen do not accept you. The priests do not accept you. You have stayed here this long only because you can divine, and they thought they would need your skill. But now you are unnecessary, your powers irrelevant. I am here."

"I will go in peace and name you Firelord, if you will make all the changes in the laws that I demand."

"*You* will name *me* Firelord? *You* demand changes?" He turned on me, his rage terrible. "You have no rights, no demands, no privileges! How dare you stand there and discuss the terms of my office? I could strike you dead now with my sword, and not one in all the world would lift a hand in your defence! You cannot change the laws! The laws have stood five hundred years, have created order out of chaos, and life where there was death."

"Life for the Chosen," I said, "slavery for the Quelled. I will make changes that will give the Quelled rights, give them honour, ease their burdens, allow them time for themselves, for education and proper homes, and — "

"Honour! Ease! Harsha, you are mad! Our very lives depend on their slavery, on their getting us the firestones! I agree with you, some of the laws are hard, and those I am prepared to change. I talked with the Firelord, of those. But you talk of reforms that sweep the whole fabric of our society into disorder! You talk of utter chaos!"

"Is dignity and a fair day's labour chaos?" I cried. "All I ask is that the Quelled be treated like human beings, with feelings and needs and intelligence! All I ask is that they work fewer hours, and are given proper shelter and food, and that their children are given a fair childhood! It wouldn't alter your Chosen lives at all! You could still lie about all day in your furs and priceless timber houses, and discuss your evil myths! Nothing would change for *you*!"

He threw the goblet on the floor, and it spun on the polished wood, spilling wine as red as blood. "You're mad!" he yelled. "Our whole civilisation is built on Quelled slavery! Jeopardize that, and you have anarchy and rebellion! Is that what you want, harsha — civil war?"

"No! And I know the lies your civilisation — "

"War is what you'll get! There's already fighting over you, fighting between Quelled and overseers, between free-thinking Chosen and the authorities. I've even heard the priests here in disagreement over you. You cannot stay as Firelord, harsha. You will cause only disruption and mutiny and bloodshed. Go home. Go anywhere you like. But I am Firelord here."

"I will not leave."

"Then I'll kill you."

I tore open the front of my garments. "My

heart's in here. Cut it out, and burn it in the holy of holies, in the fire for the Quelled. I'll die for them. But I won't give up everything for you."

He unsheathed his sword, and came close to me. His gaze met mine and held, and he was the first to look away.

"I will do this fairly," he said, "since justice means so much to you. I give you five days to gather together one hundred men who support you and are willing to fight on your behalf. In five days I will meet with them with a hundred of my men, on the plateau above the ridge east of Kasimarra. It is an old battleground. If your side wins, I will go. I swear that, in the name of God. But if I win, you go. If you refuse, you'll be taken from here dead."

"There is no justice in that," I said. "I haven't got a hundred men. I have only one."

He sheathed his sword, and gave me a dark smile. "It is fairer than slicing the heart out of a defenceless harsha. You have five days, Elsha of the Quelled. Then it is war."

He turned and strode out, his boots echoing in the hall's great darkness. The door banged behind him, and he was gone.

21

Persuasions

Maelmor came to my apartments demanding that I give them up for Zune. I refused. They could not forcefully remove me, as that would have meant touching me; so Zune was given the Firelord's guest apartments. He lived only a wall beyond me; but even though he was my enemy, and close, I did not fear that he would do me injury. His word was a Firelord's word, and he would not kill me. I was safe from him — but only him.

I went nowhere without Lesharo, and Laken allowed no hands but her own to prepare our food. We drank only wine from bottles she opened herself, which she chose from the thousands in the cellars. Lesharo and I both carried knives. I was deserted by the temple guards, and the servants abandoned me. The priests gloated. They had their Firelord now, and in their minds they had the victory.

The days crawled by, and every hour I went to the highest tower and looked for Amasai. At last, two days before the battle, I saw him approach. Like insects on the ground his army was; a mighty swarm moving slow along a far valley floor, thunderous and dark, and glorious.

While we waited, Laken insisted that I properly prepare myself to meet with him. "He's the commander of your army," she said, bending to remove my muddy boots. "And you are the future Fire Woman. You cannot hold an audience with him while you look like a slovenly stable girl."

I had been out riding that morning, and had taken a rough tumble, so her description of me probably wasn't inaccurate. She banished Lesharo from my apartment, and made me bathe and wash my hair and put on perfumes as if I were a bride. By the time she'd finished with me, I was beginning to feel as nervous as one. She clucked and muttered, and made an intolerably long task of combing and plaiting my hair. She was still fussing when I heard marching in the street. At last she was satisfied.

"I will wait for Lord Amasai in the Firelord's private library," I said. "Please make sure the fire is well fed with stones, and that we have bread and cheese and wine. And, Laken — I do not wish to be disturbed when I am speaking with him."

"I wouldn't dream of it, woman," she murmured, bowing low, then rushing off to find Amasai.

Lesharo spoke with me, briefly, while I waited in the library.

"God is good," he said, taking my hands and kissing them. "He has not only remembered the Quelled, but he has given us a Quelled diviner, and a whole army to fight on our behalf. Oh, lionheart, I feel a new wind blowing, changing the course of our history."

"Winds can be unpredictable," I said. "Pray for me while we talk."

"I pray for you every hour," Lesharo said, and left. Shortly afterwards Amasai came.

Tall and valorous he was, with his long golden hair past his shoulders now, and his brown soldier's cloak in noble folds across his army uniform. He crossed the firelit floor between us, looked long into my face, and lay full-length on the carpet before me.

"I greet you, my future Fire Woman," he said huskily. "I offer you my allegiance." He stood and stayed there before me, close, his eyes on my face. "Well, Elsha of the Quelled," he said softly, half smiling, "I never thought I'd see you in this place. And yet I was not wholly surprised when you sent for me. I came as soon as I heard, and we have travelled day and night. I hope your wait was not too trying."

"There have been anxious moments," I smiled, fighting a crazy, joyous urge to hug him. I thought how good it was to look straight in his face. He was so fine, so fair. He had changed since I last saw him. The plains and angles of his face had a slightly harder edge to them, as if he had endured much in the past year. He looked more athletic, more compelling and forceful than ever. He would be a good commander, I thought. The soldier's uniform suited him well, clothed his quiet passion with austere discipline, his gracefulness with strength. He looked less prosperous now, wearing no jewellery except the stones in the hilt of his sword. His brown cloak was thick wool, rough-woven, and fell to the heels of his high black boots. His tunic and trousers were of thick weatherproof material, plain and practical. Yet he still had that gracious, kingly way with him, that gentle humour. There were tiny lines around his eyes when he smiled, and his eyes were still that singular, unsettling blue.

"I cannot tell you what it means to me to have you here," I said.

"It means much to me as well," he said softly, fervour colouring his face. He took my hands in his. "I have thought of you every day, Elsha, since last I saw you in the kitchens of Jinnah."

I blushed, and withdrew my hands. "I've thought of you often, too," I said. "Especially these last weeks. You are so late arriving, I thought that the battle was already Zune's."

Amasai looked bewildered. "Who is Zune?"

"Have you not heard? Oh, Amasai, then it is

only by the grace of God that you are here on time. Zune claims that the Firelord chose him for future diviner. He has challenged me to a battle the day after tomorrow — a hundred of his men against a hundred of mine. The victor becomes Firelord."

Amasai turned slightly away from me, but not before I saw his face. I was suddenly afraid.

"You will fight for me in this?" I asked.

Still he would not look at me. "I cannot say, Elsha. If the Firelord chose Zune, then let Zune be the new diviner. I see no reason for conflict. If I did fight for you, and you were made Fire Woman, you would not be happy. I thought you were compelled to be future Firelord, because of your power to divine. I thought you needed me to protect you, to prevent disorder. But there is no need. Surely you cannot want this life — to be exploited for your ability, but still hated and despised. The Firelord's life is lonely anyway, but yours would be intolerable. Now that Zune is here, why not leave the work to him?"

"I don't want to be Firelord just because I can divine," I said. "I want the power to change the laws, to make a better life for my people. I need the power of the Firelord's word."

He stared at me, astounded. "By God, Elsha! You want to change the world!" He breathed a Chosen oath, then walked across the room and sat in one of the chairs by the fire. For a while he sat in silence, leaning forward with his elbows on his knees, his hands clasped, his eyes staring into the flames. I went and sat near him, on the other side of the fire.

"We will not refuse to mine for firestones," I said, "but we will not work as slaves, or be treated any longer like animals. We will live like human beings, equal with the Chosen."

"What you are telling me," he said, "is that you plan to tear down the very foundations of our way of life. The Firelord planned reforms, Elsha, and I know he had a deep and sincere love for the Quelled — but he knew Chosen minds, too, and how much he could change, and how fast. But you — you want to turn the world upside down."

"No, I don't," I said, trying to sound calm. "What I want won't change Chosen lives at all, much. But it will transform the lives of the Quelled. I want them to work reasonable hours. I want them to have time to call their own. I want their poverty eased.

"Have you ever lived with them, Amasai? Do you know how cold and drafty their tents are, how few blankets and cooking vessels they have, and how little food? You slept in the Firelord's caves every now and again, and you thought that was hardship. But his caves had wine and furs and more firestones than were needed, and you Chosen wear more garments in a day than the Quelled wear in a lifetime. Have you ever got up at dawn and eaten one paltry wheat cake and drunk some hot water with a leaf in it, and then gone into the bowels of the earth, and slaved all day? And been cursed and whipped and driven, and then gone home at night with ice in your wet clothes and your boots falling apart, to a freezing tent and no fire going, and children weeping from hunger and exhaustion and cold? And then cooked a meal for a whole family with only a cup of corn and some mouldy flour and a few miserable vegetables? And then slept for a few hours and got up at dawn and started the whole round again?

"I have. Eleven years I lived that life, with not one day to call my own. That's what I'm going to change, Amasai. Not your sheltered Chosen lives, not your feasts and your festivals and your grand houses and your wealth. Just the lives of the Quelled."

Amasai stood up and began pacing the room. I waited, agonised. I needed his support, or all was lost. He came back to the fire, crouched by the basket of firestones on the hearth, and threw some on the flames.

"I know what you want to achieve," he said. "And it's all good and just and right. But the Chosen won't accept it without a fight." He took another firestone, and held it up in the firelit space between us. "We need these, Elsha. And the only way we can obtain them is by slave labour. Who in his right mind would go willingly into those filthy mines and work under those conditions, often enough and long enough to supply every living soul with fuel?" He threw the fuel on the fire, and the move had anger in it.

"I know of a place," I said, very low, "where Quelled and Chosen work side by side in a mine, singing and joking, for as much of the day as they want, and share their firestones when they come out."

"Name it to me."

"I cannot."

"No. Because it doesn't exist. It's a dream, Elsha, an impossible ideal. It could never work like that."

"Pay the Quelled, then, for their work. Give them proper homes and food and education and leisure, in return for their service in the mines. Remove the status of slavery."

"Elsha! The Chosen will never agree to that! You live in a fantasy! The Chosen will fight to the death to defend their way of life! The most you can hope to achieve is to lessen the time the Quelled work, get them better supplies of food, perhaps, and more blankets for their beds. But as for educating them, building them homes, giving them something resembling a Chosen way of life — "

"I must, Amasai! Otherwise all my life is for nothing! Why do you think the Firelord chose me — why he honoured me and blessed me, and gave me his divining robe before he died? Why do you think he made you commander of his army? Maybe he foresaw all this, foresaw the conflicts, and knew you'd fight on my behalf. You must fight for me, Amasai, for all the Quelled. It is what he wished."

He stood up and went over to a window. For a long time he looked down across the city, his fair head bent. He came back at last, and stood in front of me. He still looked uncertain.

"You remind me of things the Firelord said; things I did not then understand. He said he believed there was another diviner, but he could not find him. He spoke of having no real choice; of compromise, and half a dream. Maybe you are right, Elsha. Maybe he did in the end mean you to be Fire Woman, and me to fight for you. But I cannot force my soldiers to accept that. Neither will I command them to fight and die for something they do not believe. If you would have them fight for you in the battle, then you must give them something great to fight for. Your personal vision for your race is not enough."

"Tomorrow morning they shall have their reason," I said.

We parted then.

That night in secret and alone I visited the libraries again.

At dawn I went to see Amasai. He had refused a fine room in the city, and had camped out on a plain with his men. The skies were barely grey when I went to their camp, and the tents were white with ice. It had snowed a little in the night, and patches of it were piled against the tents and about the tussock grass. Soldiers were already about, lighting small fires on the frozen ground outside, and heating water for washing and drinks. There were thousands of them, and their tents were pitched in straight and orderly lines, hundreds upon hundreds. The nearest soldiers watched me approach, their faces curious and unwelcoming. I wondered if Alejandro was somewhere among them, and, if so, whether he would fight for me. There was no time to make enquiries.

One of the sentries took me to Amasai's tent.

Amasai was standing over a silver bowl on a low stand, washing. He wore only trousers, and I saw that he had a long scar down his back. Steam from the water curled into the bitter air. A brazier burned on the ground in the centre of the tent, but made little difference to the temperature. Amasai did not hear the soldier announce my arrival, and his servant with him was so surprised to see me that he could not speak. Amasai finished washing his face, then noticed me. He smiled, and dried his face on a towel his servant handed him.

"I'm sorry to come so early," I said. "But I didn't want Maelmor or the priests to question me. I left before they were about."

Amasai grinned. "Why, Elsha? Have you done something unlawful? Apart from breathing Kasimarra's sacred air, that is." He pulled on a jacket, and the servant moved to button it for him. Amasai waved him away. "Leave us," he said. "I would speak alone with this woman."

The servant looked stunned, but obeyed.

"Sit down, Elsha," said Amasai, indicating a

low folding stool. "I'm sorry I can't offer you a golden chair just now. But that will come, I hope. So. What news?"

He drew a thick fur cloak about himself, then pulled up another stool and sat facing me, close. His manner was light and jovial, but I saw the apprehension underneath.

"I brought you this," I said, and took the Myth of Hamash from under the folds in my cloak.

Amasai took it to the tent entrance, unrolling it in the pale morning light. He did not speak while he read. Then slowly he rolled the scroll again, and stood for a time looking out across his army and the mountains beyond. I waited, hardly daring to breathe. At last he came back and sat down. He held the scroll across his knees, his knuckles white, as if it were a heavy thing.

"I had heard that such a book existed," he said quietly, "but I had not believed it. Where did you find it, Elsha?"

"In a concealed room in the libraries."

"The libraries are guarded — and now I see why."

"I was shown a secret way to them, through the infirmary."

"You have friends in Kasimarra, then. Be careful. Maelmor has spies everywhere."

"That is why I came here now, before day. But soon everyone will know the Myth of Hamash."

He lifted his head, looked straight into my eyes. He looked suddenly immensely weary, as if all the burdens of the world lay on his soul. "I cannot say I will publish it openly," he said, "but I will read it to my men. And then I will ask them to fight not for the Quelled, nor for a Fire Woman, nor even for right: but for truth."

He sighed, deeply. "It is a hard thing, Elsha, to suddenly know that everything I believed all my life was a lie. I am glad for your sake that we have the scroll; I grieve for the Chosen. And I fear the Quelled and the fury this will fire in them. This parchment has the power to change the world. It has already done much. Now it must undo. You must be very careful where you take it."

"I will take it nowhere," I said, standing up. "It is yours, Amasai. You have more wisdom than I have, in these things. I'm a diviner, not a strategist."

"You could have fooled me," he smiled. Then he stood also, his face very grave. "You trust me with a great thing, Elsha."

"I trust you with the future of my race, and with my life," I said.

Laken met me at the entrance to my apartments, and told me that Zune sought an audience with me. "It is urgent, woman," she said, her old face creased in anxiety. "He is very angry."

I met him in the small private library that I loved. I felt my Firelord's presence strongly here, and the place was holy to me; tonight with Zune I wanted us both to feel his influence.

Zune was very tense, white-lipped and anxious. I offered him a cup of wine, but he ignored the offer, and said bitterly: "I did not think that you would stoop so low, harsha, to buy support from trained soldiers. And Lord Amasai — what have you offered him? A high-ranking house in Kasimarra, and enough wealth to last a hundred lifetimes? From what the Firelord told me, I thought you had integrity. But you have no more honour than a spoiled woman with too much stolen wealth at her disposal. You have abused your position here, temporary though it is. You have deceived us all, harsha."

"You think this battle is unfair, now?" I asked, looking surprised. "You think I have unfair advantage?"

He swore, and came close to me, and shook his fist in my face. "I swear, whoever wins, you'll die. One hundred supporters, I said. One hundred friends. Advocates. So you bribe an army commander. I thought, until today, that Lord Amasai was honourable."

"He is," I said. "He is also my friend. I have paid him nothing. If he and his men fight for me, it is because they believe in my cause. So don't talk to me of unfairness, or lack of honour. If destiny favours me in this, then your argument is with God, not me."

He looked at me for a long time, his face sceptical at first, then hard and desperate.

"If you want to," I said peaceably, "we can settle this without fighting. Let us do our best to work together, for the sake of him whom we both loved, who called us both in different ways. I want no bloodshed. I want only a better life for the Quelled. Swear that you will change the laws, and I will walk out of here and let you be Firelord."

"You will never be Firelord," he said, his voice low and scathing. "The people will never permit it. Not a female, and a Quelled. You will be destroyed without mercy."

"Not if I am the only person in the world with divining power," I said.

"By this time tomorrow," he said, "one of us will not exist." He gave me that grim and bitter smile again, and left.

colour that I had chosen. The men were orderly and quiet, and Amasai rode up and down their lines, instructing or encouraging them.

Zune's men arrived shortly after. They came in a cloud of dust, thundering up the eastern approaches to the plateau, riding furiously and yelling as if they were mad. They gathered on their end of the field, unruly and eager to begin. Against Amasai's solemn troops, they were a wild mob. They wore no uniform, but their many-coloured cloaks streamed behind them; and their ribbons, black, they wore tied across their fore-heads. I don't know where Zune called them from; but they were a zealous lot.

I stood at the front of the ridge, with the priests and temple personnel in long lines behind me. Further back thronged the citizens of Kasimarra. They made more noise almost than Zune's men. They had musicians there, playing festive music, and some people had set up booths to sell drinks and little pies. It was not a battle they had come to see — it was an entertainment, a festival. They had no doubts that Zune would win.

Lesharo stood beside me, close. He had wanted to fight for me; but Amasai had turned him away, saying that he had five times a hundred men, all soldiers zealous to fight for a noble cause, and all well-skilled in war. Lesharo was grievously dis-appointed, but I was glad of his company. Old Laken stood a little way to our right — a public declaration of her loyalty to me. Amasai had given me a white banner, and it streamed above us, snapping in the wind. Behind us was a river of banners, all black.

Amasai's men formed in two lines at one end of the battlefield, and Amasai rode to the front and lifted his sword high.

Immediately Zune's men, almost orderly, assembled at the other end behind Zune. Zune raised his sword; then he rode forward to meet Amasai in the centre of the field. This was the ceremony that would begin the battle. For a few moments they spoke. Then they came cantering towards the ridge, to speak with Maelmor and me. The high priest and I went down onto the plateau, and stood before them. Zune and Amasai dismounted. Their horses waited behind them, impatient, puffing and stamping, their nostrils sending mists into the icy air.

Amasai came to me, his face solemn and very tense. But he smiled, and it was like a warmth on me.

"In your name, Elsha of the Quelled, and in the name of truth, I fight this fight," he said.

I replied, loud, so all would hear: "In the name of the former High Diviner, Xavier the Fourth, and in the name of God, I await your victory."

Then Zune stepped towards Maelmor. "In the name of the Chosen of God," Zune said, "and in the name of our immortal traditions and our creed, I fight this fight."

"The Chosen already celebrate your victory," said Maelmor, and tumultuous cheering broke out from the throngs. Then Amasai and Zune mounted. But before they rode away, I went to Amasai and handed something to him. It was my Firelord's sign, the divining eye, scratched over with my family sign.

"I want you to wear it in the battle," I said.

He looked at me, his eyes moist, and in silence put it over his head. Then he and Zune rode back to their men, and Maelmor and I returned to the ridge.

Amasai and Zune each gave a great war cry and rode down the grim plateau, their armies close behind, and met and clashed. It was all confusion at first, men and horses locked in terrible conflict, the clash of steel on steel, and everywhere the sound of horses in panic, the yells of desperate men, and the screams when steel struck flesh. Sometimes the dust rose so thick and high, I could see only the swords flashing, and ghostly tumultuous shapes. And always there was the noise, the hellish noise of men and animals in war.

For an age it seemed to go on. There were times when I shut it out, retreated to a quiet inner place, to keep my sanity. But then a scream more hideous than all the rest would jolt me back, forcing me to watch. I became aware that I was gripping Lesharo's hand so hard that my nails pierced his flesh. He seemed not to notice.

The dust from the battlefield carried to us on the wind, bringing sounds that were less confused now, more savage and desperate. Men fought in smaller groups, mostly on foot. The dust cleared a little, revealing the full horror of the fight. Dead and dying men and animals lay distorted on the ground. Men fell, and could not rise again. Some were killed where they lay, decapitated, or their hearts run through. The ground was black with blood, the air full of the stench of death and the agony of the living.

It was impossible to tell who was winning. The black ribbons had long since fallen off, and the white were dark with dirt and blood. Only Zune I recognised; he wore all black, and a firelord's scarlet sash. I looked for Amasai and Alejandro. I found only Amasai, fighting hand to hand with three of Zune's supporters. He was breathtaking to watch — and he was victorious. While I watched him, willing him strength, he raised his sword high above his head, and roared a command to his men. I don't know what it was he said; but soldiers gathered about him, stood straight, and fought like men renewed. And while they fought, inspired, their enemies seemed to shrink and fail. Amasai's men began to slaughter them, one after the other, coldly and methodically. I saw Zune fall, rise again, and fall a final time. Only twenty of his men were left. When they saw that he did not rise again, they all knelt and placed their swords on the bloodied ground in front of them. Amasai's men, their swords raised, surrounded them. But they did not strike those final blows. For a while no one moved, and in the silence of ceased battle, the wind brought to us the groans of the dying, and calls for mercy and help. Amasai stood tall and still, the wind blowing his dark cloak about him, and tearing at his golden hair. His stillness was more frightening than his fight.

I turned to Maelmor. His face had gone deadly white, his eyes distended and wild with disbelief.

"Zune and his men are surrendering," he said. "By God, harsha, this day our world ends."

He faced Kasimarra, and I saw that he wept. He started walking back, passing so close by me that I felt the heavy brush of his cloak, and all his grief and hate. His priests and temple staff went with him. The people of Kasimarra stayed, silent now.

I looked at the battleground again. Amasai and his men were gathering up the relinquished swords. They stood in a circle around Zune and his surrendered men, and sang a victory song. It was a verse from a Quelled myth, one that Lesharo had taught to them, and one I had always loved.

The images blurred. I was conscious of people around me moving, beginning the long walk back to Kasimarra. There were subdued sounds of horror and bitter disbelief. Some of the people, families and lovers of those fallen, went down onto the battleground to find and carry back their wounded and their dead. The sound of wailing filled the air.

I wiped my face. Amasai stood in front of me. He was very white and strained, and blood ran black and scarlet down his side. He knelt and touched the ground at my feet. He stayed there a long time. When he rose again, his eyes were moist.

"My Fire Woman," he said huskily, "I and all my men are yours, for as long as we live. Tomorrow we will stand with you when you are made High Diviner. And afterwards we will carry your laws to every place, and see that they are enforced. In all that you do, you have our loyalty."

I stared at him, dumbly. When I tried to thank him, my lips moved but no sound came. He smiled, took the Firelord's sign from his neck, and hung it about mine. His fingers lingered a moment on my face; then he bowed, and went back to his soldiers. I watched them form into much-diminished ranks, and march off the plateau and down to Kasimarra. Only ten horses were left, and those were led away. Someone — Laken, I think — took my arm, and told me to come away. I shook my head, and was left alone.

I went down onto the battlefield, among the dead and dying and those who grieved for them. The wounded were being laid on stretchers and blankets and carried back to Kasimarra to the surgeons there, to face more horror. I glimpsed some of the men as they were taken away. They had appalling injuries. A man on a stretcher was carried past me, close, and I felt waves of despair and torment from him. I glanced at his face; it was covered in blood, unrecognisable. One leg was severed to the bone; blood pulsed from the wound, and dripped through the stretcher to the ground. Impulsively I reached out, and his bearers stopped. I touched his arm, his cold hand. It was slippery with blood. Feelings tore across me — dark, powerful feelings of earth spinning and rock on fire. I was drawn down, deep down, into the force and soul of him. I released his hand and drew back, shocked, knowing it was Zune.

I bent my head to his. "Yours will be a firelord's funeral," I said, "because he chose you first; and only other men at war, and fate, chose me."

His hand moved a little, touched mine; then they bore him away. I was told later that he died just outside the walls of Kasimarra, below the high road to the Firelord's door.

After a while I realised that I stood alone. The field was abandoned, stark and desolate under a deepening sky. Vultures hung there, swooping on the corpses of the horses, and on the remains of human agony. The air stank of death. I looked towards Kasimarra, and saw a fearsome thing. The sky beyond was streaked with red. The highest towers of the temple were stained with that terrible colour, and it touched the mountains on the far horizon, tainting them the shade of blood.

I knelt down. "My God," I said, "I see your sign, the blood across the world. I don't know what it means. Tell me. If this thing I have done has displeased you — if I am not on your road — then show me clearly. And I will relinquish it all."

I stood up. My whole body shook, and I could hardly breathe for fear. I raised my eyes. The skies were livid; and over Kasimarra, its rays like tarnished gold behind the clouds, stood my family sign.

23

My Morning

I did not sleep that night of the great battle. I think most of Kasimarra did not sleep. Around midnight it snowed heavily, and the city seemed as much shrouded with disbelief and suffering as it was with snow. Even though the windows were shuttered and heavily curtained, I could hear the mourning from the houses below; the sounds of women wailing, and the plaintive tones of funeral pipes. And in the temple people lamented, and the priests grieved and tore their robes. It was more than sorrow for the dead; it was grief for the whole order of Chosen belief that was being torn apart.

Until long after midnight Lesharo and I talked. We shared a celebration meal and a cup or two of wine, and prayed together. He held my face and kissed my brand, and wept. "This is your morning, lionheart," he said, "and the great day of the Quelled."

He went to bed shortly afterwards, but for me sleep was nowhere near. I went to the infirmary and worked alongside the physicians. They still had many wounded to see, though they had worked all night and it was near dawn.

It was in the infirmary that I saw Alejandro. I had not noticed him among all the rest in that torchlit, shadowed place; but a soldier held me by the skirt as I walked past, and I looked down and saw that it was he. He was wounded in the chest, and the physicians had operated earlier in the night. A brazier burned near his bed to warm him, and in the firelight his face looked very pale. Blood seeped through his bandages.

"I greet you, Fire Woman," he said, smiling that beguiling smile of his, though he was suffering. "I would pay homage to you, but I fear that if I do, I shall fall and bleed all over your feet."

"You have paid homage already," I said, "by fighting for me in the battle."

"Oh, it was no more than any enlightened man would do," he said and laughed, though the effort made him blanch. He turned his face away, fighting a fresh onslaught of pain.

I sat on the edge of his narrow bed, took his hand, and waited while his pain subsided. He seemed more manly now; his months in the army had toughened him. The vitality was there still, the charm, the engaging boldness. But there was something else as well; a depth to him, a sincerity, that was not there before. He turned his head again and looked at me, his green eyes dancing.

"So, Elsha, you have achieved the impossible. Today you will be Fire Woman."

"I would never have achieved it alone," I said. "With all my heart, I thank you for your part in it. It was a great victory."

"It was only the first, Elsha. There will be many others, not all won on battlegrounds. The hardest battles will be fought in men's hearts, against their prejudices and beliefs. I know. I've fought there myself."

He gave me a brief grin, then closed his eyes. I stood to go, but he found my hand, and gripped it.

"Elsha, there is something else. About the myth." His face became white and strained, and he passed his tongue across his lips before he spoke again. His lips were white. "I cannot say how much it angered me. We based our civilisation, our lives, on that lie. And when people like me questioned it, saw that you Quelled were not what they said you were, they called us heretics and shoved us off to the army and hoped we'd get honourably killed. I'm ashamed to be Chosen, ashamed — " A fit of coughing wracked him, and he sweated with the agony of it.

"Don't distress yourself," I said gently. "There is no blame in you, any more than there is blame in me. We all were taken in. The fault lies with men long dead."

"But it must be put right! It isn't enough that you change laws, Elsha, that you ease the lives of the Quelled. Your ancestors were of royal blood. You owned a peaceful kingdom. You have a right to true freedom, and to claim back all your land, your houses, your — " He coughed again, and sweat poured off his face.

After a while his distress eased, and he said almost jokingly: "Have you seen the irony, Elsha? By the same power that you reform laws and improve the lives of the Quelled, you keep them in slavery."

"I have seen it," I said. "I have seen a terrible circle, from which there is no escape. We're all trapped in it, Quelled and Chosen alike. The world is trapped. And even a firelord cannot wipe away dust from the sky."

"Maybe it is already going," he said, very low. "The skies are changing. I've seen. Some of our dawns and evenings are red. Amasai says the firestones are different; they give off less smoke. I think the dust is gone, and the clouds that remain are our smoke."

Visions blazed in my head. "Then if I could find fuel that gives off no smoke at all," I said, "the skies might clear. Do such firestones exist?"

He smiled in spite of his pain. "I don't know. You're the diviner."

On my way to my room, I passed one of the high balconies that overlooked a temple courtyard, its towered walls, and the western sector of the city. Beyond the city, still dim in the ashen dawn, were the mountain slopes where the funeral pyres burned. I saw a pyre raised above them all, surrounded with banners. It was Zune's.

On the towers of the temple courtyards, priests were raising the bright inauguration flags, and from every window ledge and balcony were hung scarlet and gold tapestries emblazoned with the firelord's sign. The city, too, was being decorated. Banners streamed across the streets, and the main road into Kasimarra, my triumphal road, was ablaze with the fires of thousands of torches. I knew that in the great hall splendid carpets were being rolled out, and high on a shining dais, surrounded by fire, was being prepared a golden throne.

But in the streets the people grieved and threatened, and the air was full of menace. From the distance, and growing closer, came rumblings of disorder and violence.

I went to the holy place high in the temple, and stayed there a long time. When I went to my room to bathe and prepare myself for my inauguration, Laken was waiting for me. My ceremonial robe that she had made was flung across my bed, carelessly, and my inaugural speech, so painstakingly recorded on parchment, was torn in pieces on the floor.

"It has been cancelled!" she cried, furious, the moment she saw me. "Maelmor has said there will be no inauguration ceremony! He breaks with traditions centuries old, and revokes our greatest rite!"

My heart went cold. "He cannot do this," I said. "I won the battle. I must be made Firelord. The people cannot live without a diviner."

"No one disputes that," she said. "But listen, woman! Can you not hear the hysteria outside? It is still two hours before the ceremony, and already soldiers are settling riots. Dozens of citizens are dead, hundreds trampled or beaten to death. The temple gates are splattered with blood. If Maelmor has a civic ceremony for you, the whole city will be in chaos. There will be a small private rite, he said. Just him, ten priests for witnesses, and you. Lord Amasai has been arguing with him this past hour, saying you must have all the honour that is due to a firelord, and he will fight to win that for you. He threatened Maelmor. Oh, I have never seen such doings in the temple, not in all my life!"

"Where are they now?" I asked.

"Maelmor and Amasai? In the priests' apartments."

"Take me there."

"Woman, I cannot! Those apartments are — "

"You must! I must talk to Amasai. He fights for what is not important."

I pushed Laken ahead of me out of our rooms, and, muttering and wringing her hands, she took me to Maelmor.

He stared at me when I went in, his body rigid with shock. Then he remembered I was Quelled, and turned away. "What are you doing in these chambers, harsha?" he asked, through clenched teeth.

"I wish to speak with you about my inauguration," I replied. "For once there is agreement between us, Maelmor. Enough blood has been shed. All that is needed is a quiet place where I can make my vows before witnesses, and where you can appoint me Firelord."

"That is not enough," said Amasai, from across the room. "You are to be High Diviner, Elsha. That is the supreme office in our dominion. I will not have that honour bestowed on you furtively, as if you were unworthy. If they have to do it with my sword above their heads, every citizen in Kasimarra will pay you proper homage."

"What kind of homage is that, Amasai?" I asked. "You told me a little while ago that you would not force your men to fight for what they do not believe. How can you now say that you will force others to honour what they ardently despise? Steel does not change people's hearts. Swords bring division and death. I want harmony between Quelled and Chosen. I want equality."

Maelmor swore, then laughed bitterly. "Equality!"

"It already exists," I said, "though you Chosen won't acknowledge it, yet."

Maelmor decided to ignore that. He looked at my right shoulder. "You will be satisfied, then, with a simple ceremony, with only priests for witnesses?"

"Not only priests," I said. "Witnesses I trust. Soldiers who fought for me. I want Lesharo there, and Amasai."

"And it will be enough for you just to make your vows, and be gone on your divining business?"

"It will be enough for me to become Firelord, and to pronounce the new laws."

For an instant Maelmor's eyes met mine. "No new laws, harsha."

"If I am Firelord," I said, "there will be reforms."

"And if I repeal them?"

"Then I will not divine."

"You would not dare. You would kill us all with cold."

"The Chosen would kill us, Maelmor, with their conceit and their lies."

He stepped near me, his right hand on his sword. Amasai was already between us, his sword naked against the high priest's heart.

Maelmor ignored Amasai. He looked straight in my eyes, and said in a voice shaking with wrath: "What gives you the right to call us liars?"

"The Myth of Hamash gives me the right," I said.

Maelmor turned away, and went over to the window. He leaned on the ledge there, looking down on his troubled realm, his head bent low.

Amasai sheathed his sword, and gave me a piercing look. "Are you sure in this, woman?" he asked.

"Very sure," I said. "All that is necessary is that I am made Firelord, and that I announce the new laws. Afterwards, I would be grateful if your soldiers took those laws to every place, and saw that they were enforced."

"You already have my word on that," he said. Then he smiled, and added, with a sideways glance at the bowed high priest: "But I confess to being disappointed, Elsha. I was looking forward to a full firelord's inauguration for a harsha of the Quelled. I would like to see a victorious celebration of Chosen wrong made right."

I smiled back. "You won't be disappointed," I said. "Victory does not always come with trumpet-blasts and glory."

In the full ceremony, I would have walked from the beginning of the road into the city, through the crowded streets, and up to the great temple gates. On that walk I was to have worn a simple white linen shift, symbol of the purity of the Chosen spirit. Later, when I had made my vows and relinquished my former life, that shift would have been replaced with the magnificent Firelord's robe. I never intended to wear that white shift; I had planned to wear the grey garment of a harsha.

I don't know where Laken got that garment from; it was tattered from use, and, though she washed it several times, it remained stained from the mine. She had apologised for it, but I told her that for me this day it was perfect. Now, without the complex rituals and symbolic changing of clothes, I chose to wear only that Quelled grey.

Maelmor was furious when he saw it, and muttered something about the Firelord's office being made a mockery. I told him I was wearing the garments of the noblest people I knew. He went deadly white, and in a halting voice began the ceremony.

We were in the Firelord's private library, a place more meaningful to me than triumphal roads and halls. Here Maelmor put on me a new-made Firelord's sacred sign, and declared me High Diviner; and here I made my vows.

I wept when I made them, knowing that I gave up all my former life. I promised to serve unceasingly, to go always where I was needed, to divine whenever that was necessary, and to keep alive the warmth that sustained our people. I swore to be a fair judge and lawgiver, and vowed never to use my powers for my own gain, or to take any personal reward. I pledged my body to the firestones in the earth, my will to helping human life endure, and my spirit to fire.

When I had made the vows, Lesharo handed me the scroll of the new laws I had written. In front of five priests and five soldiers, in front of a malevolent high priest, a powerful Chosen champion, and my oldest Quelled friend, I read those laws. I wept as I read them, knowing they held the hopes and dreams I had treasured all my life; that they meant justice for my race, and a kind of freedom; that they would cause controversy and bloodshed, restoration and healing. And while I made those laws, I could hear outside the temple the dreadful sounds of strife. But I could feel the quiet of God like a shield about me, and I bound myself to him for strength; and, though I stood alone in my new calling, I held a nation in my heart.

24

Into the Light

And so the lives of the Quelled were changed; and for the first time in their history, my people had a voice, dignity, and a limited amount of freedom.

But nothing was won easily. On the second of the thrice-yearly meetings in Kasimarra, between myself and the Quelled ambassadors, the good news from the mines was still interspersed with stories of injustice and strife.

Night's lamps had almost burned out when the last ambassador stood up from the chair across the table, bent and touched the polished floor of the great hall, and left.

Wearily, I leaned back in my chair, and glanced at Alejandro beside me. He was recording on a scroll the report from the last ambassador. His writing was swift and neat, and his hands were gold in the lamplight as they moved on the parchment. Finally he signed the report, put down the pen, and sprinkled sand on the ink to dry it. He rested his head in his hands.

"The battle still goes on, doesn't it?" he said. "Every day a Chosen somewhere, somehow, violates the new laws. Much has been achieved, but there is still a long way to go, to justice."

"There can never be true justice," I said. "You told me yourself that improving the lives of the Quelled is not enough. We were a great nation, once. Strong. Free."

"God, Elsha, don't get any more ideas," he said, and slowly stood. He was smiling, but his face, for all its youth, looked tired and careworn. He gathered up the parchments, rolling them carefully. They would be given, later, to Amasai.

"Five ambassadors did not report," he added. "Either they've met accidents on the way, or their mines are in so much chaos that they cannot leave. Amasai will need to visit those mines, as well as the others where there is still discord. I have seen, sometimes, his dealings with the Chosen who will not comply with your reforms. He is hard on them, Elsha. Hard, but just. He works well for your cause."

"As you do," I said. "You are a loyal friend, Alejandro."

"No more loyal than others who love you," he said softly, and his eyes strayed across the room to where Dannii waited.

She had been talking with Lesharo, ambassador from Siranjaro, and Laken; but it was late now and the other two had retired. She sat on a velvet cushion beside a brazier, reading, her knees drawn up and her chin resting on her hand. She was beautiful in her vivid handmaid robes, with silver bracelets up her arm, and scarlet ribbons in her black hair. Alejandro had given her those bracelets and ribbons, hiding them in the caves where she and I stayed on our divining journeys. He was steward now, and never could confine himself to basic supplies. He had left gifts for us both, wrapping them in silk, and hiding them under stones and in nooks carved into walls. But the best gifts had been for Dannii, though for a long time she had not admitted it. She waited now for Alejandro, so they could have a cup of wine together before day's end.

"Take care," I said to him. "I have not yet changed the ancient laws, and we are watched every hour."

He smiled that old bewitching smile. "I am not quite so wild as I once was," he said.

I bade him and Dannii good night, and went to my room. But I could not sleep. I lay in the firelit dark and thought of Teraj.

He had written several times to me, having the letters delivered in secret, because of Maelmor's spies. In his last letter he said he was no longer in his sheltered home, but out travelling through the mines and towns, helping where the fighting was bad and the injured were many. I feared for him, out in those angry places, though I would have known if harm had come to him. He said he thought of me at the edge of every dawn, and at the edge of night; and I thought of him, too, in those times, and through all the long days in between.

I dared not visit him. I could make new laws to change conditions for the Quelled, but the time was not yet right to alter Chosen laws and attitudes that had prevailed for centuries. The laws forbidding closeness between Chosen and Quelled still stood.

Across the room, Dannii's bed remained empty, and I worried. An hour passed, and still I could not sleep. I got out of bed, pulled on my boots and an outer garment, and went to the holy place in the pinnacle of the temple. Here the walls were so high that mists formed in the roof, and the stones had ice on them. I crouched against the wall facing the altar fires, my arms crossed against my chest for warmth.

"I think I have a rebellious heart," I confessed. "Every moment of every day I break my Firelord's vows, because I cannot let go my former life. I cannot forget Teraj. And there's more than rebellion in me; there's discontent. Everything I wanted for my people, I have achieved. But it is not enough. There is still injustice, still prejudice. I feel that there is something more, something infinitely greater, that must be done.

"I was told once that there are no Quelled. But that is a lie. There will always be Quelled, as long as the world is cold and people need fire; as long as I divine. Is there a way we can survive the cold without fire or firestones, or slaves to mine for them? There must be another way. There must."

But there was none, and the stones around me grew colder and colder, and the circle of my fate more and more binding. I could no longer feel my legs or feet, and my hands pressed under my arms were like ice through the fabric of my gown. Yet, incredibly, I felt a warmth, a joy. It came from outside myself; was so real, so intense, I could almost place its source. It was somewhere near the altar, close. And somewhere, as if glad again to be in my company, someone smiled. I saw nothing; but with all of my being I was aware of him.

"Welcome," I said, smiling. "Do you like this exceptional cold? You must have fire for spirit, then. It's as cold here as it was out in the snow that day. You gave me an answer then. Can you not give me an answer now, for the world?"

And then it struck me — crashed across me in a blaze of light, and I leapt up, yelling with laughter, and ran, hobbling fast on my frozen feet, out of the holy place, and down through passages and stairs and halls, past startled guards and down to my room. Dannii's bed was still unoccupied. I ran through the halls to Lesharo's room. I threw open the door and rushed in, half falling on his bed, shaking him, yelling at him to get up. I pulled off his furs and blankets, realised he slept naked, and threw him his trousers.

"Wake up!" I cried, pulling at his arms. "There's something I want us to do!"

He stared at me vaguely, half asleep. "I can't, lionheart," he mumbled, trying to cover himself. "I've a wife — "

"Get up! I want us to go outside, into the snow."

"In the *snow*? Are you mad, Elsha?"

I made him stand, and turned around while he pulled on his trousers. Then I grabbed his hand and pulled him after me down one of the dim torchlit passages that led to the outside terraces. His bare feet slapped on the chilly wooden floors, and I could hear him breathing in the cold in painful gasps, and his hand shook. The air was frigid here. As I pushed open the heavy outer door, the raw air from outside rushed across us, cutting our skin like knives, and making our faces and eyes ache.

Lesharo gazed at me, bewildered, his breath white in the dawn air, his arms folded and shaking across his bare chest. I took his arm and pulled him further into the wind, beyond the flush of torchlight from the open door. I tore off my boots, my heavy outer dress, dropping them on the snow. My underdress was thin, useless against the freezing wind; but I hardly felt the cold, I was so elated.

"Lesharo, I want to teach you something. Put your arms down. Stop crouching like that. Stand up straight, close your eyes."

He looked distressed, but did as he was told. I

stood beside him in my thin dress, shivering from cold and excitement and joy, and took his hand. "I want you to think of fire," I said. "Imagine you are warm, enclosed in warmth, warm from your mind and heart and bones and all the way through. Completely deny the cold. It doesn't exist. The only reality is the warmth that you create. Create it in your mind, your body, and hold it there. You have far more authority than the wind or the ice. Your soul is free, transformed, strong. Your spirit is greater than anything in the world. So use it to command. Be in control. Be warm."

I don't know how long we stood there with the wind whipping about us, and the snowdrifts settling on our hair and clothes. But stand we did, and I felt warm; and after a while I felt Lesharo stop shaking, and his hand in mine was comfortable and still. We opened our eyes and looked at each other, and laughed. We looked at our feet, and saw that the snow was melted where we stood. Our damp clothes gave steam, and it rose from us in curls of silver-grey, and was torn away in the wind.

Laughing, Lesharo pulled me close to him and hugged me. "By God, Elsha, what a way to outwit winter!"

I drew away from him, new images flooding me, filling me.

"I'm not here only to be diviner," I said. "I'm here to teach every soul in this dominion what I taught you just now."

He smiled, then saw that I was serious. "I thought your other dreams were wild," he said, "but this . . . this is impossible. We weren't all born with your powers, Elsha, or your strength of will."

"It might not be an inborn power," I said, "but I believe it can be learned. And if others can be taught, then total freedom for the Quelled is not impossible. When we all have learned the warmth, we'll have less need for fire. Don't you see what this means, Lesharo? We'll need only a few firestones, for cooking and for light. I'll need to divine just a few times a year. We'll close most of the mines. The slavery of our race will be over. There will be no Quelled."

Speechless, he stared at me. His eyes were wet, and I could not tell whether it was from the cold, or because he wept.

Out on the great plateau we met, where, months before, Amasai and Zune had fought their battle. It was a bitter dawn, and the wind foretold more snow. We came in secret, safe from Maelmor's spies, to test my belief.

Dannii had chosen well. In the misty grey of first light, I saw that there were forty people. There were ten priests who were not hostile to us; Laken and other elderly temple staff; several children; craftsmen; a group of soldiers; several Quelled ambassadors; and some young people from the city, laughing and curious, and ready to dare anything.

They stood in a long line on the edge of the plateau. The gale flattened the rich fur of their coats, and tore the hoods back from their heads. All the Chosen wore fur-lined boots and gloves. The older ones were silent and tense, worried at the secrecy. When I stood before them they hushed the young people, and waited for me to speak.

"There is something new I want you to learn," I said. "It is to do with the human will, and with warmth. If you manage to learn this skill, practise it for two weeks, then see if you can teach five others. All this must be done in secret. I want to be certain that this ability is possible for everyone, before I tell Maelmor of it, and then all people. Tell only the five you will teach, and no one else. Now will you please remove your boots and gloves, your coats and hoods and outer garments; and I will tell you a new way to be warm."

Shaking, bewildered, they did as I asked. And out there on that windswept ground east of Kasimarra, in the dim dawn light, the people fought a new battle against their ancient enemy, the cold. It was a battle fought in silence, fought in the mind and heart and veins, and in the mighty arena of the human will. In the beginning there was disbelief, pain, fear, and failure. But there was courage, too, and triumph.

By morning's end they all, to some extent, were warm.

"Liberate the Quelled? Close the mines? Give up divining? Harsha, you are mad! You made vows — sacred, unalterable vows! Will you break them now, and kill us all?"

Maelmor's face was livid, and his body shook with rage.

"I do not recant my vows," I said. "I will divine, but only for a limited number of firestones. I still am pledged to giving people life and warmth. But there is this other warmth now — the fire that people have within."

"Fire within!" His face reddened, and sweat stood on his brow. He was summoning the new warmth himself, without realising it. "God forgive me," he said, "for making you the Firelord. You made a holy vow that you would help human life endure. Yet you plan to close the mines, knowing that we cannot live without firestones. They have saved us from the cold for five centuries. You cannot wipe out the necessity for them just by thought, no matter how many fools you have deceived. Your new warmth won't last. People cannot sit and contemplate heat every moment of their lives."

"They do not sit by their fires every moment, either," I replied. "And the new warmth is more excellent than fire. We have it with us always, ready to be called. We can stand in snow all night, and use it to endure. We can survive anywhere in the mountains, by our own power."

"Our own power? By God, woman — how many people do you think have that power? Two? Ten? A hundred? What happens to the rest? To those unable to call the power; to the newborns, the old, the ill, the weak-willed? You who are pledged to preserve life — do you leave them all to suffer, to freeze to death?"

"No one will suffer, Maelmor. I know there are people who will not be able to learn this ability. Many people, perhaps. They will be allowed all the firestones they need. But for the majority of us, fires will be burned only twice a day, not all day as they are now. A minimum of firestones will be used. The mines of Siranjaro, Thorn, and Raddai will remain open, and will export firestones for cooking and heating water, and for the people who are unable to warm themselves. I will divine as often as necessary, to keep those mines open. They will be worked the first half of every year by Quelled; in the second half of the year they will be worked by Chosen. Every year the mining crews will be changed; each adult will be required to mine only once in their lifetime. This is a fair way, with everyone who uses fuel doing their share of mining. Slavery will no longer exist."

"To do this, woman, you will need the entire army backing you. You may have fooled a few half-wits into believing this madness, but you will not beguile hardened soldiers. They may fight for you to keep peace, but they will not support you in folly."

"Already Amasai knows the secrets of the warmth," I said. "So do many of his soldiers. They learned it easily, because they were already used to disciplining their bodies beyond ordinary strength. This is not folly, Maelmor. It is a new power greater even than the talent to divine. It is a power we all have, if we will use it. Believe me, this skill has been well proved. Already there are fifty priests proficient in the new warmth, and able to teach it to others. Altogether in Kasimarra there are two hundred people who can summon the warmth, and keep it for an hour or more. They will be more skilled, in a month or two. I swear, Maelmor, this power is possible, proven, and a far better way to endure the cold."

He turned away from me, and was busy with his thoughts. "*Fifty* priests?" he said.

"Yes. Twelve of them are teachers in the temple school. Your students are at this moment learning the new skill."

He looked at me for a long time, straight. I saw his soul suffering monumental change, though he battled hard against it. In the end, he asked: "Could the Firelord teach the high priest this new warmth?"

"I see no reason why not," I replied, smiling, "if you are willing to stand out in the cold with me."

"Better to stand with you than against you, Fire Woman," he said, and led the way out to his frozen terraces.

Almost a year it was, before the new warmth became a part of all our lives. This could not have been achieved without Amasai and his forces.

They travelled to all the places in our mountains, teaching the skills of warmth. And several times Amasai came to visit me in Kasimarra, to tell me from his own lips how all was being accomplished.

"This past month we have gone to the last, remotest places," he said, on his final visit. "I have discovered hermits who have survived for years, practising what you call the new warmth. I wish we had known this skill a hundred years ago, or more."

"There is a right time for all things," I said.

He smiled. "I am amazed that so many have learned so willingly. People taught one another. There has been panic and confusion at times, but your friend Lesharo has an extraordinary gift for appeasing people and reasoning with them. I admire him greatly."

"From when I was a child," I said, "I saw that gift in him. When there was trouble or panic at the mine, it was Lesharo who settled it. It was for this reason that I chose him to work with you."

"And you, Elsha, what will you do, now that your divining skills are seldom needed?"

"I have work to finish in the libraries here," I said. "Alejandro and I have been recording the myth-songs of the Quelled, and this present history. The libraries are being reorganised. They will be permanently open, for everyone."

"I suppose," he said, smiling, "that you have

a display place waiting for the Myth of Hamash."

"When you think the world is ready for it," I replied.

"I will give it to you tomorrow," he said.

Soon after that talk with Amasai, my work in Kasimarra was finished. From the city now only kitchen fires sent up their smoke, and in the skies there was an unfamiliar glimmering. Alejandro and Dannii left the city, with directions to the place where Teraj lived. They took a letter for Teraj from me, saying that I would soon look on his face again. It was the most joyful thing I ever wrote.

Finally, I went to the holy place with Lesharo, and we put out the fires that had burned separately for centuries, for the Chosen and the Quelled. I said farewell to Laken, the priests, and servants who had supported me. I put extra clothes in a bag, and a supply of food for my journey. Lesharo loaded up his donkey with gifts I had given for himself and others I loved at Siranjaro. Among the gifts was a letter to my mother, and, from the Firelord's private library, a silken tapestry patterned with our family sign. Then together Lesharo and I left Kasimarra.

We parted at a crossroad half a day's walk out of the city, and we did not speak much. But as he was embracing me, he said: "You know, lionheart, those dreamer's eyes of yours have more light and joy in them now, than they have ever had."

"It's the air," I laughed, looking up. "It gets

lighter all the time, without our smoke. And it smells sweet."

"The world is lighter," he said, "because of you."

He kissed me, briefly, as an old and dear friend. Then he picked up his donkey's reins and went down the road ahead of me. I could not help thinking of that first time I ever saw him, bowed and subdued. Now, he walked like a prince. Which he was.

After a while he turned and waved, and I saw the Firelord's sign, that I had given him, flash in the strange new light. I waved back, and he turned and went on, and was hidden by the rocks along the way.

I picked up my bag and began walking a different road, to a secret place and the man I loved. Happiness fell on me like light; in my heart I flew, embraced Teraj already; and the earth itself felt warm with our joy. Laughing, I began to run. Then I noticed, in the clearer ground between the rocks, that tiny green plants grew. I knelt and looked at them, astounded. They were newborn trees.

I began walking again, marvelling, and when I looked up I saw in an opening between the clouds a space of unbelievable blue; and at the edge of it, so bright it hurt my eyes, an ancient sun.

About the Author

Sherryl Jordan is a full-time author who enjoys reading and listening to music. Of her writing, she says, "I hope through my books to bring young people something that is positive, uplifting, and joyful."

Her first book, *Rocco*, won the prestigious 1991 AIM Book of the Year Award, and her second book, *The Juniper Game*, was runner-up the following year. Two other books for young readers, *The Wednesday Wizard* and its sequel *Denzil's Dilemma*, were also short-listed in 1992 and 1993 respectively.

Ms. Jordan lives in Tauranga, New Zealand, with her husband, Lee, and their daughter, Kym.

point®

Other books you will enjoy,
about real kids like you!

☐ MZ42599-4	The Adventures of Ulysses Bernard Evslin	$3.25
☐ MZ43469-1	Arly Robert Newton Peck	$2.95
☐ MZ45722-5	Dealing with Dragons Patricia C. Wrede	$3.25
☐ MZ44494-8	Enter Three Witches Kate Gilmore	$2.95
☐ MZ40943-3	Fallen Angels Walter Dean Myers	$3.95
☐ MZ40847-X	First a Dream Maureen Daly	$3.25
☐ MZ44479-4	Flight #116 Is Down Caroline B. Cooney	$3.25
☐ MZ43020-3	Handsome as Anything Merrill Joan Gerber	$2.95
☐ MZ43999-5	Just a Summer Romance Ann M. Martin	$2.95
☐ MZ44629-0	Last Dance Caroline B. Cooney	$3.25
☐ MZ44628-2	Life Without Friends Ellen Emerson White	$3.25
☐ MZ42769-5	Losing Joe's Place Gordon Korman	$3.25
☐ MZ43419-5	Pocket Change Kathryn Jensen	$2.95
☐ MZ43821-2	A Royal Pain Ellen Conford	$2.95
☐ MZ45721-7	Searching For Dragons Patricia C. Wrede	$3.25
☐ MZ44429-8	A Semester in the Life of a Garbage Bag Gordon Korman	$3.25
☐ MZ47157-0	A Solitary Blue Cynthia Voigt	$3.95
☐ MZ43638-4	Up Country Alden R. Carter	$2.95

Watch for new titles coming soon!
Available wherever you buy books, or use this order form.

Scholastic Inc., P.O. Box 7502, 2931 E. McCarty Street, Jefferson City, MO 6510

Please send me the books I have checked above. I am enclosing $ _____
Please add $2.00 to cover shipping and handling. Send check or money order - no cash or C.O.D's please.

Name _____ Birthday _____

Address _____

City _____ State/Zip _____

Please allow four to six weeks for delivery. Offer good in U.S.A. only. Sorry, mail orders are not available to residents of Canada. Prices subject to changes.

PNT